Injury Time

INJURY TIME

KEVIN SMITH

THE LILLIPUT PRESS
DUBLIN

First published 2025 by
THE LILLIPUT PRESS
62–63 Sitric Road,
Arbour Hill,
Dublin 7,
Ireland
www.lilliputpress.ie

A CIP record for this title is available from The British Library.

Paperback ISBN 978 1 84351 949 2
eBook ISBN 978 1 84351 950 8

Set in 12.5pt on 17pt Fournier MT Std by Compuscript
Printed in Czechia by Finidr

In memory of my friend Gerry Dawe
And for Dorothea and Olwen

The cloud of infection hangs over the city,
a quick change of wind and it
might spill over the leafy suburbs.
You coasted too long.
   – John Hewitt, 'The Coasters'

All that is solid melts into air, all that is holy is profaned,
and man is at last compelled to face with sober senses his
real conditions of life, and his relations with his kind.
   – Karl Marx, *The Communist Manifesto*

1

Unmanned by his skimpy cotton mini-dress, his thick bare thighs goose-pimpling in the cool air, Fenton Conville took the proffered paper towel, and hesitated – 'You're absolutely sure?'

'Epididymal cyst. Very common.'

'Benign?'

'Nothing to worry about.' The tall, slow-moving sonographer turned his back and leaned over the sink. 'And if it starts giving trouble, we just insert a needle into –'

With a quack of alarm, Fenton hopped off the bed. 'There'll be no trouble.'

A creature, once again, of the light, the heels of his tan brogues ringing out on the marble floor, Fenton strode back along the sun-sharp corridors of the Royal Victoria. Squads of be-scrubbed and be-chinoed medics marched by, pin-striped silverbacks, stethoscopes a-jiggling, orderlies, porters. In all directions, the afflicted were in transit: in wheelchairs, on trolleys, with their tubes and canisters, the faces of the older ones variously stricken or zonked, the younger ones full of bluff or merely numb, each moving along a different, shadow-darkened road. He saw, with darting glances, chalky skin and dank hair, livid scars, bodies wasting inside cheap nightwear and fought the urge to scream.

Pausing at the open door of a side ward, he looked in. Three incredibly old men were propped up in their beds staring at a television screen on the wall, the volume up about as high as it could go. He recognized the film. 'I'm going to live through this,' Scarlett was saying, 'and when it's all over, I'll never be hungry again. No, nor any of my folk. If I have to lie, steal, cheat or kill, as God is my witness ...'

He hurried on.

Fleeing the gloom of the car park into the sunshine, he began to feel the lightness that infuses the breast of anyone who has ever dodged a bullet. He opened the car window and let the breeze wash the disinfectant whiff from his hair and clothes. He gobbled a handful of Tic Tacs, savouring the rush of menthol through his sinuses. Hospitals definitely weren't for him, he decided. With a magnanimous wave, he allowed a woman in a wheelchair to cross, then swung onto the road and powered away.

For twenty-seven days, Fenton had been living in fear. Now he was free, gone with the wind across the Queen's Bridge and on towards the dewy suburbs. The rest of the morning stretched ahead of him, rebooted and refreshed, solid again. It was the first of 183 days before he would be back in the mortal realm he had just left, for reasons he could not have foreseen.

∽

'So. Nearly there. The half-century. The Big Five-O.' Carolyn, presiding over the granite expanse of the kitchen island, shook her head, eyes bright with macabre wonder. 'I think the worm is about to turn for you.'

'Most kind. Very reassuring. Thank you, dear.'

Whatever the worm might be, Fenton thought, it could fuck right off. He opened the paper bag he was holding and released a sausage roll the size, and nearly the weight, of a gold bar. Whistling 'The Colonel Bogey March', he shoved his plate into the microwave. He'd had, he reflected, a rough few weeks. First, some anonymous glype, some absolute ganch in the supermarket car park had scobed the side of his car, a three-foot-long gash in the paintwork he feared would cost him, when he got round to taking it to the garage, a vertigo-inducing sum. A couple of days later, his mother had called to tell him his father had slipped in the bath and fractured his femur and that assistance was needed (from Fenton). This, it transpired, included helping the old bugger on and off the lavatory, a task that was to test Fenton's already tentative sense of filial duty.

Getting him onto the bowl was bad enough – most of his father's considerable weight was accumulated in his paunch – but heaving him off it while simultaneously trying not to breathe was hotter, dizzier work, and the first time Fenton nearly passed out. On the third occasion, he took the precaution of tying a hand towel, bandito-style, around his face, and this mitigated some but not all of the prevailing mischief.

Fenton's mother stationed herself at the foot of the stairs while this operation was taking place, ready to swoop in, like some specialist wing of the emergency services, to hose the scene down with Febreze. Snatches of exchange would reach her from above.

'Dad, please, what did I tell you? Don't start till I get outside. Holy Jesus ...' (door slamming).

'Fenton, for God's sake –' (muffled) 'stop making such a song and dance, it's a perfectly natural –'

'*No*, Dad, that's not natural. Believe me, *that* is not natural.'

This horrifying situation went on for a full week until the multi-toothed wheels of social care at last engaged and Mihaela and Bogdan, both from Romania, were dispatched each day in time for the 11 a.m. 'event'. Businesslike and initially cheerful, it seemed to become apparent to the two of them quite quickly that, even by the standards of lowly health-industry work, they had drawn a short straw.

And thirdly (always in threes!) the arrival of the most disturbing and time-consuming worry of all – in the shower, briskly lathering his tackle with pineapple foaming gel – the discovery of *the lump*. Despite the hot water, he had felt a chill run through him and cold sweat break on his scalp. Further feverish investigation, as he stood dripping on the tiles, brought unmistakable confirmation: a nugget the size of a marrowfat pea on his right gonad.

Top speed then, in his mutilated motor, the next morning to Dr McKenna's surgery where terror and mortification ('Just hold your – just keep that out of the way for –') had vied for dominance in his sleep-starved brain. There ensued a comprehensive run-through of possibilities and options, of which Fenton, in a state of glazed disembodiment, retained only the ramifying phrase: *prosthetic testicles*.

'So the next thing will be an ultrasound. I'll set that up for you,' said Dr McKenna, groping around his desk and squinting at various scraps of paper. 'Probably be a couple of weeks before they can fit you in, so in the meantime,' he raised his muskratty old face and grinned, 'chin up, what?'

Fenton yanked the overhead cupboard open and located the HP Sauce bottle, which was down to the dregs and made a horrible noise when he squeezed it. He carried his plate to the breakfast island.

'Listen,' Carolyn said, wagging a biro and scanning his buff-coloured thatch for signs of grey. 'While I have you, we need to finalize your guest list. I'm assuming you don't want the Sinclairs?'

Fenton studied the seething pastry in front of him. The Sinclairs bored him almost to the point of violence (especially the husband, who was a prime example of what Fenton's brother Artie referred to as a BMO – *Broadcast Mode Only* – i.e. no receiver) but the truth was, he didn't much feel like having anybody. His instinct was to skitter under his bed and stay there. Thirty had been a shock, forty a real kick in the teeth, but *fifty?* Fifty you were out there in the open, on the parched veldt, and those were live rounds in the distance. People he knew personally had *died* in their fifties. His uncle Toby had more or less exploded at the age of fifty-three – liver, kidneys, ticker, the lot. And Big Titch down at the club, he – well, Christ knows what had happened there, but he couldn't have been more than fifty-five.

With his fingertips Fenton appraised the contours of his midriff through the tight fabric of his shirt. There was no getting away from it: despite his height and breadth, he was carrying serious beef – not quite Tony Soprano standard yet, but not far off. He tried to recall when he had last not been disappointed at the sight of himself naked in front of the mirror. Ten years? Twenty? On the plus side, at least he'd ditched the fags. What a battle that had been and, if he was honest, continued to be. Three years clean next August and he still felt like a crucial part of his personality had been amputated, regularly dreamed he was smoking, on occasion, having nostrilled fumes from a passing smoker's cigarette, sensed the nicotine monster twitching and mumbling back to life inside him. Worth it, though, if only so he could climb a flight of stairs without stopping to cough up his spleen.

Unable to hold off any longer, he seized the sausage roll and munched into it, instantly scalding the roof of his mouth. He sucked air in and out very fast. Christ, the stuff was like napalm.

'Shall I take that as a no?' Carolyn regarded him over the top of her latest pair of reading glasses, which had blue Perspex frames and put Fenton in mind of the Fairy Godmother from *Shrek 2*.

'Yes.'

'Yes that's a no?'

'Yes, I don't want them.'

'Okay. So we have Bob and Una, Liam and Eileen, Ciara and Graham, Dawson and – will Dawson be bringing anyone?'

'I don't know. I'm not sure where he's up to.' Dawson's wife had died two years previously, and after a short period of mourning, he had embarked on a string of relationships with startlingly unsuitable women of varying ages.

'M'm.' Carolyn made ticking noises with her tongue. 'Newton and Bridget, I've invited Stewart from work and his girlfriend, and of the neighbours we have the Hetheringtons, the Bradfords and the McCaffreys. And your parents. Will they be bringing the Dixons?'

'Oh God, probably.'

'Right, my parents are heading up to the Glens, so that's around twenty. Next question, curry or chilli?'

'Curry ... no, chilli.'

'And the wine and so on, that's your department, and I'd say, looking at some of the names on this list,' she tapped it with her pen, 'you'll be needing a fair amount.'

Swallowing the last of his lunch, Fenton made a few calculations. It had been a long time since he had hosted so many of this particular crew at once and he was pretty confident that, if anything, their core capacity had increased since the pressure years of small children and mid-career stress, when their drinking sessions, snatched amid cyclones of coloured plastic and pushchair logistics, had been ravenous; borderline hysterical.

He thought: Graham and Bob would require beer, a lot, and later probably vodka or gin; Carolyn and Ciara Sauvignon blanc, extensively; Prosecco and probably vodka for Una and Bridget; the Hetheringtons wine and gin, at least a gallon, plus fancy mixers; his father and old man Dixon whisky (and whiskey); Liz Bradford vodka, a litre minimum; and then there was the barely quantifiable matter of red wine. Dawson, he reckoned, could probably take down a case by himself. His head a-swim with this multifoliate Venn diagram, he rose and moved to the window, where he stood staring out and performing a series of gentle belches.

The upper deck of their house had a view, through a dozen or more mature firs and sycamores, of the broad expanse of Belfast Lough. It was of bold 'modern' design, composed, roughly speaking, of a very large rectangular box with two levels (kitchen and living area, four bedrooms) perched on top of a smaller one (study, home gym, TV room, utilities) with an enclosed cobbled courtyard at the rear. It was clad in Siberian larch and embedded with much plate glass.

The site's original building, which he had managed to have demolished four days ahead of a preservation order, had been constructed in the mid-nineteenth century by a tobacco merchant wanting easy reach of the city and the pleasure of watching his cargo ships sail by from his bedroom window. The neighbouring houses were mainly of the same vintage, many of them still occupied by descendants of the linen barons, ironmasters and whiskey lords who built them. To live here had cost, and was still costing him, a great deal of money.

In good weather he would have opened the sliding doors and stepped out onto the wide balcony. This afternoon a capricious wind was flinging handfuls of cold rain against the glass, more like March than May, and the sea was in frisky form. He watched a loose gang of gulls wheeling and dipping above the slipway at the end of the coastal path where, just out of sight, a small flotilla of yachts and cabin cruisers bobbed and clanked in their moorings. Farther out, swan-white in the central channel, a Stena Line ferry sloped in the ghostly wake of the *Titanic* towards the open sea, bound for Liverpool or Cairnryan. On the far shore, below the shouldery hills and straggling estates, billows of smoke, as though drawn by a child, emerged from the chimneys of the power station and rolled slowly sideways in the wind.

The plant's days were numbered, Fenton had read in the *Belfast Telegraph*: coal-fired, inefficient. *Old* technology. It had been pumping out plumes of badness as long as he could remember. Part of the landscape. All this had to go, of course, beyond doubt now it seemed: coal, oil, plastic, petrol, diesel (filling his car sometimes he felt shifty, almost criminal), air travel, *meat*. He had to concede that his imagination faltered when he tried to envisage what was coming, the new order, but this last one, a future without animal protein, induced a sensation that teetered on panic. (The six months of veganism imposed on the household by his daughter the previous year had been a very dark time.

He had tried to blot that particular misery from his mind, but impressions flew back to him of dinner-time dread and gastric chaos, of meals that appeared to consist almost entirely of twigs and gravel.) The air-miles factor was also something to be considered, and here he was thinking of long-distance imports dear to him, namely the bosomy Cabernets of the Napa Valley and the silky Pinots of Oregon. Sooner or later, if this followed through, and Brexit, he suspected, was not going to help, he could be reduced to drinking – he shivered – *British* wine.

It was the speed with which all this had become so frighteningly urgent that he found shocking. It wasn't as if the evidence hadn't been there in plain sight – people had been moaning about greenhouse gases and global warming for decades. Unlike the slow drip of data that had eroded his sunbed empire – troublesome stats about melanomas and carcinomas and what have you – and brought it to its knees. The most recent closure had him down to just one salon now, sustained by the last (God bless them) of the death-defiers: the fact-denying, chain-smoking, steroid-munching celebrants of real-time human physicality, in all their peroxided, ultraviolet glory.

And they *were* the last of them. The new generation, his daughter's lot, had turned to the fake tan, the self-tanners, the lotions and sprays with names like Ibiza Blush and Crème Brûlée, Tenerife Teak ... Somali Warlord. As, indeed, his eldest son's crew favoured the digital over the analogue cigarette, vaping their popcorn- and apple-crumble- and – God knows – *roast-pork*-flavoured 'juices'.

He wiggled with a thumbnail at a fragment of gristle lodged between his molars. Now that he had put the testicle thing behind him, he could return to his main preoccupation: how to shore up his rapidly dwindling income. He wasn't like some of the folk in the other houses around him, people he knew of, and about, but rarely saw, whose families would be insulated for centuries to come by the riches their great-grandfathers had gouged out of the Americas and the Indies. He was second-generation money. Set up in business by his father, and following in the old man's entrepreneurial footsteps, he had done very well for himself – this was undeniable – but somewhere along the line, it seemed, he'd gone to sleep.

In the early years he had derived much pleasure, as he brought each new tanning salon on stream, from the exponential bulking of his net worth. By the age of twenty-six he had half-a-dozen shops and three rental units hosing cash into his vaults. His bank statements were a monthly treat. He had a nice bungalow in The Heights and a brand new viper-green Lotus Esprit and was whisking young Carolyn (she was five years his junior) off for weekends in Paris and Barcelona. As he turned thirty, his sunbed chain had doubled and he was upsizing to a detached stone build in The Demesne in readiness for a second child. He was young and wealthy and could only get wealthier.

But as he entered his middle years, he hit a few bumps. A foray into the stock market under the influence of a coked-up, and subsequently struck-off, financial advisor had been close to disastrous, and his feverish decision to encash his rainy-day funds in the midst of the 2008 meltdown, when they had already dropped fifty per cent, still gave him the sweats.

But the big move, the game changer, had been building the house – his Grand Design. The cash burn had been ferocious and had put him in an order of debt he hadn't encountered before: heavy, leveraged, long-term, uncomfortably invasive. Under the arrangement, the bank had dibs on half his franchise, had the right to call it in, to liquidate 'if adjudged necessary according to the bank's own principles of prudent self-interest', and this it had done – discerning the writing on the wall before Fenton had even looked up from his chicken tikka masala. This had had a grievous impact on his cash cushion.

Out in the bay, following the shoreline, Judge McCoubrey's sparkling navy-and-white motor yacht surged in the direction of the marina. At the wheel, on the flybridge – Fenton could make out his bright-yellow slicker and shiny bald head – the judge was enthroned, imperious even at this distance, and master of the waves. Once he'd dealt with his cash-crunch, Fenton was thinking, he would have one of those boats for himself. Except even bigger.

He was momentarily distracted by the sight of a string of oystercatchers stooping, pensive professors, along the water's edge. Oyster*catchers*? Was it really a case of *catching* oysters? It wasn't as if they were jinking around playing hard to get. Did those lads even *eat* oysters? Fenton did his best thinking while looking at the sea, at the birds, watching them at their frictionless, uncomplaining labour – and now, as the clouds shifted and pencils of sunlight picked out glints and sparkles on the far hills, an idea began to form.

All this. The future. The new dispensation. All that was coming towards him: he could face it (he had no choice). It was coming for everyone. Everyone had to face it. He turned from the window with purpose and, humming a little tune, made for the stairs, his den and the internet. He had research to do.

2

On Saturday morning, Clive and Hazel's number-one son brought his car to a gravel-spurting halt in the driveway to their house – the house he grew up in – a flaking Victorian villa hidden among the mossy-walled lanes above the village. The earlier rain showers had ceased and a fine mist was clinging to the magenta blooms of the rhododendrons. Fenton glanced again at his watch: 11.19. Better give it another few minutes, he thought, turning the radio up a couple of notches. It was a phone-in. The programme's host was trying to reason with a man called Ephraim from County Antrim who seemed to be proposing some kind of curfew for homosexuals.

'Sir, you can't be serious, this is the twenty-first century. Where have you been living?'

'Oh, I'm perfectly serious, boy, and I don't give a *hoot* what century it is. I live by God's law and these *people*, with their –'

At that moment the front door opened and Bogdan appeared at the top of the stone steps in his baby-blue fatigues, scrabbling a cigarette from pack to lips and igniting it in a single motion. He took a robotic succession of hollow-cheeked drags, his gaze fixed on a nearby flowerpot. Fenton allowed himself a moment or two of nostalgia, then clambered out of the car and approached the house, flashing a grin at an unresponsive Bogdan. Inside he found his mother gripping Mihaela by the upper arms and talking in firm, consoling tones. 'Okay? Do you hear me? It won't be for ever ... Mihaela, look at me.'

Fenton juked past them and down the hall to the kitchen where his father, dressed in pyjama bottoms and a pink golfing jersey, had been installed in his armchair beside the Aga, his gammy leg, in its yellowing cast, propped up on a footstool. He was engrossed in a copy of his favourite magazine, *Warmonger*, whose cover boasted a special feature on the world's top-ten tanks.

'Don't tell me – Challenger at number one?' said Fenton, making for the kettle.

'Leopard 2. Germany.' His father grunted. 'Hard to argue. Faster, more agile, longer range. A fearsome beast. Though the Challenger has better armour and its gun is rifled, making for a greater firing distance.'

Fenton popped a teabag into a cup and added hot water, then scrutinized the contents of the battered tartan biscuit caddy. 'Really?' he said. His father's obsession with the fine detail of the military world was pretty much a mystery to him: the blizzards of specifications and half-hour conjectures about the 'what if's and the 'and yet's of various battles put him into a kind of trance. When they were growing up, the old man had been an agreeable but fleeting and unreadable presence in the lives of Fenton and his younger brother, Artie, devoting himself to commerce and golf, and leaving household business and the imposition of discipline (and much had been required) to his wife. In later years, when he was in full flow about some rout at Anzio or El-Alamein, Fenton occasionally had the sense that he was somehow, belatedly, trying to explain himself.

'Mind you, you have to respect the Yanks here. The Abrams M1A2, real killing machine, very nippy despite the weight. Of course, they've also gone with the smooth-bore cannon –'

'Mm-hm.' Fenton rummaged out a Penguin. 'Listen, Dad, speaking of tanks in the field, I was wondering if I could talk to you about something.'

His father lowered the magazine and peered at his son. 'Any more of those?'

'What? Oh. Sure, have this one. Yes, I'm thinking about a new venture.'

'Really? What kind of venture?'

'A shop. In the village.' ('The village' was family parlance; it was, in fact, a small town. 'Town' was reserved for Belfast.)

'Really? What kind of shop? Here, open this for me, would you.'

'There you go … A vape shop.'

'A *vape* shop?'

'Yes.'

'You mean the weird steam things, with the funny …?'

'Well, it's not steam as such, it's vapour, and yes, it's getting very popular with the youngsters and people trying to give up smoking. It's a big growth market. I've been looking at the margins and, I have to say, they're pretty tasty.'

Fenton watched his father's face attempting to digest this information, the biscuit in his hand unbitten. 'The thing is,' Fenton continued quickly, pouring milk into his cup, 'the tanning business is dead in the water and I have to diversify, and what with one thing and another, I'm a bit overextended at the bank, and I was, uh, wondering if you could lend me some start-up cash, seed money?'

His father was examining the half-peeled Penguin as though it was an exotic fruit he had never seen before. 'Seed money?'

'Yes.' Fenton took a sip of tea. 'Just until the operation is cash-generative.'

'Cash-generative. M'm. How much?'

'Let's see, I'd need six months' rent for the premises, outlay for the initial stock. Say fifty grand?'

His father's lips formed a pantomime O and his eyebrows moved upwards. Fenton didn't like the look of it.

'I'm not sure about that, son. I mean, that's quite a lot –'

'You'll get it back.'

'Oh, no doubt, son. It's just our money is tied up, locked in, at the moment, funds, trusts for the grandchildren and what have you, and your woman has just booked us on a, well, frankly, *ridiculously* expensive cruise next year and –'

Just then the woman in question swept into the kitchen in a mode that Fenton and his father both recognized. Each adjusted his expectations.

'Right, Clive, that's the last time you have curry. I mean it. Those poor people.'

Clive of India knew better than to protest. 'Hazel, dear, your son is asking for a loan,' he said, 'to open a vape shop.'

'What? Good morning, Fenton. What's he talking about? A vape shop? A *vape* shop?' (This last in the manner of Lady Bracknell.)

Fenton set down his cup. Through the window behind his mother was a large bush, possibly blackberry, that had been trained over a rusting metal arch. It was badly pruned and seemed to Fenton to be mimicking his mother's latest hair-do. She was, what, seventy-three, seventy-four? Why did she have Rod Stewart's hair?

'Yes, I was just saying to Dad –'

'A *vape* shop?' (Again, Fenton didn't care for her tone.) 'And what kind of money are we talking about?'

'Fifty! He wants fifty K,' the armchair warrior shrilled.

'Fifty thousand pounds? Fifty *thousand* pounds?'

Fenton exhaled. He knew a beaten docket when he heard one. His best policy now, he decided, was to shut down the conversation, divert to a neutral topic such as gardening or grandchildren, make an excuse and leave. What actually happened was that, as if in a horror film, another

Fenton – in this case, snarling, *fuck-it-pull-the-pin* teenage Fenton – came barrelling up from the depths and took charge.

∽

Back in his car, breathing heavily and trying to subdue the last of his fifteen-year-old self's flailing limbs, he reviewed the previous torrid few minutes. Had he really called his mother a selfish old bitch? Goaded his father to 'grow a pair'? More horribly, had he really questioned, at high pitch, their hanging on to all their cash, given that they would probably *die soon*?

He had been under strain, he told himself; he was under pressure. But even so. He then reflected, cheeks aflame, on the style with which he had left the kitchen. He hadn't exactly *stormed* out: no door had been slammed off its hinges, no threats or insults guldered over his shoulder. He wanted to think it had been a dignified stride, at worst a petulant stomp, but no, he was pretty sure – no, he was certain – he had *flounced* out.

3

From the window of his office above the furniture show-room, Crawford Wylie (Litigation, Matrimonial, Wills and Powers of Attorney) looked out on High Street and blew again on his coffee, which was black, the milk in the fridge having turned. This discovery had not improved his humour. He disliked having to work at the weekend and would have much preferred to be at home rediscovering the joys of vinyl on his new state-of-the-art carbon-fibre-and-glass turntable (only fifty had been made; it had cost more than a small car).

His immediate view was of a section of shopfronts, including a beauty salon, an undertaker's and a Chinese takeaway, bookended at the corner, beside the crossroads, by the Coachman's Inn, with its barley-sugar windows and faux Tudor beams. On the opposite side of the intersection was another pub, The Tipsy Toad, a pharmacy, an antiques shop (though it was mostly repro) and an 'organic' deli that specialized in high-density, gluto-hypogenic flapjacks.

Just visible in the distance, beyond the rooftops and framed by the arch of the railway bridge, was a splotch of seal-grey sea. The wind, when it gusted up the street, brought a fine mizzle of iodine-scented spray. Down below, the townsfolk were going about their business, as they did every day, from butcher to baker to café to florist and all points in between, stopping from time to time for a bit of banter, a good old gossip.

The solicitor sipped his non-dairy coffee, watching their peregrinations without expression. For nearly twenty years he had been at the service of these people, taking care of their house moves and trust funds, recovering their debts, pursuing their claims for recompense, administering their oaths, witnessing and contesting their wills. They came to him at moments of gravity in their lives and he gave them peace of mind with his iron-clad bonds, deeds and codicils. And how often had he heard behind the jargon and niceties, and read between the lines of legalese, their true earthly motives: spite, greed, revenge? And how many times had he marvelled at the power of gold's magnetic fields and the haywire dances it led people to perform?

In the end, of course, it was all about the money. If he thought about it too much, it would make him sad: the husbands and wives, the brothers and sisters, the mothers, daughters, fathers, sons – at seething loggerheads forever over a few quid, a half-acre of land, a pair of chipped porcelain spaniels. (*But who gets the family Bible?*) He wondered sometimes how you were expected to maintain your faith in human nature. His own he knew to be in very poor shape.

A tune popped into his head, a song about money – by the Flying somethings, Lizards, was it? – and he hummed it. *Were* the best things in life free? It depended, he supposed, on what you wanted.

What did Crawford Wylie want? In the beginning his goals were modest, and having just about scraped through every exam he ever sat, despite putting in the hard graft, this was prudent. Through his junior years, racking up countless billable hours for his yacht-owning masters, 'competent' was as high an accolade as he could expect. But he'd kept his head down and chipped away, and at the age of twenty-seven, by dint of luck and a tangential family connection, he came under the wing of Rex Bunting, a gent of great charm and fierce integrity, who had returned to his home town after a long career in London and set up a little practice to see out his days. Rex spent most of his time playing golf and flying light aircraft, leaving 'young Wylie' to mind the shop. Four years later the old boy crashed his Albatross 190 into a sea stack off the coast of County Clare, and that seemed to be pretty much that.

And yet. Taking over at the widow's behest, Wylie set about expanding the client base and engaging new associates, eventually drawing from it a tidy income. He married, upsized to a handsome detached house near a golf course, procreated (two girls and a boy) and, by anyone's standards, fulfilled the bourgeois contract. He drove a luxury German car and had a weekend cottage in the Antrim Glens. He experienced spells of faint, vegetal contentment.

Then, in the middle of his life, he had discerned, with much puzzlement and disquiet, a great emptiness within himself, a void that yawned, as it were, in the face of material enrichment. A voice came whispering to his mind that there must be something more. He turned, as many do, to self-improvement. First, physical fitness: he began running for (or away from – he was never quite sure) his life. He invested heavily in a home gym where he sweated and suffered for several long months in preparation for a marathon which, in the event, saw him staggering towards the finish line in urgent need of paramedical attention.

Next, the esoteric lures of the East: tantric yoga, tai chi, transcendental meditation. He even briefly toyed with Buddhism. This all passed. It turned out money was what he wanted all along. In fact, it became clear that he wanted a lot more of it. As the clock ran down, he found he desired, more than anything, consolidation, depth, surplus. His ageing soul was becoming hungrier, greedier; it agitated for excess of resources – a bigger, plumper cushion. And there was something else he wanted too.

Across the street Marty McCann, re-diagnosed with cancer three months back, had stepped out of The Inn for a smoke. Wylie noted his shocking pallor in the sunlight, his diminished bulk; thought, that'll be a bit of paperwork before too long. *Ye know not the day nor the hour*, his granny had been fond of saying, *keep watch!* And there, going into the charity shop, was Johnny Baird whose mother had left him a million he didn't even know she had, and what did he do with it? Nada. Tight as a shark's arse at forty fathoms.

Nearly a year getting the probate fees out of him and then only after he had the Fox twins pull the wee chancer over for a chat. Whites of their eyes in this game sometimes.

About to turn away, Wylie caught sight of a familiar figure waiting for the green man at the lights on the corner. Boy, he'd fairly put on the weight (at school he'd been a wiry scrum-half); quite a high colour on him too. *Huh.* Smiling to himself at the coincidence, Wylie returned to his desk and hoisted the stack of folders he'd been working on to the top of a filing cabinet. Back in his chair, he took a sheet of notepaper from the drawer, uncapped his pen and, with an involuntary twitch of his neck, began to draft a letter.

> *Dear Mr Conville,*
> *I am writing to inform you of an allegation made against*
> *you by my client, that on the night of ...*

4

'Same again?'

'Better make it a half.' Fenton pushed his empty glass away. 'Driving,' he added, though no one was listening. The upstairs lounge of The Tipsy Toad was in full lunchtime swing. It was warm and just bearably noisy, and after three pints of Pilsener and a square foot of lasagne Fenton was beginning to feel a little steadier.

After the blow-up with his parents, he had gone round to see Wee Davy, his mechanic, who had stood and stared, crouched and squinted, sniffed and clucked, and drummed with his fingers on the car roof for a full minute before quoting him £800 to buff out the scratch. This had prompted quite a bit of swearing from Fenton, followed by an intransigent, and finally menacing, silence from Wee Davy, resulting in Fenton's rubber-burning departure. Thence to the new off-licence where, having assembled a shanty town of boxes containing several hundred quid's worth of birthday booze, he was informed (a little offhandedly, he felt) that the off-licence didn't deliver.

'There y'are, love. Do you want to pay for the food now as well?' The barmaid was about twenty, ebony hair scraped vertically into a clenched bun, her skin stained to hi-vis intensity. Her 'eyebrows' were large and wedge-shaped, precision drawn and heavily coloured in with what appeared to be black marker pen – what the *fuck* was going on, thought Fenton: it was like looking at a life-sized emoji.

'Yeah, why not?'

He swallowed a mouthful of beer. He'd call his parents later and straighten things out. They'd understand. He had no choice though, he realized, but to play the testicle card – use his plum-scare to leverage sympathy. Under his breath he practised a few phrases: *I didn't want to say anything … didn't want to worry you … been a bit of a strain.* Timing and tone were key. You never know – he sniffed – they might even take pity on him and advance the bloody spondulicks. But, even as he thought this, he knew it was too long a shot. So what then? Back to the bank? He couldn't go back to the bank. Not yet. Wait a minute, *perhaps* … He straightened himself on the bar stool. In his mind now was an impression of watchful energy, expensive tailoring and Ealing Studios hair: his father-in-law. Cecil McCracken. A semi-retired bookmaker and businessman, Cecil had stacks of cash. Old school, though. He'd want some kind of deal. What was the word? *Vig.* He'd need his vig. Could be a bit awkward.

'That's thirty-eight pounds forty when you're ready.'

'Fuck me. Thirty-eight quid? Seriously?' Groping for his wallet, Fenton gazed again at the human avatar. 'You sure?'

She nodded. 'And forty pee.' She consulted the docket. 'You had three and a half pints of Pilsener. That's a premium import, so it is.'

'And the food?'

'The lasagne's fifteen pounds.'

Back outside, Fenton found himself in something of a fugue state. There was a time he could have walked into any one of seven pubs (three had since closed) and had a couple of pints and a tureen of stew for a fiver. He located the wait button with his thumb. Traffic was nosing in both directions, halting every few seconds as someone left a parking space and someone else attempted to shoehorn in. He listened to the quotidian hubbub of the street, took in the swirls and eddies of passing faces, and it seemed, suddenly, that he was on an elaborate filmset among senescent, once-familiar actors. He saw his own school-uniformed ghost – cockatrice quiff and steel-tipped Oxfords – strutting towards him along this very pavement. No time at all ago, and yet ... These moments of ache were becoming more frequent, each tiny, half-grasped epiphany gone in the breeze like a breath of diesel.

Across the street a woman was standing outside the pharmacy rummaging in a small leather rucksack with the urgency of all women rootling in a bag. Having located whatever it was, she shouldered the pack and, glancing up, met Fenton's gaze and held it. For an instant she looked as though she was about to form a word – his name perhaps (or possibly just an expletive) – but, almost as quickly, she seemed to remember something and hurried off. The beeps went and he crossed, pausing to survey her retreating figure: navy puffer jacket, jeans, dark hair tied in a ponytail. There was something about the walk.

Intrigued, he changed course and began to follow her. Someone he didn't recognize tooted and waved at him from a white SUV and he waved back. Outside the post office the woman was hailed by another female and her male companion, and the three stopped to chat. Fenton turned to feign interest in the window of the nearest shop, which had been until very recently a small art gallery of the kind that sells expensive misshapen pottery and garish acrylics of overweight cats. Now a sign taped to the glass said 'Prime Retail Space to Let' and gave the contact details of a local agent. He put his face to the window and peered in at the bare interior. The unit was sandwiched between a coffee shop and an ice-cream parlour, two crucibles of leisure and pleasure – *a perfect spot for his new venture!* He stabbed the number into his phone.

When he looked up, the woman had gone but, not having any particular urgency in his day, he continued in the same direction. It was a while, it occurred to him, since he had walked the length of the village, more usually taking the bypass in his car, and now he was giving it fresh attention.

The place had lived through a few lean times over the years but only comparatively, not like some spots: there was enough fat in the Avenues and Demesnes and Heights around-about to rule out any sighting of tumbleweed. Many of these people had been trading as far back as he could remember: chemists, florists, grocers passing down to sons and daughters, other businesses changing hands but retaining the family name. Crawley's here, for instance, still a shoe shop, though Des Crawley, without an heir, was dead and gone. Fenton remembered the man's haemorrhoidal eyebags behind the *Joe 90* glasses, his tireless ingratiation, the wasteland of rejected footwear after he, Fenton (up to the age of, say, ten), had been taken by his mother to be fitted for new shoes. 'Sure, I've a pair of those myself,' Des would say when finally a decision, or more likely a state of exhaustion or imminent parental violence, was reached. This was his catchphrase, known throughout the town. Soupy Campbell, one of Fenton's schooldays gang, swore he'd once heard Des say it to a woman dithering over a pair of white stilettos.

He passed the doorway of what had been his first tanning salon, now a travel agent's, and felt a pang of nostalgia for his entrepreneurial beginnings amid the dark days of the nineteen eighties – days lit in his memory by the glow of ultraviolet tubes and the neon tans they provided. People needed cheering up back then, what with all the murder, madness and mayhem. And the rain. A nice Mediterranean tan perked you right up. It seemed it was always raining then. Constant black bead-curtains of rain. Mind you, at least that had been reliable, predictable, not like the experimental weather you got these days.

Across the street, the corner spot was still a barber's, though the cylinder with the red and white helices swirling forever downwards (or was it upwards?) above the door was gone. Fenton couldn't see the place without recalling, lump-in-throat, the occasion when his father had left him and Artie in the care of an unfamiliar assistant (to this day Fenton was unsure if the man had actually been an employee) who had visited on them haircuts of such sadistic comedy they'd had to wear woolly hats for nearly a month. In one of the hottest Julys on record. He could still picture the Saturday shoppers rearing back in horror as he and Artie ran, bristle-headed and howling, down the street, like two junior escapers from a Victorian insane asylum.

'Well, look who it is.'

Fenton turned, looked. A broad, sun-creased face was grinning at him from beneath a centre-parted shock of silvering black hair. It took him a moment.

'Jesus, Bill Baxter, how's about you?'

'Mr Conville, long time no see.'

They gripped and chest-bumped.

'Haven't seen you in, what, twenty years?' Fenton took in the open-necked shirt, the rope of coloured beads, the butter-soft suede jacket. 'You still in Spain?'

'More like thirty. Nah, been based in Kingston since … whoa, must be about two thousand and one.'

'Kingston Jamaica?'

'Yep. Irie, irie man and all that, married a local girl, set up a wee gig exporting rum, very nice, and this weather I'm shifting shitloads of medical marijuana. Wild, isn't it? All the sneaking about we had to do back then and it's all going legal. Kind of takes the fun out of it.'

'Not sure about that.' Fenton was recalling a paranoia-stricken hour behind a tree 'back then', hiding from what turned out to be a traffic warden.

'And yourself? Someone told me you died about five years ago.'

'Really?' Fenton made a show of checking his heart. 'I have no memory of it. Doing good. Still with Carolyn, kids nearly grown up. Still in business. Looking at a new venture at the moment, actually – thinking of getting into the vaping game.'

Baxter laughed. 'Fair play to you. Selling people mist – that's capitalism at its best. And tell me, what about the brother?'

'Artie? He's in Edinburgh. Quit the civil service and went back to college. Teaches history of art now.'

'Is he still at that poetry crack?'

Fenton sniggered. 'Yeah, he's even published a couple of books.'

'What's all that about?'

'Fuck knows.'

Baxter glanced around at the street, an odd smile on his face. 'God, it's weird being back here in this clean and modest little town. It's like fricken Nutwood. Here, do you remember when that,' he gestured with his thumb, 'was Ma Gilpin's place?'

Fenton did. The Tiptop Sweet Shop. He and his cohort had shoplifted its stock relentlessly on the way home from school every day for years until Ma Gilpin, a kindly frizzle-haired widow made up with old-style powder and rouge like a Russian doll, finally barred them.

'Jeez, I don't know about your crew,' said Baxter, 'but we robbed that place blind. It was terrible. Flying saucers, drumsticks, white mice. Blobs, remember them? No wonder she went bust.'

'Did she? I thought she went to live with her daughter in Killyleagh.'

'No, come on, that's like telling the kids the dog's gone to live on a farm. Listen, what about the nights up in the Glen? That fricken Special Brew. Remember Big Louie falling out of the tree? And Julie what's-her-face thinking he was dead and wetting her knickers?'

Fenton reviewed a flicker-lit montage of hormonal primates capering about in a jungle clearing high on hooch and herbs.

'Those were some wild times,' Baxter continued fondly. 'Speaking of which, I think I saw Laura Hayes earlier. Back from England.'

'Who?'

'You know, went out with Spud Murphy for a while. Coupla years below us. I thought you had a thing with her too. No? Yeah, I'm sure you did. I remember. Anyway, Fent, I'd better beat on here – flight to Amsterdam at five. Good seeing you. Next time we'll grab a jar. Hey,' he reached into his pocket and pressed a paper-rolled cylinder into Fenton's hand, 'wee treat for you.'

'Right you are, Bill. Muchas gracias.'

Fenton walked on, trying and failing to put a face to the name Baxter had mentioned. His youth had been a highly populated place, especially the teen years, with many over-lapping and intersecting groups, and much outdoor drink-ing, and then discos, house parties and girls. There were lots of girls, and Fenton had, somewhat implausibly, given his average looks and having been, by his own admission, a bit of a dick, had more than his fair share. When he looked back sometimes, it was on a fever dream of tremblings and fumblings, collisions and water slides, ecstasies and heart-breaks ... and he had a sensation of terrible loss.

He had reached the police station, shut down, deserted for several years owing to a shortage of terrorism, its win-dows blind behind their reinforced grilles. He turned left and at the end of the street entered the grounds of the old church, whose soft, dark stonework seemed to absorb both light and sound. As he walked, a mild breeze chivvied the fallen petals of cherry blossom around his shoes.

He was thinking, with a prickle of envy, about Baxter's exotic life – a pirate's life: island heat, the trade winds, rum and easy living. Apart from six months in Porto Banus when he was twenty, in failed pursuit of Spanish gold, Fenton had spent his life within a few square miles of the house he had grown up in. He had worked his arse off, raised three kids (or at least bankrolled them) and given years to the Lions Club and its good deeds. He was more or less a pillar of the community. And yet the 'what ifs' kept coming.

The church graveyard was crowded with headstones, higgledy-piggledy, at all angles, some of them barely readable. He picked his way among them: the Armstrongs, Bells, Croziers, Elliotts, Nixons (the Riding Clans, hell for leather from the Scottish Borders – *to Ulster or be hanged*) the Adairs, Blacks, Campbells, Flemings, Hamiltons, Johnstons, Pattersons, Wilsons, Whites. His grandfather, Thomas Henry Conville, who had survived the nightmare of Ypres, was here, and on the same mottled stone his grandmother, Emmeline Violet; beside them, with a marker of jade-green granite, their eldest son, Tobias, barstool legend, inventor of the riot-fomenting Lawnmower cocktail (Drambuie, whiskey, vodka, peppermint schnapps, soda water, ice), dead at fifty-three. Who would be next? Fenton wondered, and he tried not to picture his own name, etched and final.

Still brooding as he approached the car park, his attention was snagged by a trio of hipsters standing outside the tattoo parlour. Precision barnets high and slicked, curly beards of breathtaking volume and lustre, all three were engaged, between sentences, in emitting huge billowing clouds of vapour. Like three sons of Poseidon sending Odysseus a favourable wind. Each gripped in a muscular, ink-scrolled hand a vaping device the size of a mortar shell. Fenton stared in open admiration at the plaid and paisley, the cardigans, the braces, the vintage leather. Were they from the past or the future?

He wasn't sure. But he knew that here, with their tattoos, their single-estate micro-roast coffee, their craft beers, their steam-punk accessories, was his new demographic. His customers.

5

'Andrea, *for God's sake.*'

Carolyn Conville pulled the door to her daughter's bedroom shut and took a deep breath, waiting for a sensation like falling to pass. Shaking her head, she moved on along the landing. How was it possible for one person to make so much mess? How could anyone live like that? The sheer volume of detritus, the drumlins of abandoned clothing, ripped packaging and food wrappers, the biohazard crockery collection. There were things moving in there. The carpet no longer visible, how did the child even cross the room – bodysurf? Carolyn reckoned she'd seen tidier landfill sites. The boys, she reflected, were never that bad. Sanctions would have to be imposed.

She entered the master bedroom, where broad planes of cream and mint were awash with afternoon light, and padded across the deep-wool carpet, tugging off her fleece. If only Andrea would allow Roxana in there to blitz once in a while. Or at the very least turn the place over with a pitchfork. But they'd had that battle, and lost. Teenagers seemed to have so many more rights these days, or more of a sense of them anyway. More politicized. *You have no right. You can't do that. You can't tell me.* In her day Carolyn wouldn't have dreamed of going up against her parents.

In the en suite, she stripped off her yoga togs and stepped under the shower's hot monsoon. It had been a tough session, and she was still feeling the buzz. Her friend Ciara had badgered her into joining the class a few months back when her work, as a part-time legal secretary, had hit a stressful patch. The yoga helped. She wondered whether she should push Fenton into giving it a go – he'd been distinctly uptight lately – but then she pictured him in a leotard, trying to wrap his Yeti-like foot around his ear, and shuddered.

At the dressing table in front of the bay window, moisturizing, she watched a pair of white sails tacking and gybing in mid-lough and listened to the lack of noise in the house. Odd to think: another year and it could be just the two of them, her and Fenton, staring at each other across the breakfast bar. *Pass the muesli, please.* In all likelihood Conor would stay in London – that's where the big money was – Jamie would be embarked on his degree in Glasgow, and Andrea, well, who knew where the hell she would be, but she'd made it clear it would be as far away as possible from her parents. It was quite hurtful, really. Carolyn felt a tingle in her eyes and blinked it away. On the one hand, they would be freer to head off at the drop of a hat, city breaks and what have you, a fresh inrush of time; on the other ...

She stood up, hugging the bathrobe around herself, the ends of her still-damp hair chilly on her neck. She could feel the after-ache of the exercise beneath her Sauvignon belly – that final Reclining Pigeon had been a bitch – but there was pleasure in it too. She remembered the last time she had been really fit: senior school, captain of the hockey team, a blur of weightless limbs and supercharged skin, the ghost unencumbered by the machine. It had stood to her. Three kids down now, a small lump excised and one prolonged bout of postnatal blues. All in all, not too bad.

Her phone dinged. It was Stewart from chambers: Monday's session had been pushed back to the afternoon. That was good – those early starts were a pain. She keyed in a thumbs-up and an X, then deleted the X. Since they'd pulled down the big case – and it *was* big, the legal highlight of the year – the workload had become a bit ridiculous for all of them, but the bulk of the research side of things had fallen to her, and it was painstaking and time-consuming, and it had to be right, no fuck-ups. The stakes were too high. It was pressurized, but she was enjoying it. She liked being in court too, mostly, though it could be tedious, but when there were fireworks, it was a real rush. Some of the photographic evidence, on the other hand, that was hard going. That a body … someone's body … Most of the time she managed to look away.

She picked up her watch from the bedside locker. Downstairs, the courtyard door banged, and she heard the faint clank of car keys in the bowl on the hallway table. It occurred to her that she and Fenton had the house to themselves and that if he'd had pints with his lunch he might try it on. She'd have to shut that down sharpish. All nice and clean. Save it for his birthday. She propped a pillow up longwise and lay down with her back against it, crossing one ankle over the other.

Her mind went back to other Saturday afternoons in the past, when the children were young and somehow, once in a while, play dates and sporting events came into fortuitous alignment, leaving the house suddenly and erotically empty, a box of light and opportunity. There had been urgency then, like in the early days when they'd seemed to be almost constantly just an eye-beam or caress away from sexual ignition. Two healthy animals without a care. Honest to God, she thought, they didn't know they were born.

Where on earth had the years gone? There was a time, in her teens, when *thirty* seemed old, and now her husband was about to turn fifty. *Fifty!* She leaned her head forward and adjusted her towel-turban. She had been with him for most of her adult life. Only two previous boyfriends (three if you counted Kyle Scully, but that was at primary school). Fenton, on the other hand, she happened to know, had been extremely active on that front, the dirty scut, something she had once struggled not to resent. Sometimes she wondered if maybe she'd met him too soon, married a bit young, but she tried to avoid thinking along those lines. Things were what they were. *If your granny hadda had balls, she woulda been your granda*, as her father would say. Besides, starting early meant the children were nearly out of her hair (poor old Jenny Curran would be in her sixties before she got hers away) and she was still in pretty good shape, still time enough before she had to think about *that*. Ciara's friend Orla said it wasn't too bad, said she actually found it quite liberating to be free of the whole fertility thing, like a weight had been lifted. Big shrug. Pass it along the human chain. Pour me a drink. *Me-time now.* The sweats, though, the insomnia and mood swings and what have you – that was another matter.

Carolyn felt a twinge of hunger and began to think about dinner. She wasn't sure she could be bothered cooking. If Andrea was going out, maybe they'd just phone for a Chinese – yes, the baked chilli prawns – settle in and watch a film. Something with Ryan Gosling would be nice. There was music drifting up through the house: Pink Floyd's *Dark Side of the Moon* on the hi-fi. She slipped her hand inside her robe and stroked her warm clean belly. She was feeling pleasantly woozy. The window was open and she could hear the waves and smell salt on the breeze. The seasons were shifting. Summer was coming. On the ceiling near the window an arabesque of reflected sunshine flickered and fluttered like a living organism.

6

'We all have our off-days, don't be beatin' yourself up,' Cecil McCracken consoled from behind his menu. From behind his, Fenton grunted. Despite his father's best efforts, and much to their mutual disappointment, given the quasi-Masonic network it could unlock, Fenton wasn't much of a golfer. It had taken a long time, and a great deal of outlay on lessons, green fees, titanium wedges and fetishistic clothing for this conclusion to be reached. Briefly put, he was incapable of grasping, or even recognizing, the Zen moment at the centre of the moving parts – address, pivot, swing, trajectory and all the rest – that was crucial to the behaviour of the ball.

Except once. On a morning in early June in the year 2003, after a long night of fine claret, courtesy of a local tech-millionaire, and thinking of nothing much beyond lunch, Fenton had had a sudden mystical flare of *being-in-the-world* and had swung into and through the ball with such perfect certainty that he had hit a hole-in-one. It was off the seventh tee, the shortest on the course, but had nevertheless earned him a place among the silver cups in the clubhouse and engendered the impression among friends and family (including his father-in-law) that he had talent.

Unfortunately it had been all downhill from there. To the point that he had more or less given up the game. Until today, when he had risen early and donned a scarlet jumper and yellow-checked trousers and, heaving his cobwebbed golf bag into the back of the car, driven to Cecil's club for their first-ever round. Because on the links was where the deals were done.

However, Fenton wasn't sure what was happening with the deal. He certainly felt he had put his case as well as he could in between hooking, slicing and swearing his way to a twenty-seven-over-par (on the last green, a small but vocal crowd had formed to watch him take five goes at a three-foot putt) but it was hard to tell with the old boy.

'Next time we'll play the full eighteen, give you time to get into your stride,' Cecil said, setting down his menu. 'I'm ready to order. Where's that wee lad?'

Fenton continued to study the bill of fare, which seemed not to have been updated since 1972: prawn cocktail, steak Diane, chicken Kiev, *Russian salad?* and surely ... yes, there it was, Black Forest gâteau. No melon balls, though. The clubhouse restaurant was, like everything else in the clubhouse, vast and baronial, swagged, ornate, full of giant mahogany furniture – and freezing cold. A far corner of the room had been knocked through to allow for a two-way bar, on the other side of which Fenton could see several huge, ancient captains of industry, in tweed, settling themselves and calling loudly, and with the assured inflections of their class, for kümmel and gin-and-bitters.

The waiter appeared from a distant alcove and began to make his way towards the table. This allowed time for some chat about the weirdness of the weather. (As they'd teed off a light drizzle had begun to fall, the sun making rainbows of it; on the third fairway the sky was black as night and they got a right soaking; on the fifth green they'd been almost blinded by hailstones; and by the last hole it was like a mid-summer's day.)

During this exchange Fenton was once again struck by how *clean* his father-in-law looked, always looked, his chin shaved so close it was as though puberty had never happened, his pewter-sheened hair cropped above the ears and combed back hard, like some Riviera playboy in the *Picture Post*. He had switched his immaculate golfing costume for a well-cut houndstooth blazer, a pearlescent shirt with matching tie and pocket square, crisp black slacks and the kind of hand-made shoes it takes half a century to break in. He looked every inch the gent. At least, until he opened his mouth. As soon as Cecil McCracken spoke, you could hear the history, see the two-up two-down in the drenched terrace, the chimney smoke, the Lowry-esque men in the teeming shipyard, the patched-up clothes, the rickety-legged boy darting along back alleys, becoming watchful, hardening, turning resolute.

Yes, Cecil was one of those old-school self-made men. Even physically (he wasn't a large man – Fenton had a good four inches on him) there was something about the way he occupied his own space that gave the *impression* he was self-made – that is, that he had actually *made himself*. A tight wee man. And like all self-made men of that vintage, or probably of any vintage, he believed this gave him licence to tell the truth, or his version of it anyway.

At their very first meeting, a clammy, swivel-eyed sit-down at the McCracken homestead, Cecil had taken Fenton aside to deliver a harsh judgment on his (Fenton's) trousers. Laying down a marker. It's a cliché about fathers and their daughters but a cliché for a reason, and Fenton always had the idea that Cecil didn't think he was good enough for *his* Carolyn. (What had he been hoping for? A duke? A sultan?) Not *right* for her, anyhow, and, furthermore, probably suspected Fenton had had it easy, hoisted up the ladder by his well-off parents. Not self-made. Christ, he was like that guy out of – what was it? *There Will Be Blood*.

The waiter, a haunted bachelor in the twilight of his career, took their food order and returned some minutes later with drinks, an eighteen-year-old Glenmorangie and diet cola for Cecil, and a glass of dusty Cabernet for Fenton. They raised and clinked.

'Cheers, Big Ears.'

'Your very good health, Cecil.'

The wine, while not completely out of puff, had evidently been breathing for quite some time, days rather than hours, but a few gulps delivered the help Fenton needed to be alone with his father-in-law who, frankly, scared the shit out of him.

'Decent spot.'

Cecil gave the room a quick scan. 'It's not bad. Apart from' – he swerved his chin in the direction of the bar – 'all the fucken snobs. Cream of Ulster. Rich and thick.'

Fenton glanced around but the nearest diners were a good ten feet out of earshot. It was best not to let his father-in-law get started on the inequities of the class system.

'I only come for the golf – best course in the country,' Cecil continued. 'And the chicken and chips. Solid grub.' He poked at the ice cubes in his glass. 'So, is my daughter still up to her neck in murder?'

The firm Carolyn worked for was mired in a probe into police collusion with paramilitaries: a triple execution from the mid-eighties. This had necessitated her going temporarily full-time.

'Yes, she's been meaning to give you a ring, but, to be honest, when she gets home these nights she's knackered. It's brutal.'

'Waste of fucken time those tribunals,' said Cecil, wiping his mouth. 'Free money for the lawyers and no one any the wiser at the end of it. Everyone knew what the peelers were up to, course we did, paid enough of them off myself in those days. Bad business that, though.' He added the rest of the cola. 'One of those wee lads used to run messages for me, up the Grosvenor, nice fella, Everton supporter. I think he was a bit touched in the head but there was no harm in him. Had a twitch in one eye and his head jerked like' – Cecil demonstrated – 'like he was winkin' at you all the time. I heard that place when they found them was like a butcher's shop ... Ah, Jackie, good man, same again when you get a minute.' The waiter, in passing, gave a weary waggle of his head and adjusted his course towards the bar. 'Blood all up the walls, blood every-fucken-where.' Cecil gazed out of the window at the silken fairways drifting down to the sea. 'They were some dark days back then, by fuck.'

'They certainly were,' Fenton agreed. 'Let's just hope they stay behind us.'

Sipping, in reflective silence, both came to the end of their drinks. A mixed foursome arrived in high spirits and made a noisy show of choosing the best table. Fenton recognized them as being chief among the hecklers at his performance on the final green and wondered whether he should report them to the club secretary. The room was filling up.

'Don't get me wrong,' said Cecil, still looking at the view. 'Somethin' had to be done. Them boys was frightenin' the horses. I can understand it, on both sides, but it was never for me, all that sectarian crack. My da, mind you, was big into the Lodge but that was mainly to get away from my ma. No, for me it's all about the man. You stand up straight, you pay your bills, you square your debts. You do right by me, I'll do right by you. Honour, Fenton, it's a big word; it's an important word. I don't care if you're a Hun or a Taig or whatever as long as you pay your dues. Know what I mean?'

Fenton nodded and then, with relief, sat up as his tournedos Rossini and Cecil's chicken and chips trundled into view. Sometimes, listening to his father-in-law, he found himself almost unable to prevent his face scrunching into the kind of expression people make when anticipating a loud bang. Fresh drinks arrived.

'What have you there?'

'This? It's steak on top of a kind of a crouton, toast actually, and … well, it's supposed to be foie gras but this is pâté, Tesco's Finest, I'd say. But it's tasty enough.'

'Very fancy.' Cecil glared accusingly at Fenton's plate. 'Don't eat much red meat this weather. Doc says I have to watch myself, cholesterol, all that oul' bollocks. Has me on tablets. Honest to God, they're never done with this stuff. Never even heard of cholesterol in my day and now everyone's got it? It's a fucken racket.'

'Completely agree with you.'

Cecil dipped his head and went to work, fast and methodical. The old scrapper could put the grub behind him. 'What about yourself – how's your own health?' he enquired through a mouthful of chips.

Fenton wondered briefly whether to play the testicle card. 'Not too bad, thanks. Feeling a lot better since I gave up the fags.'

'Mug's game. Killed my da, as you know, hoikin' up blood all over his pyjamas at the end. Though there's a chance it could have been the boilers down the shipyard. Asbestos. Lot of them boys got sick.' Cecil was regarding him with vaguely narrowed eyes, as though crunching the odds on an ageing racehorse. 'You know, you could maybe do to sit back from the table for a while.'

'Beg your pardon?'

Cecil pointed his fork at Fenton's midriff. 'You're gettin' a bit ... you're lookin' a bit porky on it.'

'Oh. Yeah, that's since I stopped smoking. Put on a couple of pounds.'

'A couple? Think maybe we'll give the desserts a miss.'

Abandoning the remainder of his scalloped potato, Fenton began to wonder if Cecil had actually been listening out there on the course, in between his own birdies and eagles and Fenton's triple and quadruple bogies. He took a breath.

'Here's the thing, Cecil. I don't know if you've thought about what I —'

'You're not a bettin' man, Fenton, are you?' Cecil popped the last chip between his teeth and set down his cutlery.

'Um, not really, no. Used to do the Grand National for a bit of fun, you know, when the kids were young.'

'It's a mug's game, gamblin'.'

'It's been the ruin of many a young man.'

'It has, Fenton. And not just young, and not just men, all sorts, especially since all this online malarkey, people losing their houses, their livelihoods, at the touch of a button on their phone. It's fucken mad.'

'Don't you have online operations?'

'Course. I'm not daft. Doubled our profits in three years. I'm just sayin', there's no such thing as a sure thing, people take risks, there are consequences. It's a mug's game.'

'The house always wins?'

Cecil conceded a pained grin and then said, 'This "venture" you're talkin' about – I'll not come in with you. I've no fucken idea what that vapin' game's about. We'll make it a straight loan, fifty grand for six months at five per cent – would usually be a lot more but you're gettin' a discount. And you deal with front office, not with me; I don't involve myself in that any more. Victor takes care of things now – you know Victor?'

'No.'

'You don't know Victor?'

'Never met him.'

'I'll get him to call you. And Fenton?'

'Yes?'

'Remember – as they say in the pictures: this is *strictly business*.'

'I appreciate it, Cecil. And listen, there's no need for Carolyn to know about this. She has enough on her plate.'

'Say no more … You know what,' he said, pausing to frown at Fenton's belly. 'I'm think I'm goin' to have the Black Forest gâteau.'

∾

Outside on the terrace, below the clubhouse's glowering Gothic ramparts, Fenton watched his father-in-law cross the car park to his starship-sized silver car. It was not overly pronounced, but Cecil's walk retained a flavour of the street, a kind of gingerly swagger, legs slightly bowed as if to offset the discomfort of damp underpants. Fenton waved as the saloon powered towards the long driveway but perceived no response from behind the tinted glass. He turned and gazed across the fairways. The sun was shining on the resurgent earth, and there was a soft hissing in the treetops. He was breathing easier now, and the air was sweet.

7

It wasn't common to see lorries with southern Irish plates around Carnbrook Street, and it was making Victor Dougan uneasy. 'Quick as you can, lads,' he ordered. 'Move yourselves.' The vehicle in question was backed into the open mouth of a storage bay behind the old fruit market, and two tight-faced youths in grey romper suits were unloading boxes of Albanian cigarettes (KingZog Xtra Smooth) and stacking them against a wall. The lorry's driver, pale from lack of sleep, was standing to one side having a smoke.

'How was your trip?' asked Victor. 'No snags?'

The man redistributed the phlegm in his throat and shook his head. 'Do it all the time. The boys at Zeebrugge just wave us through.'

'Right.'

Victor eyed the boxes already stacked and those remaining in the lorry and ran the numbers again. Sweet enough, he thought. The fags, he had been told, were 'rough as fuck' but at the price no one on the street was going to complain. While he had little sympathy for smokers, he had to concede that the cost of smoking (legit cigs) these days was ridiculous. One of the lads down at the Welders' was a sixty-a-day man; the wife was on forty and the three kids doing twenty-plus apiece – how were they seriously expected to keep that up at full retail? Ridiculous. Not that he was in the business of charity, mind.

He turned again to the driver. 'Straight back to Dublin?'

'Ah, yeah.'

'Will you stop on the road, get some scran?'

'You wha'?'

'Somethin' t'eat, a burger or whatever.'

The man leaned aside to bark out a fusillade of shrill coughs. 'Fuck, these are rough … Ah, yeah, I'll pick sometin' up.'

'Right.'

Victor checked his watch, a chunky gold affair of questionable provenance, and motioned to his workers to speed up. He wanted to be back in the office for the 3.30 at Lingfield and he'd to call on the way and have 'a wee word' with a recalcitrant punter about his tab. His phone went and Cecil's name appeared in the window. He hesitated, then squeezed past the lorry and out onto the edge of an apron of ruptured concrete. The red granite façade of the Victorian market building opposite was cracked and crumbling, tall weeds sprouting through the curlicued iron gates. He remembered when it had been a swarming hub of noisy commerce, the rafters echoing with the banter of small trade. His mother had worked a stall there back in the day, selling nylon underwear and batteries.

'Mr McCracken, how's it goin'? ... Right, okay ... Uh-huh ... What's the term? ... And five per cent on top – very generous ... Oh, no, of course, family, I understand ... No problem, I'll handle it.'

Cecil continued, Victor nodding and half smiling. 'Well, I'll have to take your word for that, boss – sure I know nothin' about golf. What's that? Where am I now?' He edged away from the lorry, where the driver was about to start the engine. 'Just down at the dry cleaner's leavin' some things in for the missus.' The exchange grunted to a close. He put the phone back in his pocket.

Cecil didn't need to know everything that went on.

8

Fenton had a dread of industrial estates. They seemed designed to conceal everything they contained. He had been speeding up and slowing down along the same infinite road, squinting at signs, for what felt like hours. Swearing, he pulled over and rang the number.

'Liquid Skies Vaping Supplies.'

'Hi there. Is that Anthony?'

'It is.'

'Anthony, it's Fenton Conville. I'm having difficulty finding you.'

'Where are you?'

'Outside ABC Hot Extrusions, whatever that is.'

'Stay where you are.' Fenton listened to a series of borborygmic sound effects. 'Okay, look to your right.'

Across the road a young, shaven-headed man in a shiny lilac tracksuit and outlandishly large trainers was hailing him.

'It's confusing the way the place is laid out; a lot of people get lost. Anyway, you're here now,' said Anthony, leading Fenton between scaffolds of shelving stacked to the ceiling with multicoloured cartons and boxes.

Fenton sniffed. 'Smells like Willy Wonka's factory in here.'

Anthony guffawed. They arrived at a door between glass partitions that opened into a rudimentary office area where three or four young men, also in tracksuits, were lounging on flatpack furniture exhaling wreaths of vapour.

'My testers,' said Anthony, gesturing through the smog. 'These boys are connoisseurs. Come on in, sit yourself down.'

Fenton sat himself down on a swivel chair in front of a desk littered with tiny plastic bottles, dismantled vaping devices and many small metal objects.

'First things first,' said Anthony from behind the desk. 'Are you a vaper yourself?'

'No, never tried it. Ex-smoker, though.'

'Ah, well, it's not as good as smoking, that's for sure, but it's pretty much as addictive, which is what we want, right? A long-term client base.'

'That's what we want.'

Anthony did a quick drum roll with his fingertips on the edge of the desk. Barely half of his tall head was taken up by his face; Fenton reckoned there was room for another one above his eyebrows.

'Best thing is if I take you through the range of products, get you up to speed, you ask me questions, then we'll talk numbers, okay?'

Fenton opened the jotter he had brought with him and clicked the end of his biro. A deluge of technical information began coming his way.

'Watts or volts, it doesn't really matter. It's about the power, the heat, the amount of vapour. A lot of ex-smokers are looking to replicate the fag effect, you know, chest thump?'

'Chest thump?'

'Yes, that's what we call it, that hit you get here when you take a drag on a cigarette. Chest thump and throat feel, these are key … Try this one, this is the Prometheus Six, our bestseller.'

Fenton took hold of the device, which was much heavier than he expected and cold in his hand.

'Now push that button there and just puff and inhale.'

Fenton pushed, puffed, inhaled and jackknifed over in a fit of explosive coughing.

'Sorry, that was up a bit high. My fault.' Anthony was out from behind the desk, prising the device from Fenton's hand. He fiddled with the settings. 'You okay?'

Fenton wiped away tears. 'Holy shit. I wasn't expecting that much *thump*, to be honest. Or *throat feel*. Jesus, people do this for pleasure?'

'As I say, I had it a bit hot. Go again.'

This time, Fenton expelled a billow of creamy vapour and watched it disperse and sink through planes of dusty light. He felt a familiar tingle in his bloodstream. There was a sweetness on his tongue, a faint fruitiness. He coughed. 'That was better. Flavour?' Fenton asked.

'Lemon meringue pie. One of the desserts range: banoffee, pavlova, sticky toffee, you name it, they've done it. Girls love them.'

'Spotted dick?'

'You name it. Try this one.' He handed over another device, a chunkier affair with a stubbier mouthpiece. Fenton pushed the button and took in a lungful. Exhaling, he popped out a couple of passable smoke rings. He still had it.

'Chocolate?'

'Correct. Very popular. Now let me take you through the Deluxe Collection.'

Over the next twenty minutes Fenton puffed his way through several rainbows of flavour that included aniseed, blueberry, lingonberry, tangerine, sherbet fountain, spearmint, peppermint, peach melba, basil, vanilla custard, pineapple, strawberries and cream, cucumber, cannabis, cherry, bubblegum, butterscotch, marshmallow and finally tobacco, which, weirdly, was the least convincing.

While Fenton sampled, Anthony paced around delivering a lecture about coil variance, sub-ohm vaping and the esoteric art of 'cloud-chasing', of which Fenton took in very little owing to the increasing hum of blood pressure in his ears.

'Anthony, I feel a bit dizzy. Is that normal?'

'What? Oh yeah, totally. Takes a bit of getting used to, especially if you've been off nicotine for a while. Those juices there that you're trying are the highest strength; they would be for guys coming down off a forty-a-day habit. Most people would vape the mildest content, you know, just enough to keep the craving at bay.'

Fenton didn't think he could stand up. There was a film of slippery sweat on his upper lip, and he was experiencing a kind of vertigo in his solar plexus. He heard himself croaking for water.

Anthony tossed him a bottle of Ballygowan. 'Yes, it can be a bit dehydrating. Now, since you're a start-up, I would recommend you stock a wide range, but concentrate on the heavier rigs; you can buy the pens at any filling station. And you'll need a load of coils – the chronics can burn through them at a right rate of knots. As for the flavour profiles, that's your call.'

Anthony was tapping on a keyboard. 'I'm going to give you a good price – new customer and all that – and again, the mark-up's your business but you should be aiming to at least quadruple your money. Where's the shop?'

Fenton told him.

'Oh ho, Richville. What am I talking about, that's six times your money. I'll put you down for twenty grand's worth.'

Fenton's head was swimming. 'Anthony, as a matter of interest, what's the health angle on this? They seem to be getting pretty uptight about it in the States.'

Anthony waved a dismissive hand. 'Perfectly harmless. That's just pressure from Big Tobacco. They're shit-scared about the hit on their revenue.'

'You reckon?'

'Probably. I've sent you my account details. Check you're happy with the numbers and if you get a bank draft to me tomorrow I'll ship the stuff pronto. Hey, you all right?'

Fenton staggered to his car and sat with the window down waiting to stop feeling like he had chain-smoked a whole carton of Capstan Full Strength. Calculations were swarming in his head. He had already that morning signed a six-month lease on the premises at five hundred a week. If he sextupled his outlay on the vape stuff that would be a hundred-and-twenty K minus the rent, take away the capital expenditure, equalled eighty-eight, then fifty back to Cecil, plus his vig, meaning a clear thirty-five-and-a-half profit. Roll it back into another six months' stock, bring a couple more shops on line, and ... boom shanka! He craned to check his waxy, ochre-eyed reflection in the rear-view mirror, then opened the door, leaned over and boked his ring up.

∽

On Thursday morning the rain was so heavy on the carriageway it was like driving upstream through rapids, and some motorists, in Fenton's view, were not adjusting their speed to the conditions. He, meanwhile, was scanning the stations for respite from the daily phone-in inferno.

'Are facts overrated? You tell us ...'

'Would you let *your* son or daughter marry a journalist? Give us a call.'

'Today we're asking the question: Should science be banned?'

'Your last caller, frankly, was talking mad dog shi–'

When he looked up, it was to a slur of amber and crimson coming up fast between the epileptic wipers. He stamped on the brake and the car aquaplaned beneath him, the back end slewing buxomly into the outside lane to the hearty accompaniment of at least three horns. After a sickening few seconds of dreamlike panic, in the midst of which he sensed he might be about to perform the fabled 360°, he managed to wrestle the machine back onto the path of righteousness. On Crockett Street a few minutes later, he had just about unclenched.

'Ye fucken tube.'

Parked, standing beside his vehicle and wriggling into his Barbour, Fenton took a moment to ascertain it was himself who was being addressed.

'What's that?' he called.

'Back at the lights there, you near fucken hit me.' A boxy man, surely of pensionable age but with a pompadour of heavily dyed black hair, had his door open, one quivering shoe on the asphalt. 'What were you playin' at, lookin' at your fucken phone or what? Ye near had me off the fucken road.'

'Yeah, I, uh … it was a bit slippy.'

'Slippy your hole. You weren't fucken lookin'.'

'Hey, easy, there's no call for that language.'

The tone switched to incredulous: '*What'd you say to me?*' The neck was starting to go now, bantam style, as the man gauged the traffic pressure over his shoulder. He was weighing it up.

Fenton felt a pulse of alarm: a morning fist fight, in the rain, in this neighbourhood, was not out of the question. 'I'm just saying there's no need to swear.'

Down the line, someone leaned on their horn. As calmly as he could, knowing hot eyes were still on him, Fenton zipped up his coat. A fresh honk, and another, more sustained, provoked a string of guttural curses from the man and he withdrew, slamming the door. The car, a black SUV, moved, slowed, then the window came down. 'Count yourself lucky, son. I see you again, I'm gonna knock your fucken melt in.'

Regretting his lack of an umbrella, Fenton started walking, past the auto-spares depot, the discount carpet showroom, the congregationalist church ... Union flags hung like wet dishcloths from the lamp posts; silhouetted gunmen loomed rampant the height of gable ends; Masonic symbols and Red Hands flashed from the brickwork. The old acronyms were being roused from slumber by border talk, replacing the happy interim of celebrated footballers, snooker aces, plucky frontiersmen. It was perplexing to Fenton: he should have felt secure here – this, after all, was a stronghold of his tribe, crucible of shipbuilders, defenders of empire, salt of the earth – so why did he feel so distinctly unsafe?

Partly, it was mad dogs like the one he'd just encountered. What was it with these old boys who were still up for a scrap? The arthritic street-fighters still glaring and slavering at the back of the snug? You'd think they'd be done with it by now. But no, still twitchy, still ready to rumble.

The previous year he had been prompted to sign up for self-defence classes at the leisure centre after a face-off with a septuagenarian berserker in The Stocious Stoat, a misunderstanding about whose turn it was on the Sevens & Fruits. (After feeding the machine for an hour, the gnarly pensioner had gone out for a smoke to steady himself for the impending jackpot and Fenton, failing to notice the claim-staking coin stack, had stepped up and wrecked his 'system'.) It hadn't quite come to blows, thanks to an intervention by Bob, but it had been close enough that the whole pub felt storm-heavy for some time afterwards. What had shaken Fenton was the old grizzly's absence of doubt, his conviction that whatever Fenton's capacity for violence, his was greater.

The classes attended by Fenton, and half-a-dozen strangely mute twenty-somethings, were hosted by a bullet-headed ex-paramilitary named Dermot, who appeared not to have slept in several years. It was all conducted in slow-motion, which made Fenton sceptical: the key element in any bar brawl he had ever been around was the astonishing speed at which things started, and intensified. If fights were like the ones in *Crouching Tiger, Hidden Dragon*, there wouldn't be a problem. He left after two sessions.

Sunbirds Tanning Salon was located in a red-brick block above a medical and geriatric supplies outlet. Despite himself, Fenton could never resist an appalled gawk in the window at the prostheses and surgical stockings, the padded lavatory seats, the beiges and creams, the flesh tones.

Today, long-handled toe washers and bedwetting alarms were on special offer. He shuddered.

Upstairs, at the Sunbirds reception desk, Pamela was on the phone. As he entered, she waved and gave him a flash of wedding-cake-white teeth. Hooking his coat on the rack, he crossed to the coffee machine, and while it wheezed and gurgled, he took a towel from a pile beside the entrance to the beds and began scrubbing his hair. Above the door only one of the six blue 'occupied' lights was lit.

'Well, that's as maybe, Mrs Harkin,' Pamela was saying, 'but I don't make the rules, they're not my rules. No. No, it's not true what she's tellin' you ... So will we see you Friday? Right you are, love.' She put down the receiver, shook her head.

'Everything under control?' Fenton asked.

'M'm? Yeah, it's just your woman – she's agitatin' to be in here all the time, and she's already the colour of a conker.' Pamela tapped on her keyboard. 'And I noticed the other day she has a mole, a new one, the size of a Galaxy Counter, on her cheek.'

'Are you sure it's *not* a Galaxy Counter?'

'It would've melted. Anyway, how's you? You haven't been in in a while. I missed you.'

Fenton's hand twitched as he was squeezing his thumb and forefinger into the tight handle of the espresso cup, spilling a gout of java. He glanced over at his manageress, who was looking back at him with an unreadable expression.

Pamela was in her mid-to-late thirties but she dressed like a teenager, in dayglo sports gear (this morning she was in tangerine velour) and maintained an experimental interest in piercings. Her hair, dazzlingly highlighted, was bunched into a complicated arrangement of pigtails. Unlike most of their clients, she was sparing with the ultraviolet and didn't use a lot of make-up on a face that was semi-cherubically plump, in the well-fed Ulster way. As an employee, she was hyper-efficient – in the three years she'd been in charge, Fenton had barely had anything to do other than file the tax returns – and their relationship was uncomplicatedly professional. Or had been.

In the run-up to the previous Christmas, he had taken Pamela, part-timer Phyllis and Elena the Lithuanian cleaner to The Arms for a meal and drinks after work. It was the least he could do. And, he told himself, he would be home in front of the telly in his slippers by nine.

They started sedately enough, with a Randy Rude-Elf apiece (the barman's proud festive concoction – four-for-three) and chugged their way through a modest bottle of Cambodian Chablis each with their turkey-ham-and-three-styles-of-potato. The ladies proved to be surprisingly lively company, and Fenton spread his knees and began to feel increasingly magnanimous. Then, after several rounds of brandies and ports amid the puds and mince pies, Elena produced from her bag an unmarked container of Balkan firewater and poured them three fingers each. That's when the trouble started. Ten minutes later (or so it seemed) it was midnight and they were gyrating as a sweaty foursome at the Riveters Club, pushing pineapples and shaking trees courtesy of Black Lace.

Readings thereafter grew erratic, but it was certainly the case that at some time around 1 a.m., swaying back through the labyrinth from the jacks, a motor-function-only Fenton had encountered a burbling, super-heated Pamela and found himself, with scant preamble, in the velvet dark of a nearby alcove engaged in what had been known in the parlance of his youth as *a hot clutch*.

Come the harsh early light of the new year, he had lurked in the back office of the salon for a whole morning girding himself to clear the air – and failed. And as time went on, the incident became more amorphous and less explicable, sinking beneath the surface to establish itself like a restless pocket of gas under a bed of shale. For the most part he was able to ignore this twist in the dynamic, but sometimes – as now – he wasn't entirely sure what was going on.

'Yeah,' he said. 'Had a few matters to attend to. Listen, I need to do a bit of book-keeping, would you mind, uh …?'

'Updating the file and sending it over to you?'

'You're a star.'

'Not a problem. Is there a coffee for me?'

'You want some?'

As he set the cup down, she reached out for it and stroked her warm fingers along the back of his hand and, without looking up, said, 'Thanks, darlin'.'

At his tight little desk, while he waited for the computer to rouse itself, Fenton stared out of the window at the social security office and tried to work out whether he was reading too much into it: surely she had always called him 'darlin'? The problem was he couldn't recall how it had been *pre-incident*. The clinch at the Riveters had been a shock to the system: a miniature electrical storm of greedy tongues and urgent handfuls, dislocated from reality – they'd been all over each other like teenage mongooses.

Once more he congratulated himself for the rational ember in his brain that had identified her insistent *Let's go back to the salon* as probably not a good idea. Still, something had changed, and it was difficult to gauge the threat. (Carolyn had made it clear early on that she would take a dim view of any infraction, and while he doubted she would go as far as to *chop his knackers off*, he was pretty sure that having to explain a Pamela-related pickle would usher in, at the very least, a medium-duration nuclear winter.)

He clicked on the file marked 'Sunbirds Q1+' and scrolled, with the watering eyes of a farmer surveying blighted crops, through the columns and rows. There was a scuff at the door and Pamela was quickly and very physically within the enclosed space, her velour-clad lower belly at his elbow, her breath in his hair. He scrolled on, waiting for her to speak. 'Mm-hm?'

'I was wonderin',' she murmured, rubbing her hand lightly on his shoulder blade, 'if we could maybe talk about a wee pay rise.'

9

On the morning of the day before his birthday, Fenton received in the post four birthday cards, only three of them humorously cruel about his acceleration towards inevitable darkness. His brother's contribution was a stark black-and-white image of a door with a sign on it that read *Reminiscence Lounge*. The fourth one had on it a picture of a puppy pushing a little wheelbarrow containing a kitten and a mouse; inside, his Aunt Jeanie wished him a happy sixtieth.

These felicitations, however, were swiftly forgotten upon the opening of a fifth envelope. This contained a letter from Wylie & Associates, Solicitors, which was now commanding the entirety of his electrified attention. Gripping the page with both trembling hands, and struggling to see past the fizzing motes in both eyes, he tried to assimilate for a third time:

> ... *made against you by my client, that on the night of 27 August 1987, you engaged in sexual intercourse with her at a private residence in the townland of ... At that*

time, she was fifteen years of age ... stated that you were
then aged twenty ... If this were ... would constitute an
offence under Section 3 of ... statutory ... and prosecut-
able by law ...

Was it some kind of prank? He studied the envelope: good quality, local postmark, dated two days previously; the letter-heading, embossed and of a professional font, also legit; tight, fluent signature in ink – C. Wylie. The joke possibility gone, he felt a profound sick shockwave of undefined culpability rise through his body. His heart began to thump. A cold greasy sweat broke out on his forehead.

He was staring hard at the date. It rang no bell, not even a distant tinkle. But then ... thirty years ago? He thought: who can remember that far back? At the best of times he couldn't recall what he had been doing thirty days ago, sometimes thirty *minutes* ago. And why was there no name? If there was a name, he might be able to zone in a bit. He closed the door of his den and picked up his phone. A secretary put him through.

'Crawford, how are you? It's Fenton Conville.'

'Good morning, Fenton.'

'Crawford, I, uh, I have a letter here from yourself and, well ...'

'Yes?'

'Crawford, *what the fuck?*'

'Fenton, I think it's best if you come in and see me.'

'Do you? Really? Right. When?'

'Today. This morning. I could fit you in at,' he did the clicking thing, 'eleven?'

'Great, I'll see you then, but Crawford this is really –'

'I know, Fenton, I know, but let's try and keep a cool head. By the way, I'm also going to need a copy of your birth certificate.'

⁓

As he sat waiting for the solicitor, who had 'just nipped out', Fenton became aware of, and perplexed by, a burning sensation combined with a kind of tingling itch on his left thigh, high up. It reminded him of once on a train journey in the south of France when lighter fluid had leaked from the Zippo in his jeans pocket and sparked a riot in his jocks. But his Zippo was long consigned to the back of a drawer somewhere. So what was this? He stood up. Beyond the office door all was tranquil, just the muffled voice of a secretary talking on the phone. He unbuttoned his trousers, listened again, then tugged them down. Just below the hem of his underpants was a vivid patch of inflamed skin a few inches long and roughly the shape of Italy. He stared at it in bafflement.

'Sorry about that, I just had to' – Fenton hoisted up his bags; Wylie tossed a folder onto the desk – 'get something from the car.'

The two men faced each other in uncertain and proliferating silence. The onus was unquestionably on Fenton, but when nothing was forthcoming, Wylie offered a hesitant hand. 'Long time no see,' he said.

'Indeed,' said Fenton. 'How's tricks?'

'Please, sit yourself down. Not bad, thank you. Always plenty to be getting on with. And you?'

Fenton snorted.

'I was just thinking earlier,' the solicitor said, 'the last time you were here was that planning business. You ever hear any more from the preservation people?'

'No, they gave up, they let it go, and, uh, thanks again for your help with that. But, Crawford, what the hell is *this* about? Who is this woman?'

Wylie folded his hands in front of him on the desk and adopted a grave expression. 'Well, Fenton, it's what it says in the letter: a possible offence under Section 3 of the –'

'From *thirty* years ago?'

'I know, but you see, there's no statute of limitations in cases like this. By the way, did you remember the birth cert?' Wylie accepted the crumpled sheet, glanced at it and made a slight grimace.

'That's ridiculous,' said Fenton. '*Cases like this?* Who is it that I'm supposed to have … Who's saying this?'

'I'm afraid at this stage, Fenton, I can't divulge the client's name.'

'What? That doesn't make sense. If I don't know her name, how can I –?' He had a sudden thought. 'Is her name Hayes? Laura Hayes?'

'I can't say.'

Fenton sat back, clasping his hands on the top of his head. 'So, Crawford, let me get this straight. This *nameless* woman claims that I, that we, had sex – where did it happen?'

'At a house party.'

'At a house party back in 1987 – that's *three decades ago* – and she was fifteen and I was twenty –'

'Yes, she was underage.'

'And it's just her word against mine?'

'That's the long and short of it.'

Fenton sat forward again. The mysterious patch on his inner thigh was stinging now as well as itching and burning. 'Well, I absolutely deny it. Crawford, I have no memory of this whatsoever.'

'Not being able to remember something doesn't mean it didn't happen – in the eyes of the law.'

'But can't you just tell this, this woman that I deny it and get her to sling her hook?'

'It's not as simple as that. It seems it's more a case of arguing it out in court.'

'*Court?*' A flame shot down Fenton's leg and he bounced from the chair. 'I can't go to court, Crawford. Are you mad? Who are they going to believe? It'd be in the papers. My parents would shit a brick. The neighbours would … You know how tight it is round here – everyone knows everything about everyone. This stuff sticks. A nonce? I'd be fricken finished.'

'Fenton, please, you need to calm down. Have a seat. Do you want a glass of water?'

'No, I don't want a bloody glass of water.' He paced to the window and gazed, unseeing, at a colourless sky. His thigh felt like it was actually on fire. 'I'm sorry, Crawford. I didn't mean to be …' He sniffed. 'This is all a bit …'

'I understand completely. It's a bolt from the blue.'

Fenton resumed his seat and, leaning forward, head in hands, contemplated a small section of swirly carpet. Wylie maintained a sympathetic silence. At length Fenton said, 'Why would she do this? After such a long time?'

Wylie appeared to consider the question deeply. 'It's –' he tutted and sighed '– it's the times we live in. All that stuff with Jimmy Fixit, and the deejays, and whatsisname, the didgeridoo fella – it's opened the floodgates. *Payback*. It's all the rage.'

'Holy shit.'

'I know.'

Behind Wylie's head was a framed quartet of local scenes in watercolours – churches, a pub, a monument – and for a moment Fenton lost himself among them, a miniaturized ghost in a town within a town. 'What should we do?' he croaked. 'I can't go to court, and I sure as *fuck* can't go to prison.'

'Well, we could try throwing some cash at the problem,' said Wylie.

'But ... isn't that tantamount to blackmail?'

'Use of that term would suggest you have something to hide.'

Fenton felt another flash of heat down below, this time on the right. He was picturing himself in the dock, his white knuckles, his sweat-patched shirt, the rows of stony faces. Why did he already feel so guilty? 'In theory – just in theory – how much do you think it would cost me? What kind of money would it take? Ten grand?'

Wylie regarded him with what might have been sadness in his eyes. 'To be honest, I really don't know,' he said. 'That's also supposing cash would do the trick. It may be she really is set on having her day in court. But I could float it with her as a possibility. No harm.'

'Bollocks.'

'Fenton?'

'This is ridiculous. It's fricken blackmail.'

Wylie picked up his pen and scribbled some notes on a pad, then rose and held out his hand. 'Leave it with me. And look, don't be worrying. I'm sure this can all be handled. Come on, I'll walk you out.'

On the way down through the building, the two of them, Fenton without enthusiasm, exchanged snippets of news about old faces: the divorced, the ill, the dead.

'Happy birthday, by the way, for tomorrow,' Wylie said at the door, but he received no reply.

10

At the open fridge, Fenton peered in at shelves stacked with glistening beers and foil-topped sparklers, then surveyed with satisfaction the forests of bottles (there were more in boxes in the garage) arrayed around the work surfaces. That should hold the bastards, he thought. Carolyn was on the phone: 'We start pouring at seven,' she informed some-one. At the range he paused to sniff at the cauldrons of chilli con carne (nearly ten pounds of Aberdeen Angus) heaving and phutting over a low flame. Bowls and boats of crisps, crudités and dips crowded every inch of the kitchen island. He reached out and stuck a finger in the guacamole.

Against the odds (and they were mounting), he was bearing up. He was wearing his favourite shirt, pale mauve with tiny navy flowers and a decorative frill on either side of the buttons that he felt added continental panache, and his second-favourite pair of slacks, fatigued jeans with five per cent Lycra for ease of movement. His favourite trousers – taupe moleskin chinos from M&S – he'd had to discard after the lotion he'd bought at the chemist and applied liberally to his rapidly spreading rash had soaked through – not disastrously, but enough to suggest unsavoury possibilities.

The rash was worrying. A search of Google Images had taken him almost directly to the skin equivalent of *The Island of Doctor Moreau* and elicited an involuntary shout of alarm. There was also something afoot in the digestion department: groaning, gurgling, clanking – it was a haunted house down there. He had little doubt these developments were linked to the shock of Wylie's letter, which, additionally, had cost him most of a night's sleep (when he *had* slept it had been a torment of shame dreams, with one sequence involving his pursuit by a mob of villagers shouting 'Kill the bairn-worrier'). Furthermore, he was *busting* for a cigarette.

Despite all this, he had resolved to enjoy his birthday party. His Big Five-O. His Hawaii Five-O. Wylie was good. Wylie would fix it. The doorbell pealed and he heard Carolyn's greeting-people voice, laughter and then chatter ascending towards the kitchen. Bob and Una. It was seven o'clock.

∽

'So, did you hear, Fenton? The man who invented the sexual innuendo just died.'

'What?'

'Yeah, the wife's taking it very hard.'

'Oh Jesus.'

It was going to be a long night. Fenton popped a fresh premium import and took a goodly swig. They'd been joined by Carolyn's best friend Ciara and her husband

Graham, and the six of them were round the kitchen island drinking and picking at the snacks.

'Bob, that's terrible,' said Una. 'But, you know, if *you* died, I'd take it very hard too.'

'Of course you would, love,' said Bob. 'Here, has anyone seen Marty McCann recently? I saw him this morning coming out of Costcutter and that man does not look like he's long for this world.'

'Why, what's the matter with him?' Ciara asked.

'What do you think? The big C. The big C-shark. He thought he'd given it the slip last year, but it's come back for him.'

'What a shame, the poor man ... Darling, top us up would you?' said Carolyn.

Fenton did the needful, killing the second bottle of Prosecco and the first red in the process. He was pleased to see that everyone seemed to have made an effort: cleavage on display from both Ciara and Una (*mustn't look at it directly*) and combed hair on both the lads. If he was not mistaken, Graham had also oiled his vaguely Lenin-esque beard, and Bob had the pink flush suggestive of a hot bath.

'I love your shirt, Fenton,' said Una. 'Very swah-vay.'

'Like it? Got it in Palma last summer.'

Bob and Graham exchanged glances. 'How *is* the gigolo business these days?' said Graham.

'Ask your mother.'

'Speaking of gigolos,' said Ciara, 'is Dawson coming tonight?'

'I believe so. And he's bringing a new lady-friend.'

'*Another* one? God, you have to admire his stamina. How old would he be now? Seventy?'

'Oh, easily. Yes, he keeps active. At the yacht club they call him The Viagra Kid.'

The chimes sounded again, and Fenton admitted John and Linda Hetherington, his neighbours from the cross-avenue, and his old schoolmate Liam and his wife Eileen, who had arrived at the same time. Liam presented him with a three-pack of Tranquillity Briefs (Extra Absorbent).

'Does everybody know everybody?' said Carolyn. 'By the way, these are our neighbours John and Linda. They work for the BBC.'

Several of the assembly politely put on their impressed faces. 'Oh, really? How exciting. Would we have seen you in anything on the telly?' Una wanted to know.

'No, not at all, we're behind the scenes,' Linda explained, accepting a chiming tumbler. 'Production side of things.'

'Radio,' said John. 'Documentaries. Very boring. Cheers, everyone. And Fenton, many happy returns to you.'

Glasses were raised to the birthday boy who, wrong-footed by suddenly being the centre of attention, for some reason bowed from the waist and clicked his heels together. To cover in part for this weirdness, he held his drink high and shouted 'Skol!' He needed to get his act together. He switched to wine.

The party swelled – the Bradfords, the McCaffreys, Newton and Bridget, and Fenton's parents with Pixie and Basil Dixon in rapid succession. It being a mildly balmy evening, with a rumour of thunder, the doors to the balcony were opened and the smokers, the last of an endangered species, scuttled out to take the air and conspire. Dawson arrived with his latest conquest, an intense, sinewy woman in her mid-forties, glittering with chunky chrome jewellery.

'Fenton, I want you to meet Rita. She works at the health-food shop.'

'Really?' Fenton held out a hand to Rita, whose complexion signalled a major deficiency in most, if not all, the essential vitamin groups.

'Yes, she's got me on this macrobionic diet, strictly vegan. I never felt better. You should try it, Fenton, really clears the pipes.'

'Wouldn't be in your target group, I'm afraid, Rita. Very much a meat-and-two-veg man.'

'Are you, Fenton? Are you sure?' Her eyes were electric blue, the lids painted turquoise. He noticed that she was failing to ungrip his hand. 'It's never too late to change. And I could get you a wee discount.'

'You'd definitely want the discount,' said Dawson. 'Stuff's not cheap. Not cheap at all but it's worth it. You're still young, Fenton, but I'm heading for sixty – have to start thinking about my health.'

Fenton looked at Dawson, at his huge smooth face, handsome as an old stone fireplace, features unmistakably moulded by generations of ascendancy privilege. His hair, normally the colour of cigar ash, had a new, distinctly purplish tinge to it. Dawson stared back at him defiantly.

'Well, you're not in bad shape for sixty,' said Fenton, disentangling his hand. 'What do you think, Rita?'

'My Dawson? Oh, he has the body of a thirty-year-old.'

'And he keeps it under the bed,' chirped Bob as he juked past.

∽

John Hetherington was in the kitchen examining the wine bottles. 'Carolyn tells me you're diversifying? E-cigarettes, is it?' He selected a bottle and poured a glass.

'That's correct,' Fenton replied. 'But not just e-cigs – the whole range of E-N-D-S devices and accessories. I think there's a big future in it.'

'Sorry, E-N-D-S?'

'Electronic Nicotine Delivery System.'

'Ah, is that what they're called? I must bone up on this vaping lark – there might be a programme in it. Maybe we could interview you.' He swirled the wine, wafted it under his nose and tipped it back.

'So,' said Fenton, 'how are things at the Beeb?'

The producer contemplated the ceiling and did a whistling exhale. 'Not what they used to be, Fenton, I'm afraid. To quote an ex-colleague, it's all *dog-eat-dog, back-stab and leap-frog* these days. The digital generation is snapping at our arses. And bloody *measurability*. Quantity not quality. And endless historical inquiries, you know – clerical abuse, collusion tribunals and all the rest. Bores me so much I almost miss the bad old days.' He stifled a belch with a genteel finger and thumb. 'Though, God forgive me, I probably shouldn't speak too soon.'

'How so?'

'Well, you know.'

'What? Oh, you mean …?'

Hetherington hesitated, flushing slightly. 'Sorry, Fenton, you did tell me you voted Remain, didn't you?'

'I did. Better for business.'

'Phew. Yes, that almighty goat-fuck last year and the consequences thereof. Some of our, em, *stauncher* brethren are becoming distinctly unsettled by the true implications of what, let's face it, most of them voted for. It seems they didn't spot the snake at the bottom of the sack, and now they fear for their beloved *wee province*.'

'You don't think …?'

'Oh, no, not like before, and no burning buses any time soon, but –'

Just then, Dawson appeared in the doorway in mid-conversation with someone evidently trying to escape along the corridor. 'The first time I cooked it, I got a terrible dose,' he was telling them. 'Doing the Aztec Two-Step the whole night. It was like fireworks.' He entered, gave a brisk salute and loomed over the snack zone where he located a platter of cocktail sausages and, glancing quickly over his shoulder, began pushing them into his face, two and three at a time.

The producer un-transfixed his gaze and recharged his glass. 'The thing is, I actually do believe we're in the end-game. The sands are shifting. You talk to young people these days, they're not bound by the old identities any longer or by the way their parents voted. They're tired of all that.'

'Even in the heartlands?'

'Fair point. I guess I *am* talking about the middle classes. But that's part of the problem, isn't it? The more opinion atomizes among the bourgeoisie, the more the true believers feel themselves besieged. Somewhere, Fenton, in a tiny church on a desolate headland, a lost tribe is singing "Abide with Me".'

Fenton nodded to show that he got both the reference and the meaning – which he didn't – and was about to change the subject to something a little lighter when he was called away by a fresh clamour for attention from beneath his jeans.

In the glass-ceilinged side room where Carolyn tutted and swore over her indoor plants, Fenton came upon his wife with Ciara, Una and Eileen lounging on the sofas having an intense discussion about yoga.

'I swear,' Ciara was saying, 'that last one she had us doing – the Dead Parrot, is it?'

'The Reclining Pigeon.'

'Yeah, that one, that was an absolute killer. I definitely felt something go internally – like something snapped.'

'An ovary?'

Fenton, on the verge of pausing for a chat, experienced a momentary twinge in his right yarble, waved and passed on through. Upstairs in the bathroom he checked on his rash in the floor-to-ceiling mirror. He was fast coming to the conclusion that another visit to Dr McKenna was unavoidable. His over-the-counter ointment appeared to be making things worse, the map of Italy having expanded into a continent that reached nearly to his knee. It wasn't much better on the other side, and it had both deepened in colour and begun to develop a surface texture not unlike velour. And it was hot! Looking up, he caught the reflection of his own eye and held it in baleful suspension. At that moment the door opened and his mother crossed the threshold, emitted a scandalized yelp and reversed. He pulled up his jeans.

'Is everything okay, Fenton?' She was on the landing, leaning against the windowsill.

'Sorry. I thought I'd locked it. I was just –'

'It's your birthday. You don't need to explain.'

'No, I mean it's just – I wasn't –'

'Son, it's your house, you can do whatever you want. Sure, you've been at that as long as I can remember.'

'Excuse me?'

'But come here, I wanted to tell you something – we have a little surprise for you later.'

'If it's about the loan, don't worry about it. I got it sorted.'

'Oh, no, it's nothing to do with that. You'll see … Can I get in there?'

Back downstairs, trying to shake off trepidation about the nature of the little surprise, he ran into Pixie Dixon, who was appraising a Shawcross nude that hung above the hall table. 'There he is,' she said, turning to greet him, 'the birthday boy.' And she slipped her arms around his waist and pulled him to her. Before he knew it, he found himself the recipient of a wet, forceful kiss on the mouth. Her breath smelled of gin and prawn cocktail crisps. She held his face in her hands and inspected it with her tiny shiny eyes.

'Wee Fenton.' She shook her head. 'I can't believe you're all grown up.'

'Pixie, I'm fifty.'

'I know. But it seems like no time ...'

He knew what was going through her mind: a day-long boozy party at his parents' house, him in his early teens, Pixie in a gauzy mini-dress amid the coats and jackets in the downstairs cloakroom – a revelatory encounter, much reviewed at Fenton's leisure, never spoken of again.

She gave him another quick kiss. 'Have you seen your mother?'

'She's in the bathroom.'

He couldn't remember where he'd left his glass. Back in the kitchen, he registered the proliferating number of empties and noticed that the limited-edition bottle of fifteen-year-old Isle of Ulaidh he had hidden at the back of the cupboard had been discovered, jemmied open and aggressively sampled. His father and Basil Dixon no doubt. Well, he consoled himself with a grim smirk, if they maintained that kind of pace they would reap the whirlwind. He knew, from hard experience, that there was nothing – *nothing* – in the realm of self-inflicted human suffering to rival a single-malt hangover. In his own case, during the course of an implausibly long day-after, he had gained significant insight into what it must be like to be simultaneously very old and very ill. At one stage he had passed a zombie-faced quarter of an hour scrolling for same-day delivery on Zimmer frames.

'Fenton, have you seen Rita?' Dawson was at his side.

'Yes, when you arrived. Fair play to you, you dirty dog.'

'No, I mean recently.'

'No, not recently.'

'Good.' With trembling liver-spotted hands, Dawson began ladling chilli into a bowl.

'You know that's meat, right?'

The neo-vegan made a low growling noise in his throat.

Fenton circulated. His guests were mixing well – regular laughter from all quarters – and absorbing his alcohol with only minimal restraint. So far he'd had to make just one intervention ('Hey! No politics. No Brexit talk at my party'), this to Graham and Newton who were pushing each other a bit far up the octave. His house looked plush, rich textures and soft lamplight everywhere, and there were good smells around: food, furniture polish, clean hair and perfume. It was all very civilized, he thought, very *adult*. He began to stop worrying, and even managed to rise above the goings-on down below his belt.

Tucked away on the armchairs in 'the nook', he discovered his father and Basil swigging his best whisky and having manly, inappropriate conversation away from their wives. His father's cast had been removed the previous day and he was wearing a knee brace beneath a pair of voluminous, slightly greasy mustard cords.

'Still need this, mind you,' he said to Basil, tapping the crutch beside his chair.

Fenton eyed the quintuple Scotch in his father's mitt. 'You have the other crutch, though, just in case. Right?'

'Oh aye, I'll not be running a marathon any time soon. Here, tell us this, Fenton, what do you think of all this "agreed Ireland" talk that's going on? Basil says there's deals being done behind closed doors. He says Brexit's going to bugger the border.'

Fenton felt a wave of weariness pass through him. 'Wouldn't surprise me. It's kind of inevitable, isn't it? Eventually all divided countries are reunited – historically speaking. Anyway, you voted for it.'

His father raised an eyebrow at Basil.

'Not without the consent of the people,' growled Basil, who was sporting an antique-dealer-style racing-green cravat. 'Not without a democratic vote on the matter.'

'Well, that's going to happen sooner rather than later by the looks of things,' Fenton said. 'And the numbers are getting pretty close.'

'They couldn't afford us,' his father said. 'It's a small economy; they haven't got the billions to spare.'

'I'm sure they could borrow the money if it came to it.' Fenton noted, with mild interest, that Basil was becoming empurpled. 'Anyway, does anyone really care any longer? I've applied for an Irish passport, Carolyn too. And probably the kids as well.'

The two older men were staring at him as though he'd just suggested a threesome.

'They're not like us!' yapped Basil. 'It's a foreign country. Different history, different traditions and … and … and the roads are a disgrace!'

'As a matter of interest, when was the last time you were down south?'

Basil muttered something about 'the seventies'.

'I think you'll find,' said Fenton, 'the roads are more than up to European standards these days. Have been for years.'

'It's a bloody theocracy – the priests have them by the balls!'

Fenton coughed. 'Again, Basil, a lot has changed.'

'They don't understand us,' his father barked. 'Most of them have never even crossed the border. They think we're all just like the English – the *bloody English*, Fenton!'

Tempted to say something really inflammatory, Fenton instead murmured, 'Listen, gents, before you start marching round the house singing "The Sash", can I get you another drink? You look like you're running low.'

Without any intention of fetching them another beverage, he headed back towards the main throng. In the corridor he ran into Carolyn and her boss, Stewart, conversing at close quarters. Carolyn, he noted, had achieved the facial glow indicative of the fourth or fifth glass of Sauvignon blanc.

'Ah, Fenton, happy birthday,' said Stewart, extending a hand. 'How lovely to see you again.'

Stewart was a super-fit six-footer with floppy hair and a pleasant smile, related in some vague but potent way to landed gentry, and on meeting him for the third time, Fenton was confirmed in thinking he might be a bit of a shit.

'Thanks. You too, Stewart. Good of you to come. Is your partner here?'

'Yes, though I seem to have lost her. Last I saw of her she was deep in conversation with that Darwin fella.'

'Dawson?'

'Dawson is it, with the big face?'

'That's him.'

There was a pause.

'I was just trying to persuade Carolyn here to go full-time permanently,' said Stewart, 'but she's playing hard to get.'

'Oh?' Fenton looked at Carolyn, who looked back at Stewart.

'Yes, she's a real asset.' Stewart reached out and gave her upper arm a quick rub. 'She could go all the way.'

'Really?' Fenton felt a need to assert himself. 'What do you think, darling? Would you like to go all the way?'

'Fenton, stop it.'

Confident he was finding his form, the birthday boy returned to the conservatory and – 'Room for a wee one?' – with much squeaking of springs and protecting of drinks, squeezed onto the swing-sofa between Ciara and Una, who were lamenting the absorption of their teenage offspring into the digital underworld.

'Sometimes I look at our guys,' Una was saying, 'when they're staring into their phones, which is pretty much all the time, and it feels like we're in some kind of sci-fi movie, you know, like they're plugged in to an alternative universe or something, receiving instructions from their alien overlords.'

'I hear you,' said Ciara. 'Same with our two. Total screen-slaves.'

'I think Andrea used to play that on the piano,' said Fenton.

'Play what?'

'Screen-slaves.'

'Are you pissed? Where *is* Andrea?'

'She's around somewhere; she has a friend sleeping over. They're probably in her room staring at their phones.'

'And Jamie – I can't believe he's in Kenya, it's *so far away*. You must miss him terribly.'

'Missing *him*? I'm missing a lot of money – trip's costing a fortune.'

'Is it a real orphanage?' said Una. 'I mean, are the wee elephants actually *orphaned*?'

'Yes,' said Fenton. 'Their parents have been killed by poachers. For their tusks.'

'Bastards. And does Jamie get to feed them and everything?'

'Yes, with big bottles of milk. I have pictures here, hold on.'

They stared into Fenton's phone.

'That's *so* cute,' said Una. 'What a lovely thing to do.'

Fenton was enjoying being sandwiched between the two women. The heat and softness of their relaxed bodies, their smell, the proximity of their breath made him feel very safe.

'I know,' he said. 'I fricken love elephants,' and – he couldn't help himself – he began to weep.

Una leaned her head on his shoulder. Ciara took his hand and squeezed it.

'Don't worry,' Una said, 'Jamie will look after them. They'll be okay.' She rubbed his leg, triggering the rash. 'Everything's going to be all right.'

He felt a rumble of thunder deep in his groyles.

～

Husky and hot, and in need of air, he stepped out onto the balcony where Liam and Bob were just recovering from a bout of hysterical laughter. Dabbing his eyes, Bob proffered a cigarette.

'Sure I gave them up. Three years ago.'

'One won't kill you.'

'Carolyn will, though, if she catches me.'

'Are you a man or are you a mouse? It's your feckin' birthday.'

Fenton faltered and fell, fired up and took a long pull, consciously enjoying both chest thump and throat feel. It was delicious. He gazed out through blue smoke across the water at the starry decks of the evening ferry, at a creamy gibbous moon tilting above the hills, and listened to the soft collapse of waves on shingle. A moment immortalized by life-threatening fumes. How could he ever have given these up?

'Here, Fent,' said Bob. 'How does your man Dawson do it?'

'You mean *literally*?'

'No, just the women. The raw numbers. Every time I see him, he's got a new one. He's about a hundred and fifty years old and he's running a harem. It's unbelievable.'

'Bear in mind not all of them are, you know ... top drawer.'

'Well, he's doing better than me,' said Liam. 'Last time I suggested sex to Eileen, she burst out crying.'

'M'm,' said Fenton, squinting. 'Probably not a good sign.'

'What about you, Bob? You getting any?'

'What, sex?' Bob wicked his dog-end down into the foliage. 'Not so much. To be honest, these days it's more like a kind of medical intervention. Never easy with young kids running around – they're like a nookie SWAT team, kicking the door in just when you're about to, you know. It's uncanny. They seem to sense it.'

'I remember well,' said Fenton. 'Requires a lot of play-date juggling.'

Liam grunted. He and Eileen had agreed not to have children. Or, at least, he had.

'Here, I watched that Arnie movie last night,' he said. '*True Lies*? Remember it? From the nineties?'

'His wife doesn't know he's a spy and then she gets caught up in it? And there's Arab terrorists?'

'That's the one. Horrible film, but tell you what – that Jamie Lee Curtis.'

'Oh yeah.'

'She's smart, she's funny and, my God, that body.'

'Oh yeah. Thighs that could strangle an orca.'

'But even the body stuff,' Liam continued. 'She's somehow kind of ironic with it.'

'Not a conventional beauty,' said Bob.

'M'm, s'pose not, but I personally find her very attractive. She could strangle my orca any time.'

'I dunno,' said Bob.

'I think she's attractive to men,' said Fenton, 'in the same way Kevin Bacon is attractive to women.'

For some reason this observation resulted in what broadcasters term 'dead air'.

Bob shook his cigarette pack and fished for his lighter. 'Oh, here, Fent, ran into Big Roy down the street earlier and guess what?' He held up a small plastic bag of white powder and waggled it. 'Fancy a wee birthday treat?'

'Come on, Bob, I gave that up too, as well you know. By the way, for your information, I read the other day that cocaine increases your chance of a heart attack within the hour by two thousand per cent. What do you think about that?'

'Fake news. Liam?'

'Fuck, yeah.'

The pair of them moved towards the lamplit interior, leaving Fenton alone on his balcony. On his birthday. An observer of this solitary figure might have concluded that here was a man struggling with an internal conflict, by the way his brow was furrowing and his lips were forming unvocalized words, by the way the fingers of his right hand clenched and unfurled. He turned on his heel and hurried after his mates.

Over the course of the next hour, he danced inappropriately with every woman in the house except his mother, drank a whole bottle of wine, smoked five cigarettes, held brief but highly compressed conversations with everyone except his parents and Basil Dixon, and managed to collate more or less all his CD collection by genre. Taking a breather at around eleven, he was summoned to the front door to find Artie and his wife Rosie embracing Carolyn, who turned to him with delighted eyes.

'Surpri-eeeze! Look who's here.'

Artie, who had, at some time in the year since Fenton last saw him, grown a quasi-professorial beard, stepped forward and gripped his brother by the shoulders. 'Hey, bro, how's being old working out for you?'

'Cheeky bastard. You're not far behind me.'

Rosie, slightly plumper but otherwise unchanged apart from a few silver hairs, hugged him. 'Sorry we're late – flight was delayed. How's your party going? You drunk yet?'

'Not quite.'

'We'll have to fix that.'

⌇

Round midnight, a group of men in the latter stages of inebriation gathered in the downstairs den to try out the complimentary vaping devices and e-juice samples Anthony had given Fenton. Almost immediately, Basil Dixon broke the Prometheus Six by pressing all the buttons at once and was insisting on taking it apart with his penknife. Graham and Bob were working their way through the dessert flavours. Unpleasantly reminded of his overdose earlier in the week, Fenton took charge of the whiskey bottle and joined his brother on the sofa, away from the fumes.

'So how are things up in Edinburgh?'

'All good. Cold. That wind down Princes Street would cut the bark off you.'

'You should be used to it by now. What is it, seven years? And what about the kids?'

'Grand. Ben's landscape gardening business is taking off, and Liz is loving her course, especially the design stuff. Where's Andrea, by the way? Haven't seen her.'

'She was around earlier. She has a friend staying over; they may have headed out.'

'Tell me, how are the folks doing? I've called them a few times over the last while, but between our mother's dodgy ear and that crap phone they have, it's all "Hello, hello, can you hear me? Is there anybody there?" It's like a fucken séance.'

Fenton glanced up the room at his father, hunched over the table with Basil, poking at the now dismantled vaping rig. 'Same as ever. Both mad as fish. And dealing with your man's busted leg was no picnic, believe me.'

'Oh, I believe you.'

'Though, I have to admit, Bogdan and Mihaela have borne the brunt of it. That poor bugger Bogdan even did half an hour on Dad's toenails and only threw up twice.'

Some kind of disagreement was occurring at the table. 'Fenton, do you have any fuse wire?' demanded Basil.

'Jesus ... NO.'

'I can't make head or tail of this thing!'

'God's sake,' said Fenton to Artie, 'the man was decades at Shorts designing fricken missile components and he can't fix a simple vaping device.'

'Well, to be fair, he is completely langered. Pass the wicksy there, would you? I haven't caught up yet.'

'You still writing the old poetry?'

'Trying to. Hoping to have another collection out next year.'

'Artie, what the fuck is that all about?'

His brother laughed. 'Very good question.'

'Seriously, does anyone even read poetry these days?'

'*It's hard to get the news from poems,*' Artie began, '*but people die daily for lack of what's in them* – or something.'

'Come on, Artie, don't be at the quoting. Not the quoting.'

Something metallic ricocheted off a glass lamp farther up the room. 'There was nothing wrong with *analogue* technology,' bellowed Basil.

With a sigh, Fenton lay back on the sofa and let his head loll. Much as he had tried to suppress the dread that had recently come to dwell in his gut, it was there, a submerged beacon, sending out constant pulses of foreboding. He needed to share, to make sense of it.

He and Artie had not been close as brothers, neither in childhood nor for most of adulthood. As teenagers they had been careful of the magnetic fields between their respective social groups, or at least Artie had; Fenton just did whatever he wanted. And this had included sustained and systematic bullying, mental and physical, of his younger brother for much of their early lives, something that, in moments admittedly both rare and fleeting, he regretted.

Artie had, for his part, it seemed to Fenton (although he didn't know how or when), managed to outrun him, to become impervious to his scorn and belittlement, and even to make Fenton feel he was the one leading the meaningless life. This had been the case for a long time, but at some point – after they had both undergone the mortality check of fatherhood, he supposed – an unspoken truce had occurred.

He leaned heavily forward. 'Listen, Artie, do you remember a girl called Laura Hayes? From way back? Went out with Spud Murphy?'

Artie massaged his new beard for a while. 'Don't think so. I remember a Norah Taylor, from Caproni's, great wee dancer, and there was a Maura Hewitt on the go at one point – your man Soupy Campbell had the hots for her – but Laura Hayes … no. Why?'

Fenton outlined, with great relief at the unburdening, his predicament.

'Holy shit, thirty years ago? That's rough.'

'Tell me about it. It's doing my head in.'

'And is it possible that this actually occurred?'

'I honestly can't remember. It was party time back then, the wild frontier, you know yourself.'

'I do. But … it's possible?'

'M'mm? Oh …' Out of nowhere, and with a distinct crawling sensation on the surface of his rash, he was picturing a smiling girl with big teeth, a gap between the two front ones; a party in a house with high ceilings. A girl called … Claire. 'Who knows.'

11

Something happened then: a bang, without apparent external cause, that Fenton concluded must have been within his own head. His eyes were open and he was lying on his back. Above him, the night sky crackled with a billion bluish stars, and for a few moments he had the sensation that he was staring down at them rather than up. When this passed, he ascertained that he was in the garden beside the summerhouse, flat out on the old green sunlounger, his hands gripping the cold metal frame on either side. He could smell creosote, and earth, and the resiny scent of conifers. Somewhere in the darkness, a nocturnal creature was making an odd whirring, clicking sound.

Fenton didn't know what had hit him. Or rather, he did: the contents of Bill Baxter's gangsta-strength roll-up. His guests having departed in the early hours, and feeling pleasantly knackered and drunk, he had ambled down into the garden for some quiet post-party communion with himself. Hauling out the sunlounger, he lay down. The sky had cleared; the night was still and warm. He remembered the joint in his shirt pocket and, with Bob's lighter, sparked it up. He recalled thinking, after a couple of draws, *Christ, that's a bit strong*, and after a couple more being unable to move his legs. And then it was as though the whole world rushed into his skull. Stars and all.

Once, at Alton Towers he had been persuaded by his eldest to ride the rollercoaster they called *Nemesis*, and midway he had genuinely feared that he might implode. What happened behind his eyes was of comparable velocity. The faces raced at him like meteors out of the darkness, vignettes of promiscuity blossoming and dissolving at light speed: snogs, hot clutches, quickies, tremblers, one-nighters – in bedrooms, bathrooms, cars, bus shelters, bird hides, on carpets, lawns, sofas, beds, behind doors, curtains, sheds, against walls, trees and, on one occasion, a soft-drink dispenser. There was a babble of voices also, or rather a multitude of murmuring choruses that rose and fell in volume, too layered and indistinct to make out the words. There was a time when such a drug-enhanced rush from the vaults would have induced a Buddha-like smirk of satisfaction, but now something wasn't quite right: the voices were off-key, and, rather than fond, fleeting recognition, he was searching the faces as they flew past, as they in turn searched his. Claire's was among them. *What had he done?*

With some difficulty he unlocked his seized-up fingers from the lounger frame and, with much writhing and rocking, managed to stand up. What century was it? In the moonlight, the garden around him was suddenly and indisputably alive, the lawn flowing silver, the deep shadows beneath the trees and bushes breathing out darkness, each coral cluster of cherry blossom illuminated from within. The creature, some kind of bird, churred again a garden away, and the hairs tingled on the back of Fenton's neck. He listened. The sound had sharpened the quiet of the hour, not even a car on the road, the sea stilled.

He pictured the little sweep of coast, the moonlit black water, the dreaming houses, the town, its streets emptied of people, its doors locked, exhaling after another day, another week, another reckoning of the balance sheet. He thought of the hills behind the town and the view down across ancient woods to the rooftops and church towers, the playing fields and gardens, the crescents of the shoreline, to the glimmering bowl of the Lough itself, perpetually changing and unchanged. And he imagined all the people in their beds, soon to reawaken and begin moving again along the pathways that made up their lives. From above, he saw a swarming diagram of phosphorescent trails, layer upon layer, day upon day, accelerating into a madly dense, scribbling mass that made him feel dizzy. He thought, *And then it stops*.

୕

'Fenton,' Carolyn's voice was disembodied, submarine. 'What is that?'

'What? Nothing.' He snuggled in, his chin nuzzling her bare shoulder, his forearm resting on her naked hip. Her neck was misty with sleep-heat, scents of brine and alcohol. He felt her micro-tilt away from him, tighter into the foetal position.

'Don't be at it; it's way too early.'

'I know, but …'

'But what?'

He moved closer, reached so that his arm lay the length of her thigh and his fingers curved round her knee, gently stroking the soft indentation. He felt her leg muscle flex, thought how the hockey years had stood to her. He breathed into her hair. It tickled his lips.

On the floor beyond the bed, in the granular dawn light that seeped round the edges of the drapes, he could see the black puddle of her discarded dress, the tangled tights, the double knot of underwear. He saw her swaying towards the bed, wine-blurred, stripping herself of tiresome bonds, naked at last. It was girlish somehow, this abandonment. Still girlish, this woman he had married. After everything.

'I love you,' he said.

She made a noise in her throat, low down, half-sceptical, half-pleased. 'Haven't heard that in a while.'

'It's true, though.'

She twisted around to look at him. 'Do you think my head buttons up the back?'

'What?'

'I know what you're up to.'

'Hey, come on. I mean it.'

He kissed her mouth. She was watching him with barely focused eyes, a glycerine shimmer. He slid his hand to her hip and squeezed her to him, kissed her again, and this time met a lazy tongue.

'All right then. But don't expect me to do anything. I have a terrible hangover. And don't you dare give me that rash.'

No matter how many times it happened, he was amazed afresh at the way it was always new, always a revelation. The shocking reality, the *now*-ness of it. How it seemed to be an outrageous thing to be doing (*This* ... in *there?*) and yet made perfect sense. His wife was breathing hard through her nose, her hands lightly but hotly on his sides. He couldn't remember the last time his body chemistry had been this awry. He had the sense that all his trace elements were being dragged and gathered into a point by an irresistible magnetic force. His mind teemed with cleavage, perfume, music, stars. He pushed himself up so he could look at her, but her eyes were shut in a frown of concentration, and when he tried to kiss her, she turned her head and made a whistling sound with her lips.

'What're you doing?' Her voice was tight. 'Why are you stopping? *Don't stop.*'

'Buffering,' he croaked. 'Just buffering. Don't move, *don't move.*'

But she did move, gripping his arms and shunting her hips with the urgency of a prospector finally realizing a panful of gold, and as the wet sparks flew, Fenton could hear nothing but the popping of his synapses and the clanging of his heart. For a few endless seconds his lump, his rash, Cecil McCracken, the money, Crawford Wylie, inchoate guilt, fear of death: they all went away.

12

When Fenton rose from his bed, the sun had already traced three-quarters of its arc towards noon. He checked his rash, showered, dressed and descended to the kitchen, where he stared for some time at the devastation wrought by his guests. On his way to the car, he met his daughter and her friend Zara coming up the driveway.

'Hi, Dad. Did you enjoy your party?'

'Great, thanks. Where you guys been?'

'Down to the shore. Where you going?'

'Just to get the paper. Need anything?'

'No thanks. Hey, should you be driving?'

'Whaddya mean?'

'Your eyes. They look ... weird.'

'Thanks. Hi, Zara. Andrea, do me a favour and take a cup of coffee up to your ma if you're making some.'

'Has she got a hangover too?'

Fenton pulled the car door open. Andrea was giving him a look, *the* look. Her mother gave him the same hard stare from time to time: quizzical, wondering, slightly sad.

Both of them had the power to knock him off his stride; both could wind him up by increments so subtle it was as though he was under attack from the spirit world. And yet they were like the pulp in his teeth – if he was out of kilter with either of them, something ached in his core, and it had to be fixed.

'Judge not, lest ye be judged, sweetie,' he said.

Zara, who seemed to have replaced her eyelashes with dead tarantulas, sniggered.

He fastened his seatbelt and, a little disorientated, reacquainted himself with the machine's controls. Sunshine was bouncing around the cockpit, hurting his eyes. He scrabbled his shades out of the glovebox, put them on and engaged the ignition.

The long avenues, as he drove, were rivers of neuralgic leaf-light. A couple in blazing red fleeces, walking their dog, waved at him. He put the window down and let cool air buffet the side of his face. A flickering collage of images from his party presented itself for review, and he had to conclude that, all in all, he had got away with it; more, it had been a success. He pictured the lads, confronted by their various Sunday scenarios, taking their tentative first steps, reaching out with trembling fingers for blister-packs, for coffee, and smiled to himself. It had been an event. They would remember it.

Swinging onto the carriageway, he misjudged the speed of an oncoming van and received a full-blooded blare of horn, which had him jangling and swearing all the way to the shop. To compensate, he marched straight to the baked goods section and set about the Danish pastries with the tongs. He was, he realized, ravenous.

He dropped his treats and the dead weight of the *Sunday Times* on the counter. The youth manning the checkout had old-style acne on a scale Fenton hadn't seen for years. Decades, in fact. Not since Jeremy 'Beano' Hynes in fourth form, who'd once had to go through a whole term bagged up like the Elephant Man.

'You know, a couple of sessions on a sunbed could help with that,' he said.

'Sorry, with what?' The kid glanced up.

'With the, uh,' Fenton indicated with nods of his head, 'with the acne.'

The register did a flurry of chirps and beeps.

'What acne?'

'Righty-ho. Can I tap?'

'No.'

Fenton remembered when the shop, which stood alone on a plot set back from the carriageway, had been the old post office. As well as stationery, it had stocked a small range of convenience foods and had been the nearest source of sweets and comics when he was a boy, a mile's walk from home. It was presided over by Old Tommy, a parboiled, portly man with a squirrel-hair toupee and a gingery lampshade moustache, who gave the impression that running a post office was the best job anyone could have: '*More* stamps, Mrs Johnston? Oh ho, those love letters are fairly flyin' out!' 'Big fat parcel for you here, Mr McNabb, and what's this, a *Do Not Puncture* sticker? Oh ho!'

One morning, Fenton was rifling through the rack looking for a *Whizzer and Chips* when the door burst open and two youths in leathers and balaclavas entered, one of them waving a revolver which he put very close to Old Tommy's face, demanding that the cash from the till be transferred, *fucken pronto*, to the bag the other one was holding. Old Tommy just stood there as if frozen solid, and there was a strange drawn-out moment of no sound (though Fenton could hear the twang of his own pulse), just the four of them absolutely motionless in a shopful of morning light. Then the one with the gun biffed Old Tommy on the snout. That did the trick. Twenty seconds later they were gone in a fading whine of motorbike, and Old Tommy was yammering down the blower to the Royal Ulster Constabulary, blood caking all over his moustache.

Fenton had to give a witness statement, which made him feel very grown up. The cops said it was more than likely 'a fundraiser for the boys'. Not long after, Old Tommy jacked it in.

Fenton wondered whether they'd ever caught the two lads. He stood beside the car, massaging the varicose veins on his temples and scanning the headlines: *Brexit 'divorce chaos' looms*; *Middle East peace hopes fade*; *Veteran DJ denies sleaze claims*; *WWI bomb found up pensioner's flue*.

John Hetherington maintained that there had always been roughly the same amount of bad things and violence happening in the world; it was just the speed and efficiency of the modern news machine that made it seem worse. In the olden days, he contended, a man had to clamber up on a horse and slog twenty miles to the next village to impart an urgent snippet, an outbreak of glanders, say, or an escaped pig. We were in danger of overdosing, he said. Fenton certainly felt that, of late, his own news machine had been working overtime.

Not far from the house, on a whim, he turned off onto Cuchulain Avenue – which would take him home via a sweeping loop along the shore road – and ran smack bang into a police checkpoint. He watched as a cop waved him down and a big rozzer face loomed at the window. They exchanged a few pleasantries, about the weather, about the contents of the paper bag.

The peeler leaned in. He seemed intrigued by Fenton's eyeballs. 'Late night, sir?'

'No, not really, a few friends round. It was my birthday, you see.'

'Oh, very nice … Just pull your veckle in over there for me, sir.'

He pulled in behind the meat wagon, a dusty white Land Rover with its back doors open. Two officers, one male, one female, were perched on the tailgate having a right old giggle. He drummed on the steering wheel, wondering whether a Danish quickly wolfed might improve his chances, but just as he was groping for the bag, the policewoman hopped down and approached, tugging a package from her trouser pocket. Behind her the other cop cupped his hand round his mouth and coughed what sounded to Fenton very much like 'blow job'.

'What did he say?'

'Who, sir?'

'Your colleague, it sounded like –'

'Oh, don't worry about him, sir.' She turned and mugged reprovingly in the direction of the wagon. 'He's very bold. Now, have you ever been breathalyzed? No? It's very simple. Just take this tube between your fingers and give a good hard blow for me.'

Fenton blew good and hard. His sinuses crackled and something popped in one of his ears, triggering an oceanic roar. The policewoman inspected the device with eyes that first narrowed, then bulged. She glanced back at the meat wagon. 'I'm going to have to ask you to step out of the veckle, please, sir.'

Down at the cop shop, amid the sour odours of coffee, sweat and fear, a second test produced an even more impressive blood-alcohol score. Wylie, not pleased at being extracted from a round of golf, took care of the paperwork.

'I think I can get you off with a six-month ban. Best we can do,' he told Fenton as he drove him home. 'A quick court appearance, a fine, and your name will be in the paper, but that can't be helped.'

Fenton stared out of the window. He was still coming to terms (not least with the fact that the peelers seemed to have nicked his pastries). It had started to rain, giving the shaved fields and chamfered hedgerows a dreary Sabbath look. Vast grey clouds lay piled up on the horizon like great tufts of biblical beard.

For some reason this part of the province made him think of the American mid-west. Protestant heartland, abstemious church-going folk: Baptists, Lutherans, Pentecostalists, Episcopalians – *born again*, a lot of them, whatever that meant – Methodists, Quakers, Brethren, Presbyterians, Free Presbyterians, Reformed Presbyterians. *New Improved* Presbyterians. It seemed the only thing they could agree on was that they weren't Catholic. Numbers dwindling now, of course. The youngsters weren't buying it.

In the distance was a huge red barn, most of the side of it taken up by white lettering: *BE NOT DECEIVED / GOD IS NOT MOCKED / FOR WHATSOEVER A MAN SOWETH / THAT SHALL HE ALSO REAP.* It had been there for ever. He remembered seeing it as a child, on the way back from Sunday visits to his grandparents, wondering at the length of ladder required and at the dedication of the painter. Some God-fearing farmer presumably. Praying for rain. Or for it to stop. While he had been fascinated by Old Testament imagery in the Bible classes at primary school – the colourful robes and epic beards, the parting of seas, the smiting and terrible vengeance, the sheer power and scale of it all – religion had never been Fenton's bag. It wasn't that he was incapable of spirituality – seasonal change, Christmas-tree lights, certain passages of classic rock by the likes of Rush, The Who and Santana, these often produced in him strange hankerings – it was just that he couldn't work out what the deal was if you didn't believe in heaven. Where was the quid pro quo?

'Crawford, you have to tell me who this woman is,' he said.

Wylie groaned.

'Is it the one I said before, Laura Hayes?'

'Fenton …'

'Come on, Crawford. Is it Symington? Is her name Claire Symington?'

'Fenton, you know I can't name names.'

'Tell me again why not.'

'Lots of reasons. Client confidentiality. Sub judice rules. And you might try to contact her.'

'So what? I could reason with her, I could –'

'No can do. Strictly *verboten*. They'd have me up in front of a tribunal. Have you thought any more about settling?'

Fenton said nothing. He was thinking. During his rocket-sled trip through inner space on the sunlounger, he had visited the year in question and a few more faces had wobbled into view. It would be a process of elimination.

13

'Do you have a minute?'

Carolyn, at her desk by the window with its view, rain-beaded this morning, over the silver scurry of the Lagan Weir, looked up. Stewart was in the doorway with his (admittedly winning) earnest schoolboy face on, holding a fluorescent orange Post-it between the finger and thumb of one hand and flicking it rapidly so it made a sound a bit like a propeller. In truth, she was thinking, she didn't really have a minute. Every lawyer on the team, it seemed, was in increasingly urgent need of documents and reports, and 1987 was proving a particularly troublesome year to retrieve: classified material, missing files, dossiers that were so redacted, some of them, that only prepositions remained. Deadlines were piling up. And the new intern – Christ on a bike – he was as much use as a waterproof teabag.

'Sure. What's up?'

Stewart approached and seated himself on the chrome-and-leather chair opposite Carolyn's desk, leaning forward with his elbows on his knees, still flicking the Post-it, but at a more meditative pace. The sleeves of his pale-blue button-down Oxford shirt were rolled up, revealing smooth, veiny forearms. 'We've had a possible breakthrough.'

'Okay.'

'Yeah.' He wafted the square of paper. 'Suspect C has provided a name. I think he wants to make things right with the Lord or something, you know, clear his conscience, because it's not going to get him off the hook to any significant extent, but anyway, he says this guy was a prime mover – made him sound like a real psycho – and if we can track him down there may be a way to compel him to testify. Which, as you can imagine, would be a real boost, given the way things are going.'

'Mm-hm.'

'Obviously, we're tied up with Officer A for the time being, not to mention Officer B, but if we could get this off the blocks and at least in the works – well, I think it could be worth something. Down the line.'

'Okay. So …?'

'So, would you be an angel – I know you're up to your eyes at the moment, but could you do a deep dive' – Carolyn's jaw tightened, she hated that phrase – 'into the database, see if you can trace him: police reports, criminal record, anything that could be used for leverage. You know the sort of thing.'

'Sure. I'll give it a go. Maybe not right *this instant*, but … leave it with me.'

Stewart flashed his full-beam smile and rose. He placed the paper carefully on the desk. 'We still on for a quickie after work?'

'M'mm?' Carolyn was staring at the Post-it.

'Quick drink? Merchant's?'

'Oh, um, yeah. Just a quick one.'

'You're a star.'

He moved off, closing the door behind him with a respectful click. Carolyn picked up the square of orange paper and held it at half arm's length, assessing the name that was written on it: black ink, capital letters – a name that was familiar; a name that had been in the margin of her family's life for many years. *Victor Dougan.*

14

The house, when Fenton saw it, was just as vast and complicated as he remembered, with its turrets, Gothic eaves and oriels, and the high oculus window glaring down at him as he crunched along the gravel towards the hunched stone lions. He patted one of them on his way up the steps and paused in front of the muscle-bound door to catch his breath. It had been a forty-minute walk with a steep hill at the end of it and his rash (it was psoriasis, apparently) was burning bright, the ointment prescribed by Dr McKenna yet to exert a grip.

He turned and looked over the acreage of tiered lawns and gigantic vegetation, the crumbling follies. It was coming back to him ... that summer ... this garden. Her parents safely on the Côte d'Azur, the garden had become the epicentre of a party scene that, while not quite Gatsbyesque, was nonetheless excessive. He lost himself for some moments in a miasma of barbecue fumes and Embassy Regal smoke, Heineken foam, a strobe-lit frenzy of dancing, Madonna exhorting them to get into the groove – over there beside the monumental fountain, a fat moon overhead and Chinese lanterns wafting colours through the trees.

It had been a low-pressure thing with him and Claire, *casual*, a dance of wide circles, finding each other, unplanned, here and there across the summer, and always grateful for it. They'd had a few laughs: she liked his 'devilish' eyebrows; he liked the gap in her teeth and her 'buttery' hair. They'd canoodled outside pubs, taken it further at the odd house party. Once, again by chance, both out for a cycle, they'd met in the country park and ended up having sex in a bird hide, against the wall, finishing just as half a scout troop thundered in behind them. And then autumn came, the leaves fell, and the dancers receded. It was as simple as that. He had no recollection of a formal ending, no pangs. There had surely been no rancour.

He pressed the bell and a few minutes later heard clumping footsteps. The door opened, and a very tall man in his seventies, carrying an axe, surveyed him from under raptorish eyebrows. Fenton took in the stained graph-paper shirt, wire wool sprouting from the neckline, the waistband of the crackling canvas breeks just below nipple level.

'Hello there, I wonder would Mrs Symington be at home?'

'Are you here about the tree?'

'The tree? No, no, I'm not.'

'You're not from the council?'

'No. I'm not.'

The man, who had an unusually flared philtrum and donkey-ish teeth, stepped aside, pointing over his shoulder with a thumb. 'Ottoline is in the Long Room.'

As Fenton entered, the man exited, slamming the door behind him. Fenton glanced around at the vaguely familiar hallway: heavy-gold-framed paintings, tapestries, a Louis Quatorze mirror the size of a small swimming pool. He took a couple of creaky steps on the parquet. 'Hello?' There was no sound beyond the usual faint yelps and groans that emanate from the more distant rooms of old houses.

He paused at the expanse of table beneath the mirror, where a collection of framed photographs jostled for space between an ormolu clock and a marble bust of a periwigged composer. Most of them were black and white – the really old, silver-vapour kind where everyone's trousers appear to be on fire – and mainly of bearded men in frock coats and women with hats and parasols under tropical suns. Several of them featured in their background ranks of sparsely clad, unsmiling black people. Others were on a sporting theme: both sexes in tennis whites, silver cups being hoisted, polo mallets brandished. And here – he had a mild shock of recognition – was Claire, in colour, posing in graduation gown and mortarboard in the arch of some hallowed portal. Her hair was cut short but there was no mistaking the big-toothed grin. He looked around for a more recent photo of her, but oddly (he thought) there were none.

He tried the first door and peered in at a room dominated by an enormous chandelier dulled to opacity by a century of dust and insect death. A grand piano slumbered under a tarpaulin by the bay window. Bales of manila folders tied with string were stacked on a knackered chaise longue, beside which a painted wooden statue of a black youth in a bell-boy outfit, complete with pill-box hat, proffered a tray of flaking refreshments.

The next door revealed a dining room, dark with mahogany and bristling with candelabras. At one end, a dresser bore a museum-like display of bygone kitchenalia: salvers, cloches, chafing dishes and the like. The air was haunted by scents of stale beef fat and doused embers. He creaked onwards. At the end of the hallway, at right angles, a wide staircase led up to a towering stained-glass window depicting a medieval knight and his wife accepting flowers from hideous sprite-like children. Just beyond, a couple of steps descended to another door, which was ajar.

He pushed at it and entered an improbably long, narrow oak-panelled room. This was not, in any way, familiar. In the distant shadows he could see flames fluttering in a grate and, in an armchair beside it, the likelihood of a human form. He set off along what seemed like about a quarter mile of parched oriental rug, avoiding eye contact with zebra, baboon and warthog, and many an eland and impala. These people were no friend to the fox or the stag either.

He went over his story. He was an alcoholic ... It had taken a long time to admit ... His recovery programme required that he ...

'Mrs Symington?' He had arrived, a little out of breath, at the hearth. The woman in the armchair looked up from a sheaf of papers, on which were scrawled copious additions and subtractions. She had one of those prow-shaped faces, with eyes that sloped downwards at their outer edges, handsome in a way that made Fenton think of a cheetah. She was wearing an ivory-hued shirt, with the sleeves rolled up, that matched almost exactly the shade of her lustrous hair, and a man's watch with a big white dial. Her lower half was concealed by a bristly tweed blanket. Disconcerted by her stare, he said again, 'Mrs Symington?'

'Are you here about the tree?'

'The tree? No, no, I'm not.'

'You're not from the council?'

'Afraid not.' He realized he wasn't sure how to begin.

'Bugger. Well? Are you here to rob me?'

'No, not at all; of course not. I –'

'Just as well, there's no money, only all this,' she waved a hand, 'this old rubbish. There's a bit of jewellery, my mother's, but it's locked up in a bank. I don't think people appreciate how much it costs to keep a house like this going.' She flapped the papers. 'It's like trying to breastfeed a bloody dinosaur. You know we damn nearly froze to death last winter?'

She glared at him, and Fenton gave a brief strangled laugh he hadn't heard before. 'No, I'm here to … It's about your daughter.'

'Claire?'

'Yes. I'm an old friend of hers.'

'Really? I can't say as I recognize you.'

'Yes, as a matter of fact we went out together for a while, a long time back. Thirty years ago, actually.'

Her frown relaxed. 'Oh, well, that explains it. Claire had lots of boyfriends back then, I mean *lots* – I wouldn't have known a fraction of them. And, of course, Esmond and I would have been away on the continent a lot, on business and what have you – couldn't be helped. I'm afraid she might have run a little wild. Mind you, there's nothing wrong with that. I was a bit of a girl myself in my time, went through them at a right old rate. Young people these days are so sensible, so *boring*, don't you think? Sit down, why don't you – you're making me uncomfortable standing there like a big sausage. And put something on the fire.'

He did as he was told. It occurred to him, as he tossed a briquette into the grate, that it was much cooler inside the house than out. Before he sat down, he spotted, through the window, the man who had let him in, braced on the lawn, apparently remonstrating with a large elm tree.

'Yes, the thing is, I was wanting to get in touch with Claire and I wondered if you might have a contact address. You know, her email. I searched the internet and I can't find her.'

'Get in touch? With Claire?'

'Yes.' Fenton shifted in his leather bucket seat, triggering a sustained twang deep in its innards.

'After thirty years? You're not one of those stalker types, are you?'

'No, nothing like that.' He geared up. 'The truth is I'm an alcoholic. It took a long time to –'

'Nonsense!' His hostess rocked forward. 'There's no such thing as an alcoholic. Some people like to drink a lot and other people don't, and some people can't afford it – it's as simple as that.'

Knocked off his stride by this pronouncement, Fenton faltered. 'No, it's true. I have … I have a disease. I'm on a programme.'

'Well, I've never seen it. When Esmond and I lived in South Africa, we drank almost constantly, and so did everyone around us. I don't think I ever saw the Townsons draw a sober breath. We'd start before lunch and carry on from there. Every day. For years. Didn't do us a bit of harm. Mind you, the humidity was disgusting and the locals were itching to kill us, so you needed a stiff drink. These days I have a three o'clock rule' – Fenton checked his watch – 'but that's for budgetary reasons. We lost a lot of money in two thousand and eight, you know, an awful lot. Bloody Esmond. Took his eye off the ball, the daft bugger. I really think he might be losing his marbles. Do you know what he did the other day?'

While his hostess expounded on her husband's 'borderline imbecility', Fenton fought the urge to stand up, drop his trousers and go to town with both sets of fingernails on his rash. Instead, he attempted to outstare the fiery eyes of a particularly pissed-off macaque that reminded him of a politician from the seventies.

'… his bare buttocks. And he doesn't even *like* oysters.'

Fenton waited a few beats, then continued. 'So, as part of the recovery thing, the, uh, thirty-nine steps, I have to apologize to all the people I let down in my life due to my, uh, excessive drinking, and Claire is one of the people on my list, so if I could just get –'

'Apologize? You silly man, don't you know you should never say sorry for *anything*. Ever. It's a sign of weakness, a fatal character flaw.'

'Sorry,' said Fenton.

'I saw that fool prime minister, whatsername, on television the other day apologizing for some nonsense in India a hundred years ago, *a hundred years ago*. For God's sake, what's next? Slavery? The Potato Famine?'

'Actually,' Fenton began, 'I think we –'

'What did you do to her?'

'Pardon?'

'Claire. What on earth did you do that was so awful?'

Incredibly, he hadn't anticipated this question.

'And another thing.' She pointed a bejewelled forefinger at him. 'Who *are* you exactly?'

This one he could answer. 'Oh, sorry, Fenton's my name, Fenton Conville.'

'Conville?' Her eyes fluttered.

'Yes.'

'That's not a common name. Are you anything to *Clive* Conville?'

'Yes, yes, I am. He's my father. Why, do you know him?'

She gave a bark of laughter and, turning to smile at the fire, didn't say anything for such a long time that Fenton became thoroughly hypnotized by the metronomic thunk of a grandfather clock on the other side of the room. Old stuff, he decided, gave him the willies.

'Gosh, it's been …' The memsahib's palely rouged lips quivered. 'I haven't thought about that man, your father, in years. Absolute yonks. Of course we were very young, probably too young given what, but, oh, he was so handsome – I presume you take after your mother – and so suave.'

'Wait a minute … *my father?*'

'We used to go up to the jazz at the Maritime Club – Jimmy McDonald was still playing then – and dance our absolute socks off. Your father was a fabulous dancer. And another time he took me down to Portrush for the weekend in his car, a Hillman Hunter, I think, or a Ford Anglia, I can't remember, blue anyway, or white. Do you know, I'm not sure we left that hotel room the whole weekend.'

Fenton managed to un-dry the inside of his mouth. 'What happened?'

'I beg your pardon? Oh, you mean … Well, it was very short-lived. My parents didn't approve, thought he was a bit below the salt, would never amount to anything, the usual stuff, and then, of course, I got knocked up by Esmond. Tell me, did he marry that Gibson girl? Heather, was it?'

'Hazel. He did.'

'Poor man.'

'Excuse me?'

'I knew he had an eye for her, but I always rather suspected she was in love with that Dixon fellow, the one who designed aeroplanes.'

'*Basil?*'

'That's the one. There were rumours.'

'Wait, *Basil Dixon*?'

'Yes, him. Are you married, Fenton?'

'What? Oh, yeah. A long time.'

'Happily?'

'I love my wife, yes.'

'I dare say. Children still around?'

'For a while yet, probably.'

'M'mm.'

'What?'

'Oh, nothing.'

'What?'

'It's just, you might find it different, Fenton, when the offspring have gone, when the smoke clears, as it were, and it's just the two of you looking at each other and thinking, *really*? Is it just you? Your face? For eternity? It happens a lot, take my word for it.'

'No, I don't think so. As I said, I love my wife.'

'Oh dear. Love? Love is a cruel biological trick, Fenton, played by nature so we carry out our duty to propagate the species. Once that's done, the soup goes cold.'

'Oh my God.'

'Think about it. If it were purely lust by itself, no one would hang around to raise the little buggers. No, it's an illusion, I'm afraid. Esmond and I haven't shared a bed in thirty years. I hate his face.'

'Oh my God. Anyway, I've taken enough of your time, Mrs Symington, if I could just get Claire's contact details, I'll be –'

'I'm afraid it wouldn't be of much help to you.'

'How's that?'

She gazed over his shoulder up at the tall window, and Fenton, zooming back to the photo in the hallway, knew with sudden conviction what was coming.

'Claire's dead. She died in a car crash outside Melbourne fifteen years ago. On her thirty-second birthday. She and her husband. They were on their way to a barbecue. Fortunately, they were childless. A small mercy.'

With a mechanical gurgle the grandfather clock emerged from its trance and, with all the time in the world, delivered itself of one, two, three deafening chimes.

Mrs Symington sat up. 'Ah, cocktail hour. At last. Where's Esmond? What about you – would you take a glass of something?'

'Whisky, please. Large.'

After choking down a double own-brand Scotch so raw and rough he'd wondered if he might have been better rubbing it on his rash, Fenton made his excuses. A taciturn Esmond Symington showed him out. In the hallway the old man paused to tap on a misted barometer that was hanging on the wall. 'The glass is falling hour by hour,' he intoned. 'The glass will fall for ever.'

'Is it?' said Fenton, confused. 'Does it?'

'But if you break the bloody glass you won't hold up the weather.'

Time stopped for a second. Fenton edged towards the Brobdingnagian front door. 'Okay. Well, thanks.'

He shot down the stone steps and didn't look back.

15

Hazel Conville tugged at the half-open drawer, wrestled it from side to side and pulled again until it squeaked and slid out. A rub with a candle would fix it but she never remembered to do it. She removed three tablecloths and set them on top of the dresser: her mother's heavy, cool white linen, rosebuds and shamrocks in delicate braille. Napkins, placemats and tablecloths in the top drawer, sheets and pillowcases in the next – still good after all these years.

The fabric gave off a clean smell, seemed almost to breathe it out. It took her back to her childhood, to the stout slate-roofed farmhouse amid the drumlins: scents of carbolic and bleach; the daily labour of the scullery, sheets being hoisted like sails up to the ceiling to dry. She thought of foam cascading down scrubbed steps, the coal glittering in its shed. She saw her mother's forearms, pink as hams, her floury hands, the starch-stiff apron. *Remember, Hazel, cleanliness is next to Godliness.*

An hour to go, three tables to set up and still half a mountain of sandwiches to finish. It was her turn to host the

Bridge session. At least the cakes were bought and waiting: Victoria sponge, always popular. Fifteen years they'd been meeting now. Though it really hadn't been the same since Paddy died. There was something special about a Bridge partnership, and their alliance *had* been special – verging on telepathic. Wee Maisie wasn't a bad player but sometimes she was a bit wild with her bids, didn't think it through. There just wasn't the trust she'd had with Paddy.

His funeral had been a quiet affair, attended by what was left of his family and a dozen card-players, on a morning of shrill sunshine in early spring. It was the first time Hazel had been at a service in a Catholic church, and she'd been surprised by how self-conscious she felt, how much of an interloper, been taken aback also, sniffing the musky incense, by the silent clamour of disapproval that rose within her from deep in the past.

She'd long stopped going to church, corrupted by that heathen Clive, but, growing up, it would have been obligatory, as much a social occasion as a spiritual one, a chance to catch up with friends and neighbours you might not otherwise see from one end of the year to the next. That was important when you lived in the country. It was also a kind of confirmation of allegiance, a show of faith, of solidarity, though she wouldn't have thought about it like that back then. Nor did she recall anything explicitly said about why she shouldn't enter a Catholic church: it just *wasn't done*.

Anyway, it had been a lovely service. She'd liked how they had put a deck of cards and his accountancy certificate on the coffin. Good with numbers. The priest had made a point of saying that. Always a head start in Bridge, Paddy said. She was good with numbers too: got her first job, at eighteen, in the Bank of Ireland in Enniskillen after coming top in the county in arithmetic. Since it was thirty miles away, she'd had to stay in a boarding house (run by Mrs Earls, she remembered the name) and there was another lodger there, a boy called Conor, who had come up to be apprenticed to a tailor. He was a year older than her, tall, with curly brown hair and a slight hesitancy of speech, and he was a Catholic. After a few weeks of covert glances and shy smiles at Mrs Earls's table, he had asked her out to a dance, which was about as much excitement as she had ever known.

One evening, after a trip to the cinema, she had arrived back at the boarding house to find her father and brother standing in the hallway, her packed bags at their feet. Her brother was staring at the floor. Her father's cheeks were flushed and his eyes were blazing. 'Keep your coat on, Hazel,' he said. 'We're taking you home.'

She often thought about that silent journey, away from the street lamps and out into the dusk of the countryside, along winding lanes between damp hedgerows, past sheets of glimmering fields. It was only when the car pulled into the yard and the stopped engine was ticking to a rest that her father spoke again, in a low voice: 'Hazel, what are you playing at? A *papist*?'

Three months later, two weeks after her nineteenth birthday, she left the farm for good for a position at the bank's head office in Belfast. What a shock that had been: so crowded, so noisy. Sharing a house with three copy-takers from the *Belfast Telegraph* (they were *wild*, those girls), drinking cocktails and dancing the weekends away at The Plaza, the Orpheus, at Romano's and, her favourite, The Maritime Club.

That was where, one evening in February (or was it March?) 1966, she'd first met Basil Dixon. She could still picture him, debonair at the bar in his double-breasted suit, chin in the air, surveying the girls on the dancefloor. And he spotted *her*, picked her out. He bought her a drink, a spar-kling perry, and they danced the rest of the evening. And went on dancing every weekend for weeks, until he went off with someone else. Just went off, without so much as a word … She hated him then, but didn't show it, didn't make a fuss. It all seemed so silly now. Anyhow, there was Basil's friend Clive, a much more solid proposition, and that became a thing, and before she knew it, they were engaged.

She looked up from the counter and gazed in an unfo-cused way into the greenery. Even at this remove, she could not explain where her head had been that early September afternoon when Basil Dixon had unexpectedly turned up again, in his new car – a metallic-grey Humber Sceptre – and taken her off to a hotel on the Antrim coast to drink champagne, and afterwards … Two weeks later she had married Clive (with Basil as best man) and waltzed off on honeymoon. And the following May, she gave birth to her first son. There was no certainty (how could there be?) but she had never shaken it, the dim but persistent shame that lodged in her conscience like a skelf.

More and more these days, she found herself drifting back to the fields around the farm, the side-meadow in early summer full of forget-me-nots and buttercups, ragged robin, the dog roses pink and white in the thicket hedges, the mayflower holding its late snow against the air. She heard the unending music of the stream at the bottom of the pasture – so cooling in hot weather – and smelled the almondy scent of meadowsweet, the mushroomy perfume of the woods in October. These impressions were sharp and real, but the days and weeks, the years, wheeled and spun until the colours ran and were a blur.

She cut the crusts off the final round, sliced it into triangles and set them on top of the others. Moist crumbed ham from the butcher, freshly planed. Plenty of butter. Paddy had appreciated the lunches – they always made extra so he could take some home. He had struggled after the wife died. Hazel sometimes wondered how Clive would cope if she went first. He barely knew the recipe for toast. As for keeping the place clean and tidy, that was another matter, and one that didn't bear thinking about.

Washing her hands at the sink, she found herself imagining her own funeral, in the little church at the end of the village where Clive's people were buried. It was full up now that graveyard, had been for quite a while, but anyway, cremation was the modern way. Much cleaner. Once you're dead, you're dead, and just throw the ashes round the rose bushes.

She wondered what kind of turnout she could expect. Decent enough probably. She pictured rows of faces, mouths moving in song, a few pausing to dab away a tear. *Where is death's sting? Where, grave, thy vic-tor-y?* She'd always been fond of that one. Nice tune. She hummed it as she dried her hands. *I triumph still, if Thou abide with me.* Yes, she'd have to make sure they sang that one. As for the rest of it, they could say and do what they liked.

16

'Christ, Aaron, what the –?'

Fenton had stepped into an old London-style fog. A real pea-souper. He windmilled his arms. At the counter, a startled Aaron, bat-like in his baggy black hoodie, was also flapping at the air. As he edged forward, Fenton could make out two other monkish wraiths lurking to one side.

'Bloody hell, Aaron, the place looks like it's on fire … Hey, who are these guys?'

Aaron was out of his chair fumbling with items on the countertop. Fenton noted the wastepaper bin full of empty e-liquid bottles.

'Oh, hi, Mr Conville. These guys? Uh, this is Tilt and that's Lamp. They're just sampling the juice, some of the juices.'

'Go on, lads,' said Fenton. 'On your bikes.' Scowling in their cowls, the lads shambled out. 'Fuck's sake, Aaron, what did I tell you? You can't have your mates in here all the time sucking up the stock. You gotta *sell* the stuff, right? *Right?* Look at me: how many sales today?'

Fiddling with the drawstrings dangling from his hood, Aaron frowned at the card machine. 'A wee bit slow so far.'

Fenton assessed his surroundings. The Planet of the Vapes fit-out had been quick, basic and cheap, and looked every penny of it, like those pop-up shops that sell sparklers and plastic skeletons at Halloween or inflatable crucified Santas from Thailand at Christmas. It needed sexing up. He'd get back to Anthony, see if he could wangle some promotional gear, posters, or flashing lights, or something.

'Mr Conville, I was, like, wondering ...'

'What?'

'Like, it's really boring in here by myself all day, so it is, and I was wondering, like, do you think could we maybe get a Nintendo? Or an Xbox?'

Fenton shot a quick glance at the black-peppered nose, the spatulate chin, the covert eyes. An ex juvenile delinquent, Aaron had been assigned as his mentee via a Lions Club do-good scheme a couple of years back, Fenton having been 'tasked' with teaching him basic business programs on the computer – spreadsheets and what have you – without much success. In (unsolicited) return, Aaron had introduced and addicted his mentor to online gaming, specifically *Relentless Evil: Entrail-Eaters V*, a xenomorph-annihilation epic (forty-six levels) that had consumed about two-thirds of Fenton's waking hours for nearly four months. At the expense of both work and family (and personal hygiene), rarely out of his pyjamas, his nervous system synced with the green pulse of the motion tracker, he had stalked his cosmic foe through the seeping subterranean tunnels of a hundred God-cursed planets. In the later stages, monster-fear had annexed many of his sleeping hours as well and he'd had to concede, in retrospect, that for several weeks he may actually have been clinically insane.

'No, I don't think so, Aaron. Just look at your phone, like everyone else.'

∽

Upstairs in The Toad, Fenton's younger brother was already perched at the bar with a Black Bush-and-water, a paperback open before him on the counter.

'Ah, Mr Polanski, so glad you could come.'

'That's not funny, Artie ... Pint of stout, please.'

Artie closed his book. Fenton craned and squinted. '*Coming Up for Air*. George Orwell. Any good?'

'Very good. Probably not for you, though.'

'Why's that?'

'Little in the way of sex or violence and, crucially, no pictures.'

'Ha ha. What's it about?'

'Basically, a fucked-up middle-aged man on a journey into the past, trying to get back to his childhood, to a simpler, more carefree time.'

'Sounds a bit lame. You know, Artie, sometimes I wonder – what is literature actually about?'

'Whoa. That's a pretty big question. *Seriously?* Well, if I really had to generalize, I'd probably say something like, it's about the miracle and, uh, mystery of human consciousness and its journey through the, uh, chaos of happenstance.

Something like that. Or, in more standard form, love and death. What was the last book you read?'

'Um … I think *The Da Vinci Code*. A few years ago. Most of it anyway. You read it?'

'No. But I do recall a review that described it as "almost *ingeniously* bad". You should probably read more good stuff.'

'Why's that?'

'Why? Because it's liberating to see the world through a skilful writer's mind. It invigorates and illuminates; it nurtures imaginative tolerance and diminishes, temporarily, the intense loneliness of being human in this vast, empty universe.'

'Artie, can you *hear* yourself when you talk? Come on, grab that menu, I'm eating my hands here.'

They took their drinks over to a booth beside the street-side windows but after a couple of minutes Artie declared the grumbling and squawking of a nearby speaker to be too much, so they moved.

'Don't be starting,' said Fenton. 'You're getting just like the old man.'

'Whaddya mean?'

'He's never done whingeing about music in public places.'

'And he's right. It's driving us all nuts – cumulative stress. They've done studies.'

'You're getting old. Ah, hi there. A Big McIlroy with bacon and cheese, please, chips, no salad. Artie?'

'I'll have the soup 'n' wheaten. Thanks.' Artie flapped out his paper napkin and laid it on his groin. 'A Big McIlroy?'

Fenton gestured at a row of framed portraits on the wall, the largest of which, in bilious acrylics, was of the celebrated golfing hero. 'You can't get away from him these days.'

Artie scrutinized the artwork. 'M'm, the naïve school. Georgie Best, he's unmistakable ... Mary Peters ... Mary McAleese? ... I assume that's Hurricane Higgins ... Is that Winston Churchill?'

'Van Morrison. You see him floating around the odd time.'

'Is *he* on the menu? Should we get a side order of astral leeks?'

Fenton took a long pull on his pint. 'So, back to Sconnie Botland tomorrow?'

'Yep, early flight. I'm lecturing at noon. "More Bricks Than Kicks: The History of the Turner Prize".'

'Rather you than me. I don't really get art.'

'You surprise me. And yet you've a few nice pieces in the house.'

'Carolyn's the one with taste. Fancies herself as a bit of a collector. Have to rein her in sometimes, though, with the online auctions. The stuff's not cheap.'

'*If you have two loaves, sell one and buy the white narcissus.* Sure you've heaps of money.'

'M'mm.'

'What?'

'Oh, just everything. Kids are bleeding me dry. Conor was on the blower the other day looking for a deposit for a flat he wants to buy, the cheeky bastard, and that's on top of his fricken college fees … Did you hear I'm going to lose my licence?'

'Yeah, Mum told me. That's a bollocks.'

'It's a shag is what it is. Reduced to public fricken transport.'

'What's wrong with public transport? Are you too far up the evolutionary ladder to take the bus?'

'I don't like it. The people. Coughing and sneezing all over the place. Yapping on their phones. The body odour. And there's always some deranged wino or jabbering space cadet who makes a beeline for the seat next to me. I'm like a magnet for them.'

Artie laughed. 'Jeez. Hey, any progress with the, uh, with the time-bomb problem?'

'The what? Oh, no, not really. I've to see Wylie this afternoon. He seems to think cash is the answer, pay to make the bastarding thing go away, but I'm hoping to avoid that obviously.'

'Have you discussed it with Carolyn?'

'Of course not. Are you mad? And don't mention it to Rosie either.'

Artie stared hard into his drink. 'I don't know. It seems odd to me.'

'What?'

'Well, that you can be accused of something you can't remember by someone whose name you don't know. It doesn't add up. It's fishy.'

'I agree, it's outrageous, but Wylie explained it to me – sub judice and all that. It's the world we're living in now. Ah, here's the grub.'

They ordered another round and set about the business of de-foiling and sachet-ripping.

'Anyway,' said Fenton, hefting his cushion-sized burger in both hands, 'I've come up with a few names, a few possibles, and I'm going to try and get in touch, head it off at the pass.' Squaring his shoulders, he clamped in, tore and chewed. 'In fact, I've already crossed one off the list.'

'Oh yeah?'

'Yeah. Do you remember Claire Symington?'

'Posh, big teeth?'

'That's the one. Turns out she died fifteen years ago. Car crash in Australia. Very sad. How's the soup?'

'Textbook. Righteous Ulster broth. Barley and everything. How's the burger?'

'Fully leaded.'

'You never worry about your ticker?'

Fenton ran a quick inventory. 'Think I'm probably more concerned about my liver.'

'The liver's overrated.'

The drinks arrived, and Artie requested more butter. 'Well,' he said, 'I really hope you can work this thing out. It's a well-known fact that paedos get a very rough ride in the nick. As it were.'

'That's not funny, Artie. Speaking of which, what about your shenanigans with that maths teacher – what was her name?'

Artie reached for more pepper, coughed. 'Miss Mehaffey.'

'You were definitely underage.'

'That's different.'

'Remind me, how old were you?'

'Sixteen.'

'And she was?'

'Twenty-seven.'

'Lucky bastard.'

'Come on, she lost her job, just avoided jail by the skin of her teeth. *And* I failed my maths O level.'

Fenton sniggered. They ate in silence for a while, then discussed the eccentricity of their parents, and from there speculated about the grisly mysteries of old age until it became too depressing.

'Raining again,' said Fenton. They gazed down at umbrellas blooming in the street, at the pavements spattered and darkening.

'*Blessed are the dead that the rain rains upon*,' Artie murmured.

Fenton dispatched the last third of his burger and began picking at the chips. 'So, do you think you'd ever come back? To live, I mean.'

Artie set down his spoon and looked out at the low-hanging sky. 'Back to the *wee Province*,' he said, softly, as if to himself. He cleared his throat. 'I don't know. It's strange. It was so refreshing, so liberating to get out of this place, away from the baggage, the ghosts, the binary code of church-or-chapel, the chuckies and the not-an-inchers, the pinhole vision, the demagogues, the ancient grudges, the *endless* whataboutery … to be somewhere normal, where people just get on with it, where the past isn't always sucking at your feet like quicksand, where there isn't any of that *sure-I-knew-your-da* stuff.'

'Tell me about it.'

'But then – it's odd – after a while you sort of start to miss it, the unspoken codes, the shortcuts, the not having to … to be able to pass over in silence. It's very specific, you know, being from this place, having been formed by what happened here – it's not like being from Glasgow or Glamorgan or … fricken Finchley. Other people, they can't know, they have no idea. They remember the headlines, the footage, the slogans, and you're either a victim or a jack-booted oppressor, and obviously a lot of bad stuff went down, but there was so much that wasn't like that, yet when you try to explain it, you see the eyes glaze over –'

'Artie, you were hardly on the front line.'

'True, but does that make my experience invalid? No, it doesn't. Anyway, what I'm trying to say is that you start to miss the shared history, grim though it was, the word hoard, the nuances of, yes, I'll say it, *identity*, that it seems to me become increasingly important as you get older. I think a lot of people as they age, whether they're conscious of it or not, come to a point where at some level they're trying to get back to their roots.'

'Wait, I feel a song coming on.' Fenton made the hand-scribble sign for the bill. 'Well, thank you, Professor Conville – most fascinating – but we'll have to leave it there. Next week on *Really Long Answers to Simple Questions*, we'll be talking to Sir James Windbag about whether he'd like a biscuit. Fuck's sake, Artie, I only asked if you'd ever come back.'

'Okay, all right, the answer is: not in the foreseeable future. But who knows.'

Outside, they stood surveying the street. The rain had stopped, but the lower air still hissed with wheels moving on surface water. From the library roof a gull was declaiming in a tone that was both belligerent and self-pitying.

'I'm headed that way,' said Fenton, pointing. 'Wylie's office is up there.'

'Right you are,' said Artie. 'M'm, Crawford Wylie. Didn't you and your mates bully him senseless at school?'

'Nah, not really. Routine stuff for every junior. He took it in his stride. It was character-building.'

'Yeah right. I seem to remember you made his life a misery. But anyway, thanks for lunch, I'm not sure when we'll be back next but hey ...'

They embraced. Fenton felt the warm thud of his brother against him, flesh and blood, the force field between them momentarily neutralized, and had a brief dizzy sense of time evaporating elsewhere.

∽

The news from Wylie wasn't good.

'Say that again?'

'A hundred.'

'A hundred *thousand* quid?'

'That gets you a signed, cast-iron non-disclosure agreement. Rock solid. Clean and final.'

'Not a chance, Crawford. Not a hope in hell.'

'It's a lot, I admit,' said Wylie. 'But, Fenton, think about it, it could get very messy if this thing goes live.' He rose and replenished his cup at a side table. 'Top-up?'

Fenton waved it away. 'Come on, who is she? Can't you at least give me a clue?'

'A clue? How many were you getting through back then?'

'Crawford, can *you* remember the details of thirty years ago?'

'Yes, actually, I can. I was in my bedroom building Airfix models and listening to my Hall & Oates records.'

'Ah.'

Wylie sat down again, angling himself so he could cross his legs. He took a slurp of coffee. 'Listen, for what it's worth, I agree with you, it's a lot of money –'

'It's bloody ludicrous.'

'It is, it's too much, but it's an opening gambit. I'm pretty sure we can get it down to something more reasonable. In fact, I'm confident we can.' He flipped open a leather-bound desk diary and studied it. 'I'm across the water at a conference for a week and then in the Algarve for golf. I'll get back on it after that and give you a call, probably the end of next month. There's no need to hurry this.'

Fenton stood up. His head was as light as a balloon and, down below, the Big McIlroy was squirming and kicking like a restless baby.

The solicitor set down his cup. 'Oh, and Fenton, there's one more thing. She's talking about, uh, calling your wife' – his face expanded in pained apology – '*for a chat.*'

17

As the plane banked, Artie gazed down at the city, and remembered a line from a poem about how Belfast from the air looked like a radio with its back ripped off. Didn't all cities? Pre-digital anyway. He squinted. Yes, he kind of got it: the circuit board of streets, the domed civic buildings like capacitors, the industrial zones blocky with transformers. The silver solder of the river.

Unsquinting, he took in the red-brick terraces, tight-ranked, sheened with Bangor Blue slate, the Victorian crowns of algae-green, the white jumble of new estates scattering to the slopes of the hills. The shipyard's mustard-yellow cranes were toy-like in the vast maze of docks and quays. It all looked so peaceful in the gauzy morning sunshine.

He didn't often think about the city that defined home. He preferred not to, and since moving to Edinburgh he rarely looked back. No one wanted to look back. (He ran into them from time to time, émigrés, refugees like himself, and they registered each other – regardless of background or tradition, he had noted – with a kind of Masonic ping, and their ears strained for the inflections and modulations of speech that unlocked codes deep down in the marrow.) But for a moment, as the undercarriage retracted with a thump, he heard, unwillingly in his mind, the explosions, the downpours of rubble and glass, the shouting, the cries, recalled chaotic footage of countless sudden ruptures in the quotidian, the sharp crack of gunfire, the heart-pounding to and fro of opposing forces in narrow streets.

He thought of all the people stopped in their tracks, cancelled without warning, by bomb or bullet: the judge gunned down outside the church, the policewoman atomized at the twist of a car key, the child felled by a stray shot off the brickwork. How would we live, he wondered, if we knew the date and the place, the exact portion of time remaining? And he imagined them, all the ghosts of the Troubles, continuing on their way as though nothing had happened, moving among the living, in their own neighbourhoods, greeting friends, buying a newspaper, thinking about lunch or a walk in the park.

Completing its circle, the plane gained height above the lough, and Artie craned to see the shoreline, and the village beyond, and what might have been the top of Fenton's house, but he couldn't be certain because of the trees. He went back over the conversations they'd had about Fenton's situation. No doubt about it: his brother was in quite a pickle.

The cabin was buoyant with light, and the sun through the window was warm on his thighs. Beside him, Rosie was running a quizzical eye over the safety instructions. He watched the quiltwork of fields and hills skim by beneath, the glints and flashes. Already he was feeling the peculiar lag he experienced each time he left the old turf, a kind of hangover, a sense of something unrealized, a detail, a clue missed.

'Well, that's me up to speed,' said Rosie. 'Though how you're supposed to get your head between your knees' – she patted the seat in front of her – 'there's no room.'

'Least of your worries,' said Artie, failing to not picture the panicked last seconds before impact, the shattered fuselage, the deluge of fire. Still, flying was the safest way to fly, as someone once observed. 'If it comes to it, I'll probably just put my head between *your* knees.'

'I honestly don't know whether that's funny or not,' his wife said.

He fished a book out of his rucksack but didn't open it. Sometimes, this weather, he found he was exhausted by the prospect of more words. His thoughts were still fluttering around the days just gone, the familiar world re-entered, how comfortable it had felt: the plush lives in the airy, solid houses, the merchant class at its well-earned leisure. Yet as a young man he couldn't wait to get away from it, from what he regarded as an artificial construct, a weird, refracted version of an imagined English shire, with all its stultifying certainties, its picnics in the sun. It couldn't last. The old order was crumbling. Time was performing its sleight of hand. Fear was consulting its watch.

His parents' generation, he suspected, were the remnants now of an assumed gentility specific to an enclave more or less homogenous in both religion and class, though religion was barely an issue in that warm bath of affluence in which the ancient oppositions – Protestant, Catholic, Planter, Gael – appeared to have dissolved.

It was an irony, he felt, that these terms came into sharper focus the farther away you went. In Scotland, he often found himself at a loss as to how to define what had formed him. Still, somewhere at the core of it was an inchoate pride in a flowering of engineering and scientific prowess that had long since faded and died: Belfast as a powerhouse of industry, a crucible of ideas and debate, 'an Athens of the north'. It had all gone before he was even born. Instead, he had arrived just in time for a hot mess of madness and murder.

They had ascended into the blankness of the cloud realm. As the engine tone relaxed into steady white noise, he was pondering the poet Derek Mahon's lines about returning to his native place after years of exile. If he had stayed and lived it 'bomb by bomb' would he have learnt what was meant by 'home'? That distracting half-rhyme of *home* and *bomb*.

'Do you think we'll ever go back?' he said.

'You mean for good?' said Rosie. 'Like, to live?'

'Yeah.'

She stared past him at the vapours of the upper air. Her parents had been dead for ten years, her siblings long scattered. Her childhood in the terraced streets east of the River Foyle, with their gable-end murals and hopscotch grids, seemed like a dream now. 'I don't know. Can you ever really go back?'

Artie wondered if he should tell Rosie about Fenton's predicament. It was probably inevitable that he would. It was too juicy not to share. But not yet. His brother had always coasted along, frictionless, insulated, adept in the material world. Okay, so his father had provided the seed money, guided him through the early days, but once up and running, he had done well: big house, flash cars, fine wines. A pillar of the community? Not quite, but not far off. And now the whole shebang was under threat.

And what *about* that threat? Artie didn't know much about legal matters, but this, well, it seemed a bit rum. So long ago, so vague. So dangerous. On the other hand, with Fenton, the way he was back then, blundering around acting the maggot and being an entitled prick, it wasn't possible to rule anything out.

'Rosie,' he said. 'Wait till you hear this ...'

18

Fenton was slumped in the armchair in his den, more or less poleaxed by the effort of memory. His recollection – and it was impressionistic, the colours out of register like old cine-film footage – was of a long slim girl with brown curls and sleepy eyes waking beside him on a sofa bed (the overall viewpoint is low down, so maybe one of those futon-type fold-outs). Nearby, glass doors are half-open to a garden or patio, letting a warm breeze waft between gossamer curtains. There is no movement elsewhere in the house, though a languorous bass thrums in the floorboards ('Walking on the Moon' by The Police, he thinks). They are kissing. She wears a black Live Aid T-shirt, the one with the rainbow guitar on it, and, as she's heading for the bathroom, red pants.

Foraging for breakfast in an off-kilter morning-after kitchen: coffee and toast amid tidelines of empty cans, drumlins of dog-ends. Other faces drift in and around. The liberation of being outside, dressed and young, with the ground surging under their feet and the broad avenue of the day open ahead of them. They wait for a train on a deserted platform, smoking cigarettes beside a derelict stationmaster's house. It was vaguely – what was the word – *romantic*, he thinks: birdsong in the treetops, the hum of the train in the rails, soft summer light. Her name was Sally. Or Shelley. Or maybe Sandy.

Fenton was spending more and more time wondering about himself, about his behaviour. *And* about his memory. Was it bad that he could remember so few of their names? It was certainly real (and often urgent) at the time. Mutually, he believed. Not that it was *all* opportunistic and fleeting. He'd gone steady three times, the longest being a year – Tanya Martin, a pocket Venus with a taste for verse, who had led him a tempestuous (and mystifying) dance before dumping him three days ahead of his A levels for the school groundsman's son, whom Fenton had always believed to have a learning disability, but who it turned out was some kind of promising poet. This had had quite an impact (on his exam results also) and he had nursed the blow to his ego for several months before falling into the arms of Donna Lynch, a conchita-eyed daughter of the Armada, only to dump her on Christmas Eve for festive high jinks with the sensational Janine Trimble. There was no doubt about it: he'd been a right slippery-dick. (But had he been a predator?)

୰

Two days later, standing in front of the bookcase in the living room looking for his old paperback of *The Da Vinci Code*, his eye snagged on the spine of a Collins dictionary. It came back to him: *Sandy. Sandy Collins.*

He hurried on down to his den and fired up the desktop. After half an hour (there were a lot of Sandy Collinses) he found her CV on LinkedIn. She worked for the Irish arm of a multinational hedge fund. A senior position. He ran his eye down her work experience. An impressive career. London School of Economics. A year at Harvard. And then he saw it: her date of birth. With a hot scalp he performed a quick calculation. The summer in question, she would have been ... He groaned. There was an email address.

While he was at it, he searched again for Laura Hayes, but there were still no viable matches. She probably went by her married name now, he told himself. Or did some people simply leave no trace?

Dear Sandy,

I'm not sure if you'll remember but we knew each other briefly back in 1987. I hope this doesn't seem wierd [He paused. The word looked weird – how did you spell *wierd*? He spellchecked] *weird but there's something I would like to talk to you about, and if you could spare the time, I would very much appreciate a meeting, whenever and wherever would suit you? I totally understand if you can't but it would be a great help if you could.*

Best wishes,

Fenton Conville

P.S. I'm not a stalker!

He pressed Send.

19

Above the glittering cranes and gantries at the end of the lough where the city began, the hills were damply plush beneath a film of haze, and the sky was flax-flower blue beyond them, faint racks of cloud like smears on a hastily wiped table. The 10 a.m. Belfast-bound train was flexing along the embankment, gleaming like a toy fresh from its box. In the park, as they passed, the trees seemed to positively shimmy in the morning sunlight, and banks of radiant blooms spelled out the news: summer had arrived.

Fenton saw all this, but as through a glass darkly. He sniffed. He was trying to recall when his life had been uncomplicated, when he had moved through the world unbeset by presentiments, had last not woken to a swarm of fears and burdens (not least a late-night text from Pamela at the salon suggesting they discuss her pay rise *over drinks*).

'Did you hear what I said? Fenton?'

'What? Sorry.'

'Are you all right?' Carolyn darted a couple of sideways glances. 'You seem a bit mopey. Is it because you're fifty now? Has the worm turned?'

'I honestly don't know what that means. It's nothing. I'm fine.'

Carolyn, on a day off, was driving them into the village to leave the car with Wee Davy, who had agreed to buff out the gouge for a (marginally) revised price. 'So a couple of hours, you think?'

'That's what he told me. You meeting Ciara?'

'Yep. A massage, followed by coffee and cake.'

'You're good to yourselves.'

'We're worth it. What about you?'

'Oh, a few messages and then I'll maybe dander over and check on the justified-and-ancients.'

~

His first port of call was Planet of the Vapes where, to his pleasant surprise, Aaron was actually dealing with genuine customers. Anthony had come through on the promotional gear and the counter was now pulsing with spangling displays for various brands of juice and hardware, including the mighty Prometheus Six. Along the shelves were hundreds of little plastic bottles labelled in sweet-shop colours. To one side, for the comfort of waiting vapers, was a heavily scuffed leather sofa that Fenton had had Aaron and his mates lug from the Oxfam up the street, and on this a couple of pompadoured, pewter-suited hipsters were lolling, puffing away as though on fine cigars. Fenton loitered briefly to bolster himself with a few dopamine-pings from the cash register.

Next stop was the pharmacy for a fresh tube of rash ointment. He handed over his prescription and it was taken away into the hallowed fluorescence of the dispensary where, it seemed to Fenton, an alternative time zone was at work (something similar pertained in the recesses of hardware stores). What were they *doing* back there? Why did it take so long to locate some pills (or screws) and drop them in a paper bag? Idly, he browsed the condoms and deodorants, before moving on to the depilatories. Other script-hostages stood around with folded arms and vacant eyes. He examined the foot powders and bunion plasters.

As he was scrutinizing the feminine hygiene products, someone entered his space. 'It is! I *thought* it was you.' Half-squinting, half-grinning at him was a well-dressed woman with tightly cropped gunmetal hair and Barton Fink glasses. 'Oh. You don't remember me, do you?'

He took a step back. 'Ah, for goodness sake, of course I do.' He didn't. He reached out and cupped her elbow. 'How the hell are you?'

'Not bad, not bad, strugglin' on, you know yourself. What about you?'

'Good, good, just,' he gestured vaguely and they both regarded for a suspended moment an array of vaginal moisturizers, 'uh, waiting for a prescription. Lucky I'm not in a hurry.'

'Oh, I know, it takes for ever in here. What *are* they doin' back there?'

'God only knows. Drinking cocktails or something.'

She laughed. 'It's been an absolute age.' She cocked her head to one side, appraising him from behind her goggles. 'Last time I saw you was at Wendy Scott's party, in the back garden, the pair of us gettin' up to no good if I remember rightly.' She laughed again. 'What were we like?'

'Wendy Scott,' said Fenton, as if in a dream.

'Aye, Bendy Wendy. Saw her at a reunion a wee while ago – gettin' married for the *third* time, the besom. And do you remember her mate Gemma McConkey? She just sold her candle company for, like, a squillion quid. Anyway, here, I'd better scoot.' She leaned up and kissed him on the cheek. 'Good to see you.'

She hurried along the aisle and into the bright flurry of the street, and Fenton stared after her, assailed again by a sense of time out of sync like a slipping clutch.

Outside, a provincial morning was well under way: people with small dogs on leads, aproned merchants, elderly couples moving at aquarium speed; smells of coffee, bread, butchery. There was a delivery taking place at The Stoat, the air clanging with the seismic impact of beer kegs on concrete. He tucked his ointment into his jacket and headed towards the junction, slowing to peer in the window of the bakery. All this walking he was doing, could he not justify a quick sausage roll (or maybe a fifteen or a coconut slice)? But the queue was back nearly to the door.

On the corner he ran into Dawson, encased in tweed in spite of the weather and gazing about him with imperious grace. The older man gave a slight start when hailed and looked momentarily furtive before recovering.

'Ah, Mr Conville, it's yourself. You came up on my blind side there. How are you this fine morning? How's the rash?'

'Wait, *what*? How'd you know about that?'

'Oh, I was talking to Sharon in the chemist's last week and she said you'd been prescribed some pretty serious skin cream.'

'Fuck's sake, is there no privacy round here?'

'Just running a few errands?'

Fenton explained about the car.

'Most unfortunate. That could cost you.'

'Seven hundred quid.'

'God's teeth.'

'I know. What about you?'

Dawson indicated with a toss of his head. 'Miriam's just getting some cash. Sorry, Miriam *McCann* – you heard about Marty? Very sad. Funeral was last week.'

A slim, soft-featured woman, Valium-eyed, with sunglasses atop mulberry-tinted hair, arrived in front of them securing the clasp of her handbag. She gave Dawson a wan smile and nodded at Fenton. Slipping his arm under her oxter, Dawson said, 'Miriam, I was just telling Fenton what a professional job they did on the funeral. It was rather lovely, wasn't it?'

'Really sorry to hear about Marty,' said Fenton. 'I hope you're managing okay.'

'Thank you. I've been taking it very hard.' Her voice was barely more than a squeak. 'But Dawson has been very kind. I'm in good hands.'

Fenton looked at Dawson, who gravely moved his eyebrows around. 'We'd better be off,' he said, 'before it gets too busy. Miriam's treating me to a pot of tea and a cherry scone at Archibalds. Have you tried their scones, Fenton? I recommend them. Good luck with the motor.'

∽

Fenton exited the village via the Old Kissing Bridge, cutting across the playing fields and out through the wrought-iron gate onto Pevensie Road, with its vicarage-style villas dozing behind laurel hedges, and at the end turned up the laneway that opened into Lilliput Close. As he approached the house, he spotted his mother and Mihaela lounging on garden furniture under the pergola, laughing and smoking cigarettes. He faltered. He hadn't seen his mother smoke since he was a child.

'Morning, ladies.'

They stopped laughing.

'Oh, hello, Fenton,' said his mother, hiding her cigarette down the side of the chair. 'Didn't expect to see you today.'

'No, I was in the village having a dander and a wee pockle round the shops and thought I'd call by. What's going on here?'

'Just taking a break. Mihaela came to check on Clive's leg and guess what? She's fixed the washing machine. Saved us a fortune. Back home she worked as an engineer. She says there are as many women engineers as men there.'

Mihaela took a robust pull on her fag and grinned at him. 'It's good to know how to fix things, Vintan,' she said.

'And Bogdan's coming next weekend to build me the gazebo your father's been promising for the last ten years. What do you think about that?'

'That's marvellous,' said Fenton. 'Where is the old man?'

'At his hobbyhorse. The professor's here. They're playing soldiers in the den.'

Professor Augustus Kirkpatrick was a retired historian who lived in a baronial-style house farther up the hill, with a seldom-seen younger man referred to exclusively as 'the nephew'. He and Clive had collaborated on the construction, recently completed, of a diorama depicting the Battle of the Boyne and were now re-enacting stages of that day's conflict and debating the various strategies of the generals. (Fenton had never heard the word before and Artie, when told on the phone that they were working on their diorama, suggested Dioralyte. They planned to recreate Waterloo next.)

Fenton rather liked the professor. He said clever stuff but wasn't a smart-arse about it, and with his fluffy white side-hair, shiny pate and round glasses, he looked exactly the way professors were supposed to look, or at least the way they looked in films and comic books.

'Righty-ho,' said Fenton. 'By the way, I can see you hiding that cigarette.'

His mother brought her hand back into view. 'Just keeping Mihaela company. Don't say anything; you know what he's like.'

'Your funeral.' He waved at the air. 'God, those smell rough.'

His mother coughed richly. 'They're from Albania. Mihaela gets them cheap.'

He moved on, entering through the side door into the kitchen, and stood for a moment listening to the tick and groan of domestic machinery. A tap was dripping. A radio moithered distantly. He sniffed: food had been recently consumed. His mother, a decent cook of hearty traditional grub, had abandoned the stove a while back in favour of ready meals in plastic trays, and the reek of something gloopy, super-heated in the microwave, hung in the air. The secret of her legendary roast potatoes would die with her, he thought grimly.

He made his way upstairs and along the landing, past the paintings and bric-a-brac of his childhood: the porcelain spaniels – could they be worth anything, he wondered (there was a Steinway baby grand piano in the sitting room that was definitely worth something) – the Asian woman with the green face, the China basin on its pedestal, still brimming with asthma-triggering potpourri.

In the den, Clive and the professor were poring over the Artex terrain of the battlefield, with its hillocks, ravines and trees, and the famous river twisting through it. The scene was heavily populated with cavalry and infantry, the dragoons and musketeers armed with tiny matchlocks, flintlocks, swords and halberds. Prominent amongst them, on one side of the water, was a scarlet-tunicked King William astride his rampant milk-white charger; on the other, in black, on an ash-dark steed, was King James II. Fenton stood at the open door and watched the two men submerged in their miniature world, their heads full of the sounds of battle.

'Allocating so many troops here,' the professor was saying, pointing, 'was the key tactical error.'

'He overreacted to Billy's flanking manoeuvre,' said Clive. 'Nerves. Put a lot of pressure on the boys at Old-bridge.'

'Outgunned,' the professor agreed. 'Having said that, William should really have had them at Duleek.'

'M'm, he made a few mistakes. And losing old Schomberg early on must have been a big blow, don't you think?'

'Certainly it was. Shot in the neck by who, Clive?'

'By Cahir O'Toole of Ballyhubbock.'

'You are correct, sir.'

Fenton entered the room and was registered with the barest of glances and grunts. The diorama, which sat atop an old card table, measured six square feet, and dominated the centre of the room. It had taken the two men several months to model and paint, and several more to source and assemble the figures, and while Fenton had initially snickered and sneered at their labours, he had to concede that the finished article was rather impressive.

'So,' he said, 'the sun rises over the Boyne once more. The Glorious Twelfth of July.'

The professor cleared his throat. 'Actually, Fenton, it didn't *technically* take place on the twelfth.'

'Really? Should someone tell the Orangemen?'

Clive weighed in. 'It's all to do with the Battle of Aughrim, Fenton, which did take place on the twelfth and which was the decisive clash in the Williamite war in Ireland. But at the Boyne both kings were physically there on the battlefield, so it's more … what's the word, Kirky?'

'Totemic?'

Fenton's grasp of seventeenth-century Irish history was sketchy (for him, as for many of his peer group, the whole Orange thing was a gaudy anachronism, something that fizzled on in dusty village halls, kept on life-support by humourless old men performing arcane ceremonies in spooky regalia) but seeing the scaled-down arena, with its gradients and obstacles, the swathes of combatants locked in their suspended dynamic, it seemed suddenly fresh and exciting. He almost felt something resonate. 'Right. Okay, so what's happening now?'

'Well,' said Clive, edging the King William figure forward, 'Billy's got to get his Dutch Blue Guards across the Boyne here – they're a crack force but the river's quite deep and James's men have the advantage of the slope. Meanwhile, in the centre here, his commander-in-chief, the Duke of Schomberg, is about to catch a bullet. Kirky, would you mind moving the duke?'

Fenton watched for a while. The professor's fingers, handling the tiny figures, were slender, strangely young, he noticed, the nails trimmed and buffed, and he couldn't imagine them loading or even holding a real firearm.

'Here could have been another turning point, don't you think, Kirky?'

'Absolutely. Heavy casualties. The Huguenot troops took the worst of it. They were lucky to hold out. Didn't you tell me your people were Huguenots, Clive, in flight from persecution?'

'Apparently. Though I doubt they were at the Boyne. Then again, they could have been.'

Fenton was beginning to experience a nebulous disquiet. It had something to do with history, or rather his lack of grasp of it. He understood that the battle these two men were looming over like gods had been important – how could he not? – but he wasn't quite sure why it was *still* important. If he thought about it, he supposed it undeniable that his kind had benefited from the outcome of William's campaign. The privilege of power opened up opportunity – everybody knew that. (What was that line Artie came up with? *Bliss was it in that dawn to be alive / But to be Protestant was very heaven.*) The old money – the *really* old money – in his neighbourhood no doubt owed something to whatever carve-up had ensued, and the imbalance had obviously rankled on down through the centuries, but that's just what happened in history, wasn't it? The boot could well have been on the other foot.

Growing up, he had only ever witnessed one outbreak of sectarianism, when Soupy Campbell had called Spud Murphy a 'Fenian bastard' for drinking his last can while Soupy was off in the bushes with Wendy Scott. Spud had retaliated with 'bluenose dick', but it had simmered down quickly, and never resurfaced. There had also once been some tension between Bob and Liam over Liam's insistence on calling the Falkland Islands the Malvinas, but this too had been eclipsed by more pressing adolescent business.

Fenton marvelled that anyone anywhere these days could still be bothered to think in the harsh terms of the pre-peace years and yet someone somewhere was testing the tension of a goatskin drumhead, someone somewhere was polishing the emblems on the sash their great-grandfather had worn. Fresh shockwaves were shuddering through the labyrinth.

He checked his watch. Wee Davy would be done with the car by now, he reckoned. Time to go and pay up. This thought triggered the weight of the Wylie business, and then the smaller but only marginally less nagging matter of his loan, and he looked with a jag of envy mixed with something like resentment at the two old men with nothing to worry about beyond the fate of some toy soldiers. A minute later, trying to extract a two-wheeled cannon for closer inspection, he managed to knock over a whole troop of Inniskillings, and his father ordered him to leave.

20

Carolyn and Ciara were stretched out on their fronts, six feet apart, emitting little grunts and groans as the masseuses worked on their sheeny backs. The air was fragrant with ylang-ylang oil, and sounds of birdsong and the trickling of water into a mountain rock pool emanated from a hidden speaker. After a while Ciara said, 'Hey, did you hear about Gina Bradley?' and Carolyn, in a thick sleepy voice, said, 'No, what about her?'

'Ooh, wait till you hear this. Brian, you know, holier-than-thou, big-in-with-the-church Brian? She caught him doing a line with one of his exes who got back in touch on Facebook.'

'No way!' Carolyn was chided back into relaxed mode by the diminutive masseuse. 'How'd she find out?'

'Left his email open, first time ever. She'd suspected for a while, so she was on the lookout, doing some deep recon, and then there it was, in black and white on the laptop, planning to meet up with her in a hotel in Portrush, the dirty hallion.'

'Wow, I would never've … So what's she going to do?'

'Oh, she's gone full metal jacket. Best lawyers in town. Poor bastard didn't know what hit him.'

'That's terrible.'

'I know. I know. Makes you think.'

The background speaker transitioned to gently cascading Tibetan bells. Outside in the street the sound of traffic was dreamily distant. Carolyn groaned. 'Oh that's great, a bit lower, yes there, m'mm … You'd never suspect Graham of any of that carry-on, would you?'

Ciara snorted. 'I doubt it. He's more interested in bicycles than women these days. Anyway, I'm getting to the stage where I'm not sure I'd even care. It would take the pressure off me. What about your Fenton? Seem to remember he was a bit of a lad back in the day.'

Carolyn was quiet for a minute. 'I dunno. He has been a bit weird recently, but you know Fenton, he doesn't give much away. I really don't think he'd risk it, though. He'd be afraid of what his parents would say.'

'Speaking of which,' said Ciara, 'how's the gorgeous Stewart?'

Carolyn twisted up from her padded face-hole and looked sharply in her friend's direction. 'Ciara, that's not funny.'

'Hey, hey, take it easy. It's not like there's anyone listening.'

'You're a bad bitch.'

'Come on, I'm only messing. How is work? Any movement with that thing?'

Carolyn settled herself again. 'Not much. It's a very slow process.'

'Are you sure you're probing hard enough?'

'Ciara, for God's sake!'

Carolyn tuned out and had a bit of a drowse while the masseuse kneaded her calves. She'd rather Ciara hadn't brought up work, trying as she had been not to dwell on the name that had most recently bubbled up from the depths, setting off a perturbing thought process. About her father and his business activities and what part that man (and she was certain now it was him) had played over the years. Always there. Always in the wings. Quiet, menacing Victor. She had been wrestling with whether to bring it up with Stewart, given that it might represent some kind of conflict of interest, but something in her was resisting. What was it? A fear, she supposed, that he would judge her, think less of her if she revealed the connection with her family. Anyway, sure it was early days yet. No smoking gun. Would she mention it to Fenton? M'mm, maybe. Then again, maybe not.

21

Gus Kirkpatrick was thinking about something Clive had said earlier, about how he wished he'd had a chance to go to war. 'Wouldn't you have liked a crack at it, Kirky? The camaraderie, the taking part in history ... Don't you feel we missed out? As men?'

Well, the answer to the first was a definitive *no*. Kirky felt very strongly that he wouldn't have liked the battlefield at all, felt very fortunate, in fact, to have been able to read accounts of its terrors and horrors in the safety of libraries and hushed wood-panelled rooms. The second was a more complex question, and here he mused on his friend's fascination with war craft – the machinery, the mobilization of forces, the firepower – the way his eyes gleamed and he became fervent when discussing strategy and tactics, his serious expression like that of a boy being allowed his first beer.

The professor had met many men in whom he divined consciousness of something unspent, of valour, courage, strength untested. (And women too, though on this general subject he was no expert.) It was possible that deep in the heart's core everyone hankered for a cause – to commit and prevail on the side of righteousness, to bathe briefly in flames of glory. These *lives of quiet desperation*, who had never blown up an airfield of enemy aircraft or scored the winning penalty for their country. History was full of ordinary people galvanized by circumstance into becoming extraordinary, finding within themselves, when the cry went up, a capacity for feats of utmost bravery, of cunning, of violence.

He flipped shut *The History of the Decline and Fall of the Roman Empire (Vol. II)* and, with pistol shots of cracking cartilage from both knees, rose and wandered over to the hearth. 'In times of peace the war-like man attacks *himself*.' Who had said that now? Camus? Kierkegaard? 'Better to die on your feet than to live on your knees.' There was another one. The Mexican. Zapata.

On the mantel was an array of photographs in maple frames and he gazed at one in particular, reaching out a finger to minutely adjust its angle. In profile, against a backdrop of levelling sands and bleached stony hills, his father, Lieutenant Colonel Bertram 'Bertie' Kirkpatrick (DSO), his hand resting on the grooved barrel of a Vickers machine gun, squints into the sun. He's lean and scruffily bearded and, incongruously, given the almost palpable heat, wearing a woollen jersey. On his cap is a badge emblazoned with a winged dagger. He looks so young – what would he have been then, twenty-seven? – and yet there's a gravity in his expression that foreshadows the older man.

Not that much older, though. The professor recalled the moment he found out that his father had died. His first term at Cambridge. The tap at the door, the crackling telegram paper. The words had hit him with an almost physical force. It transpired that this man who had laid waste to German airfields on night raids in the deserts of Egypt and Libya, parachuted behind enemy lines in Normandy, captured an entire Italian garrison, had drunk-driven his car off a County Down pier in the early hours of the previous morning. He was forty-five years old.

In a way, though it was certainly a shock, it wasn't actually a surprise. Like others who had found their métier in the adrenaline-drenched real-time of combat, his father had been unable to settle in the horse latitudes of civilian life. A brooding, restless presence, he would disappear for days, sometimes weeks, returning exhausted, hungover, often nursing the results of a bare-knuckle encounter in some bar or other. But he was always gentle with his son, his only child – his 'little soldier'.

Gus had only one memory of his father smiling. An afternoon visit to the playground above the lough shore, a sultry brine breeze, not many around. A rare à deux outing. Gus was at the top of the slide, his father on a bench smoking a cigarette. It was so high up! His stomach ached with trepidation. He checked once more that his father was watching and launched himself down the chute. Much faster than he expected, so smooth it was like falling. Then he was in the air and skidding across the tarmac, and his knees were bleeding. His father was already there, gripping his shoulders, pre-empting the tears. 'It's not so bad. You'll live.' The smile. A smile directly from the eyes, connecting with the pain, absorbing it. 'Chin up, my little soldier.'

What would Lieutenant Colonel Kirkpatrick have made of his son's sedentary, uneventful life? An insulated observer, a shade among the carrels? He moved to the window and gazed out at the garden, where late sunshine hung in gilded suspension over the flowerbeds and hedges, barely a flicker of air in the trees. 'The nephew', with trouser bottoms rolled, was a little way off, intently deadheading the roses with a pair of duct-taped secateurs, his slim arms already bronzed. The thinning patch on his crown, amid the brown-grey curls, was becoming ever more monkish. And what would his father have made of *this* arrangement, still *sotto voce* after nearly thirty years?

The professor turned back to the room, to its shapes and shadows, and crossing again to the hearth, stared at himself in the mirror above the mantel, his fingertips resting on the cold marble.

22

Dear Mr Conville,

Ms Collins has asked me to pass on her reply to your recent email.

She says she does remember you, and would be willing to meet. I have arranged a lunch booking at Temps Perdu on Jury Street for 1 p.m. on Friday, 12 June. I hope this suits. If you are unable to make it, please let me know as soon as possible.

Yours, etc.

Fenton didn't recognize the restaurant, or the street. He scrolled down. 'Bugger.' Her office was not, as he had unthinkingly (and perhaps tellingly) assumed, in town, but a hundred miles away, in Dublin.

Wee Davy was hesitant. 'Why don't you just get the bus or the train?' Fenton explained his aversion to public transport. 'Can the missus not drive you?' Fenton said Carolyn was in London for work, which was true. She had flown out that morning, with Stewart, on tribunal business, and wouldn't be back until Saturday.

'Okay, but I'll need cash. And you're payin' for the petrol,' Wee Davy said.

The next day, when Fenton opened the door to the courtyard, he was dismayed to see not one but two faces staring up at him. The one that wasn't Wee Davy's had a flopping piston of a tongue, and mad assassin's eyes, and belonged to an enormous dog whose huge head was encircled by a white plastic cone, giving the impression of a fearsome carnivorous flower. Both visages were at almost the same height. (Had he ridden here, Fenton briefly wondered, on its back?)

'Who's your friend?'

'This is Sniper. He's to come with us,' said Wee Davy, slapping the end of the lead against the beast's rippling shoulder. 'I can't get anyone to mind him and I don't want him tearin' out his stitches.'

Fenton eyed the rivulets of drool dripping onto the cobbles. He had nothing against dogs – he had been chief mourner at the funeral of the family pet, a pug-Jack Russell cross named Algy – but this thing was a monster. 'Okay, but we're taking *your* motor.'

'Nah, we'll have to go in yours, mine's runnin' rough.'

'What?'

'Clutch. Just started on the way up the road.'

Fenton swore.

Twenty minutes of significant exertion followed. The creature, used to Wee Davy's van, required much cajoling, manhandling and application of its owner's boot to install it in the back seat, where it immediately set about trying to remove, without benefit of its teeth, the blanket intended to protect Fenton's upholstery. It was still bucking and scrabbling as they crossed the river onto the Westlink towards the motorway.

'Christ, he doesn't give up easily, does he?'

'He'll settle in a minute.' Wee Davy glared in the rear-view mirror. 'Pain in the arse.'

A minor accident on the approach to the Broadway Roundabout slowed the traffic to a crawl, allowing Wee Davy time to glug from his litre bottle of SunnyD and both of them leisure to contemplate the city's largest example of public art, a huge geodesic sphere-within-a-sphere constructed from white steel tubes, on the underpass ahead.

'I quite like it,' said Fenton.

'It's stupid,' said Wee Davy, suppressing a belch. 'Waste of money.'

As they surged onto the M1, Sniper, having at last arranged the back seat to his satisfaction, wedged his cone between the headrests and directed his hot breath into Fenton's ear. They were in the outside lane, cruising at about eighty.

'What's he …? Why's he …? Why did you call him Sniper?'

'I didn't. I inherited him. I was lookin' after him for an oul' lad on the estate got put inside a couple of years ago for whaddya call it … *historical crimes* – one of those tribunals – and never came out again. Cancer. Now I'm stuck with the bastard.'

'I see. And the stitches?'

'Broken glass. Mad shite jumped into the sister's aquarium tryin' to get at the fish.'

'Jeez.'

'As I say, pain in the arse.'

Fenton fiddled with the air conditioning, as much to counter the pungent sirocco of Sniper's breath as to cool himself down. The morning sun was asserting itself. He switched on the radio and idly scrolled along the stations. Every other song comprised the same anguished vocal style: pop-and-crack percussion, four-square melodic chorus, procedural middle eight. It was as though they'd all been designed on the same computer program. In between were songs that sounded like they'd been assembled from bits discarded by the successful bands of the seventies and eighties (he preferred these).

He remembered the shock to his solar plexus the first time he heard the Sex Pistols erupt from the family radio, one Saturday afternoon in the late seventies. Even at the age of nine he could tell something dangerous had broken free and was across the threshold, confirmed by one glance at his father's gorilla-faced incredulity above the slowly descending newspaper, turning to a look of genuine fear, his mother more or less sprinting across the room to flail at the Off button.

He turned to Wee Davy. 'Any requests? What kind of music you into?'

'Country.'

'Like Johnny Cash?'

'Johnny. Or Patsy. Or a bit of Tammy.'

Fenton twiddled on, without success. They listened for a few minutes to a discussion about the hydra-headed chaos summoned up for Northern Ireland by the referendum result, but when the opposing party leaders, triggered by beliefs phoned in by Norman from Tiger's Bay, started bellowing slogans at each other, Fenton switched it off.

'Muppets,' said Wee Davy.

'Who?'

'All of them. The whole lot of them.'

'The politicians?'

'Aye. Sittin' around on their arses doin' sweet eff-ay on taxpayers' money. Should be sacked. We don't need them.'

'We don't need government?'

'Sure, we haven't had any government for months and have you noticed any difference?'

Fenton conceded that he hadn't (in fact, if anything, things seemed to be working better than usual) but how long could it go on? Surely anarchy would eventually enter the vacuum like a riptide of fire. There was definitely in the air – he had sensed it for some time – an impression of frames and brackets coming loose, of scaffolding falling away, of ground no longer solid. Globally.

The financial crash of a decade ago had been his first experience of a shock to his adult world view – finding himself gripped in the pre-dawn hours by the luminous-eyed fear that his money might not exist by morning, wracked by visions of shuttered, defunct banks. Up until then he had never questioned the idea that these overarching structures were in the vice-like charge of expert grown-ups with everybody's best interests at heart. Now he knew the truth: no one – none of these people – gave a fuck. It was a free-for-all. *Give a man a gun and he can rob a bank* – he had once read, on a fridge magnet possibly – *give a man a bank and he can rob the world.*

'Well, we've only ourselves to blame. We voted them in.'

'Not me,' said Wee Davy. 'Never voted in my life.'

'Really?'

'Never. Waste of time. They're all as bad as each other. You want somethin' doin', you do it yourself.'

Fenton semi-dozed for a while, the sun spangling through his eyelids, and thought about his upcoming meeting with Sandy Collins. He wished he had a better idea of how the conversation might go. It was making him nervous: he was aware of soft implosions and subsidences in his gut.

A few miles before the speed-limit signs were due to switch to kilometres, they pulled in to a services area, and while Wee Davy topped up the tank, Fenton hit the jacks (hard) and bought them a coffee each. When he came out of the shop, Wee Davy had parked the car at the edge of the forecourt and was standing squinting down at houses, steeples and a meandering, cloud-reflecting river.

Fenton handed him a cup. The mechanic's slicked-back quiff of mahogany hair – Fenton sometimes wondered if he combed Swarfega through it – was glistening in the sun, his sleeves rolled up to reveal smudged blue tattoos on gnarly forearms. He nodded in the direction of where the road climbed into the hills. 'Do you remember havin' to stop at the army checkpoint up there?' he said.

Fenton did remember: weekend jaunts with the lads to Dublin in the late eighties – nights drinking Smithwicks, smoking stubby heavy-calibre Major Extra Size, queuing for Big Macs at Ireland's only McDonald's, gargantuan morning-after fry-ups in Bewley's Oriental Café – required first the gauntlet of scrotum-tightening scrutiny by edgy, tooled-up soldiers on the brow of that hill. And he also recalled the feeling of escape, of unfurling lightness, as they barrelled away on the road south, across the border, down into another country, into another – or so it seemed – time zone.

'Well, it was still there the last time I went to the Free State.'

The Free State? Fenton was beginning to wonder if Wee Davy was a lot older than he looked. 'That's a while back. You might find it's changed a bit since then.'

They cruised down through the borderlands, between drumlins and forested slopes, big white new builds where once had been the decaying houses and outbuildings of abandoned farmsteads, registering without comment the signpost for Warrenpoint, a dark marker on the map of the Troubles. The once-infamous Crossmaglen, Fenton mused, was only a few miles to the west, in the idyllic-sounding Orchard County. He wondered whether its macabre home-made road sign – *Sniper at Work* – was still there or on display in a museum somewhere.

Not far beyond the shadows of the Cooley Mountains the sky began to darken, and by the time they reached the

Boyne Valley, rain was pixelating the windscreen. Fenton tried briefly to translate what he'd seen on his father's diorama to the sweep of fields passing on his left: the to and fro of thousands of shouting men, the terrified horses prancing amid the chaos of artillery fire and cannon smoke, the unearthly lulls; blood on the grass, the cries and groans of the fallen.

The rain increased in velocity and volume as they neared the Irish capital. On the outskirts, confused by a traffic system much altered since his last visit, Wee Davy took a wrong turn and Fenton had to resort to his phone to try and get them back on track. This led to some ill temper and swearing, as well as tense silences at an infeasibly long series of red lights.

A short time later, giving in to the dictates of Sniper's bladder, Wee Davy swung into the car park of the Brian Boru pub. Fenton watched as the dog, oblivious of the pelting rain, led its minder on a leisurely reconnaissance of the area before favouring the rear alloy of an Audi A4 with a urine release lasting approximately three minutes.

Breathing heavily, Wee Davy arrived back in the driving seat. While his shirt was saturated, his hair appeared untouched. 'Gimme a minute,' he said. Fenton checked his watch. Still plenty of time. Behind him, the beast was working through some form of rigorous dressage that entailed optimal contact with the upholstery. It then shook itself violently, rocking the car on its springs and soaking the whole of the interior.

They started off, but as they edged towards the road, a meaty-faced man wearing a bouncer suit and holding an umbrella stepped out and halted them with a white-gloved hand. Other similarly attired men walked by at a solemn pace. A black limousine nosed past. 'Funeral,' said Wee Davy. 'Bugger,' said Fenton. On the far side of the road a line of mourners filed along, some struggling to stay beneath shared umbrellas, others resigned to a drenching, hair slicked to the skull.

The sky darkened further, suffusing the scene with a heavy aubergine light. And then, the rhythmic clatter of hoofbeats, and into view came two huge black-plumed horses pulling a Victorian-style hearse complete with side lamps and a top-hatted driver sitting high in the rain. 'Fuck me,' said Wee Davy. 'Jesus,' said Fenton. If he had seen one of these before, it had been in a ghost film or a nightmare. It drew level, and they took in at close quarters the obsidian depths of the paintwork, the Gothic crenellations, the polished jet of the casket behind silver-etched glass. The top of the carriage frothed with wreaths of cream and vermilion flowers, which seemed only to accentuate the impression of indelible darkness. Following in the hearse's wake were more black cars and more people in silent procession under the ceaseless downpour.

'Gangster,' said Wee Davy. 'Bet you any money.'

'Why d'you say that?'

'For a start, take a look at some of these guys ... them'uns over there for example.'

A trio of shaven-headed men, boxer physiques testing the seams of their hired suits, stood on the far pavement assessing the vicinity with quick, wary movements. One of them was eyeing the northern registration plate on Fenton's car.

'And also, drug dealers love all that *Godfather* shit when it comes to a funeral. All the drama … You know these boys are shootin' the bollocks off each other every twenty minutes down here? It's wild.'

'I know, it's out of control, I watched a documentary,' said Fenton. 'And all the nicknames, The Blacksmith, The Hairdresser, The Weasel, The Gouger … Is there one called The Clamper?'

'Dunno. Do you think they still get a church send-off?'

'Looks that way. It would have to be one hell of a forgiving God, mind you, to receive some of *these* lost sheep – a merciful Lord indeed.'

'Ach, away out of that,' said Wee Davy. 'Sure, once you're dead, you're dead. Right, that looks like the end of it.'

As they made their way down the hill towards the Liffey, the rain began to ease and a portion of sky glimmered turquoise above the quays. Around O'Connell Street, flocks of tourists in dripping ponchos trudged in the direction of the General Post Office to take pictures of bullet holes. Fenton consulted his watch again. He was cutting it fine. Bloody funeral.

On the bridge they hit yet another red light and he gazed down at the river, which was swollen and choppy and had a mauve-ish hue to it. A couple of storm petrels hovered, high up, where the Liffey curved past the financial district towards the ferry port and the open sea. Next stop Holyhead.

They found a parking space on the fifth level of a multi-storey, and while Wee Davy let Sniper loose on the front grille of a Toyota Yaris, Fenton confirmed the location of the restaurant and gave his hair a quick primp in the light of the vanity mirror.

ᔕ

Temps Perdu was below street level, down some steps. Fenton stood for a moment at the top, leaning on the metal rail and wishing he had a cigarette. It was a strange appointment, surely, by anyone's standards. He descended and entered a realm of soft leather and expensive light. A sinuous maître d' in a matador-tight outfit led him through a series of archways to an alcove behind an illuminated wall of wine bottles where Sandy was already seated. She was on the phone and held up a forefinger as he sat. He napkinned himself and opened the menu.

'*Nein*, Klaus, the liquidity isn't there, our client is not comfortable … *Nein*, you're not listening to me …'

Fenton recognized the curls, still dark, still glossy, but scissored brutally straight and short across the fringe, a style he usually characterized as 'asylum cut'. In her case it was chic, a statement of modernity, and was backed up by a deftly tailored chalk-stripe jacket. Her face, though much better preserved than his, and practically make-up free, was more problematic: he had pictured freckles. He turned his attention to the bill of fare, which was a single sheet of sparse French and, as far as he could tell, contained no reference to meat.

'You *do* that, but let me know before the New York bell. By email, *ja*. Okay. *Danke*.'

She set the phone on the tablecloth. Her expression was bemused, curious, but with a wingbeat of cold suspicion. 'So. Fenton. Fenton Conville. Here we are, and where are we?'

Now that he was looking at them, and to his slight surprise, Fenton remembered exactly the large dark eyes, their soap-bubble lustre.

'Sandy. Sandy Collins. It's been a long while. Thank you so much for meeting me.'

She continued to stare at him, nodding, apparently lost in an audit of time past. A waitress materialized at Fenton's side, all ears.

'Listen,' Sandy said, 'I'm against the clock, so I think we should just have the set lunch; it's quicker. What will you have to drink?'

'A glass of house red would be great.'

'I'll take a Perrier. Thanks.'

The waitress withdrew and Fenton, in a space empty but for faint clinkings and tinklings from the background, had a sensation of free fall. He felt the urge to blurt out something, but he wasn't quite sure what it was.

'So,' he said.

'So.'

'So how long you been in Dublin?'

'What? Oh, yonks. Fifteen years? I was in London for ten years, so yes, fifteen. I didn't mean to stay so long, but you know how it is.'

'And are you up the road much?'

'Up North? Not very often, my parents –' Her phone went. 'Sorry, I have to … Hello? Yes, Wario, thanks for getting back. I know it's late there but I wanted a word about the Damashitoru position.'

Ten minutes later Fenton had drunk his wine and dispatched his starter, which consisted of a lozenge of root vegetable about the size of a pencil sharpener and three speckled beans glistening under a pixie-cap of white spume. Sandy was still on the phone, but had managed to put away two beans.

'*Arigatou*, Wario, I'll leave it with you. *Oyasumi nasai* … Apols, where were we?'

'You were saying you don't get back up North much. Do you not miss it?'

She sighed. 'I do from time to time, but my partner's been based in Brussels the last couple of years, so I tend to head over there when I'm free. And you, you're still …?'

'Yep, still scratching around on the same piece of ground – mortgage, kids, the whole deal. You any children?'

'No.'

The main course arrived. Fenton contemplated a circle of alternating yellow and green blobs within which was what appeared to be a purple carrot and two disks of shaved cauliflower. Writhing in an earthenware dish on the side was some kind of seaweed.

'Looks good.' Fenton grimly dipped his head.

'So, have you something to say to me?'

'Uh, yeah.' The carrot had an ice-lollyish texture and was the most intensely *vegetal* thing he had ever eaten. He dabbed a bit in a blob. It didn't help. 'It's a little awkward, actually. It's, uh, about that time, do you remember, when we, uh –'

'Spent the night together?'

'Yes.' He munched a frond of bladderwrack, releasing what seemed like a quarter pint of the Atlantic into his mouth. His gorge rose.

'What about it? Um, are you all right?'

'Excuse me.' He wiped his chin and stuffed the iodine-stained napkin under his knee. 'I wanted to apologize.'

'Oh yes?'

'For … well, you know, for …'

'What exactly?'

'Well, the thing is I'm afraid I may have taken advantage. You were very young, *too* young, maybe, and if that's the case …' He took a deep breath. The earlier compulsion to blurt now found free rein. Sandy set down her fork and leaned back while Fenton babbled about his shock at receiving the legal letter, the precariousness of his financial situation, his standing in the community and his good works, his abject regret for the disgraceful behaviour of his youthful self … All the while, Sandy fixed her gaze on a point just beyond his left ear, which was disconcerting.

'Wow,' she said at last. 'That's – sorry, I have to take this.' It was Marsha from New York and she was excited. 'Marsha, you're going to have to slow down ... The source, is it solid? ... What's the upside, and how long do we have?'

Mopping his brow with his cuff, Fenton tried to compose himself. He felt strange. Unburdened yet vulnerable. Off balance. This intimate act of eating, with this woman he hadn't seen for thirty years and barely knew, their only connection a tiny, distant pocket of shared time, and yet who seemed close, familiar. He felt a long way from home. He felt irrelevant.

'I'm really sorry,' said Sandy, tucking her phone into her bag. 'Something's come up. I'm going to have to jump back to the office. But, Fenton, just about what you were saying there – and it seems you're in quite a predicament – for a start I wasn't underage –'

'But it says on LinkedIn –'

'Are you *sure* you're not a stalker? Look, everyone lies about their age on those things. And anyway, nothing happened – I suspect you'd had too many lagers – but you see it wasn't actually anything personal. I was just working something out for myself, something I'd been wrestling with for a while, and if it's any consolation, you confirmed it for me once and for all.'

'You mean you're not into men?'

'Yep, and very happy with it.'

'So it's not you?'

'It's not me.'

Fenton looked down at his plate.

'Hey.' She rose, tossing a length of chartreuse silk around her shoulders. 'I'm not going to lie to you' – she held out her hand – 'this has been weird.'

～

On his bench in the shade on Stephen's Green, Fenton chewed the kebab he'd purchased after leaving the restaurant and watched the ducks squabbling over rounds of white pan, frisbee-ed into the pond by a man and his young daughter. He was pretty sure bread wasn't good for ducks. Nor was the kebab, in all likelihood, good for *him*, but after the practical joke played on him at Temps Perdu, he was friggin' eating it.

He thought, with another flush of outrage, about his dessert, a densely layered wedge of asbestos cake in a puddle of beige emulsion (he'd managed barely half of it) and tried not to think about the truly astonishing bill he'd stared at in disbelief for several minutes. Further insult came with his discovery (in tiny print below the logo) of the phrase *gastronomie vegetale*.

And after all that, he was back to square one. The shark was still there, down in the depths, cruising around, biding its time, intent on biting off his legs. There would be blood in the water, and what then? The disastrous scenarios unspooled in his head once again. Prison time. Possible divorce. Small-town ostracism. Probable exile. He shivered. It was hideous. It would have to be fixed. He would have to fix it, that was all there was to it. But how? The shark was not visible.

Meanwhile, the bread bag was empty, and the girl was disappointed that the ducks were dispersing, no longer within her magnetic field. She wanted it to go on. More bread was required. She was on the verge of full-scale petulance, her father leaning over, gripping both downy forearms. The girl reminded Fenton of Andrea at that age, something in the obstinacy of the posture, the unnerving inner stillness while nuclear options were reviewed. Andrea had come through it (the early teens were another matter) but for a while she had wrought mayhem. For most of her fourth and fifth years, in fact, she had been terrifyingly impervious to any kind of sanction as she laid waste to family outings and suicide-bombed her own birthday parties. Once, in the park, after a torrid stand-off, Fenton had called her bluff and strode on at a brisk and determined pace, expecting at any minute to hear panicked bleating in his wake. Instead, when he at last lost his nerve and turned, she was receding into the horizon towards the carriageway like a miniature Road Runner, save for the trail of cartoon dust clouds. He had his full cardio that day, and no mistake.

His phone pinged: Wee Davy declaring himself back at the car. Fenton made a few wrong turns finding the car park. The streets were so crowded, he couldn't see where he was going. The cafés were full, the pubs spilling out, people lounging under awnings, laughing, quaffing, smoking. They couldn't all be tourists. *Why were they not at work?* And that smell everywhere, the yeasty, treacly ghost of toasted barley that gusted downriver from St James's Gate and along every alleyway. A beverage with its own invisible, airborne advertising.

Wee Davy had succumbed. 'I only had five pints, but s'prolly better if you drive.' He was crouched down, one hand on the side of the car, supervising Sniper's lunch, a foot-long meatball sub.

'I don't have a licence,' Fenton reminded him. 'That's ... that's the whole point. Five pints?'

'Sure the Irish cops can't touch you and I'll be right as rain by the time we get to the border.'

'*Five pints?*'

'I've driven on five before, no problem. I think the stuff must be stronger down here.'

Fenton paid the incredible sum demanded by the ticket machine, and they set off. Wee Davy blethered non-stop all the way to Balbriggan: about his visit to the Leprechaun Museum, where he'd learned how leprechauns differ from fairies, elves, goblins *and* pookas ('they're actually little *people*'); about the Irish fella in the pub who bought him a jar and told him the story of his grandfather who'd fought at Messines Ridge in 1917 ('My granda was there too!') and risked his life digging two men out from under the rubble of an exploded landmine, one of them minus an arm, the other a leg; about the woman who'd chatted him up in Merrion Square park while Sniper was having a crap, who couldn't get enough of his accent ('She was all over me like a rash; thought I was gonna have to go home with her'); about how friendly everyone had been.

As he checked again in the rear-view mirror for peelers, it struck Fenton that, all in all, Wee Davy had had a grand day out. He further reflected that, including various sundries, such as deluxe ice creams for Sniper, he was down about five hundred quid.

'So how did it go with your fancy woman?'

'It wasn't anything like that,' said Fenton. 'I knew her years ago. We were just catching up.'

'Yeah, right. So does wifey know about this trip?'

'Not exactly.'

'Will you tell her?'

Fenton considered. There was no plausible untruth for having his mechanic drive him to Dublin; Andrea didn't know where he'd been; there was no money trail, he and Carolyn having had separate accounts from the start (Carolyn's earnings had for many years provided the family's holiday fund). 'Probably not.'

Wee Davy made a strange sound, and Fenton realized he had never heard him laugh before.

'Seriously, it's not what you think.'

'Sure, sure, hey, it's none of my beeswax. Whadda they say? When the mouse is at, wait, no, when the cat's not ...'

Fenton decided Wee Davy was still pissed. 'If you must know, I was looking to find out some information. I'm in a bit of fix. Someone's trying to hurt me. Someone from the past.'

Wee Davy went quiet. 'Listen,' he said after a minute, 'if you're havin' a problem, I can maybe help you out.'

'How's that?'

'Just … I know some people, a few lads from the old days, boys you wouldn't want to mess with, if you know what I mean. Just say the word.'

It was Fenton's turn to laugh. 'Yeah, thanks, that's very good of you but it's not that kind of problem.' And with a touch of bitterness he added, 'Unfortunately.' And then, before he could stop himself, 'When you say *from the old days* …?'

'Ach, sure I was young and foolish; you get mixed up in things.'

Now that he thought about it, Fenton remembered hearing rumours in the pub, hints about Wee Davy's 'involvement'. Did he really want the details? But it was too late, Wee Davy was off and running. And it turned out he'd been quite the young defender. True blue. Fenton listened with growing disquiet as his driver-turned-passenger unburdened himself.

An enthusiastic participant with the York Road Tartans in weekly street fights and mayhem tours to Ibrox ('We were teenagers, the crack was mighty'), Wee Davy found himself at the age of eighteen the worse for wear in the top room of a pub up the Shankill Road, putting one hand on a Bible and the other on a Luger and pledging to resist and repel by all means necessary the encroachment of republican violence on the Protestant community ('It was nineteen-seventy-two, things were seriously kickin' off').

He was 'active' for seven years. 'Started off with fundraisin' mainly, you know, collectin', whatchacallit, *insurance* from shops and businesses, settin' a wee fire if they didn't cough up, moved on to pullin' the odd post-office job.'

It got worse. Of course it did. But thankfully, Wee Davy wasn't too specific ('We met force with force … we were on a war footin' … you did what you were told'). And then, he was nicked. A botched carjacking on the Woodstock Road (he managed to ditch the rod) earned him fifteen months inside. This gave him time to have 'a wee think'. He concluded that he was on a bad path and should probably make a clean break.

'It's not that easy but. They don't like people hangin' up their boots. They lean on you, they pressurize you. I had debts. I owed money to one of the top boys – this guy was a real psycho, and he held it over me, he said right, one last job and you're on your way. Fair enough. But it turned out to be a big one – takin' out a judge. I'd only been the getaway man before, never pulled the trigger. There was no way. It just wasn't gonna happen. I went along with it till the mornin' of the hit, then I took the boat to Liverpool. And I never came back for five years.'

'Jeez. And they left you alone?'

'Had to keep the head down. Some people have long memories. But there's a few retired boys on the estate, and there's no problem. The peace deal changed everything, sure. They're still hard men, though, especially after a wheen of pints.'

'Do you regret it?'

Wee Davy stared out of the window for a long time. 'I have the odd bad dream all right, but I did what I thought had to be done at the time. And let's face it, none of your lot was gonna get their hands dirty.'

'My lot?'

'Aye. The middle class.'

Fenton felt he'd better leave it there.

23

Tugging the knot tight, the man from the council (Conservation Department) – a dark, lean plaid-shirted thirty-year-old of pensive demeanour – eased the coiled rope from his shoulder and let it skitter down through the branches. This was as much as he could do until the lads with the machinery arrived. They took their own sweet time those guys: coffee breaks within coffee breaks. The man loosened the harness strap and twisted around, crossing his legs over and leaning back against the trunk so he could look out through the desiccated foliage.

At this height, he was level with the tallest turret of the house and had almost a hundred-and-eighty-degree view over the treetops of the neighbourhood. And what a plush and pleasant vista it was: tiered lawns and ivy-clad walls, summerhouses and gazebos; topiary. It was like one vast garden spread across the plateau, overlooking the distant roofs and spires of the town and the sparkling sweep of the lough beyond. The trees, and they were plentiful, were in mid-blaze – yellow-and-auburn golds, daubs of crimson – swaying together so gently their element might have been water rather than air.

Down below, at the far end of the lawn, the old boy, Symington, was attempting to keep his ancient trousers up while hobbling around herding fallen leaves with a clapped-out leaf-blower and making a right hames of it. Wasn't that the gardener's job? Maybe they were too mean to pay one – Symington had got quite shirty when told he'd have to share the cost of taking down the elm.

A passing breeze made the tree creak, and he glanced up at the clumps of dead growth, clawed like arthritic hands around the twigs. It was a shame. The thing was mature, standing for a century he reckoned, and one of the last survivors of its kind. Its preservation tag, the aluminium corroded now, the numerals just legible, was like a medal pinned to its trunk. He never liked to see a tree felled, young or old, but sometimes it had to be done. This one was tricky – hence the rope: it was perilously close to the ornate glass conservatory that was just about clinging to the side of the house.

House? The place was bigger than a lot of hotels. Sixteen windows, not including French doors. Most of those on the upper floor were blinded by shutters, but the one nearest him had neither shutters nor curtains and he could see into a large bedroom, its flower-patterned walls festooned with posters of pouting, lion-maned rock stars. On one side, above a bed with a sheeny marshmallow-pink cover, a menagerie of soft toys wrestled together on a shelf. Unquestionably the lair of a teenage girl.

In one of the ground-floor rooms a woman was seated in an armchair with a rug on her lap. He could make out little of her except for the impression of a cloud of silvery hair and that she was gazing up at the tree in which he was perched, but at this distance, and shielded as he was by the scintillations of the bower, he doubted he was visible. Nonetheless, the single-minded quality of her contemplation spooked him.

His phone chimed twice in succession, and he extracted it gingerly from his tool belt. The boys, he learned, were just having a coffee and would be on their way asap. The second message was from his father, telling him the word from the lawyers was that the inquiry could be heading for deadlock. Not enough evidence, unreliable witnesses – *might not stand up*. If it was right, this was terrific news.

They'd all been fretting about the strain on the old man's ticker, which hadn't been the best even before he retired. A lot of his ex-cop pals had health problems too. All this digging into the past, trying to dredge up memories from thirty years ago – it was stressful: who did what and on whose say-so; who had looked the other way; was that a nod? Had that been a wink? X would know but X was dead. So was Y. Z was dead too, or maybe never existed. *Whatever you say, say nothing*. At this remove all was Chinese whispers, smoke and mirrors, ghosts and vapour. The truth was pretty much gone with the wind. His father was a good guy, he was sure of it – a good guy caught up in a bad do. He sent a fingers-crossed emoji and put away his phone.

It was a clear bright morning, the first dry day for nearly a week, which was a bonus – slippery branches were a bollocks – and milder now after the early chill. At the far side of the garden the old boy was setting fire to a heap of leaves and brush behind a box hedge. The smoke rose and began to perfume the air. In the middle of the lawn was a three-tiered stone fountain, long dormant; a pair of wood pigeons were prowling around in the lower basin, alert, proprietorial – he could hear their faint fluting ruminations. He checked his watch. Nearly eleven. Where the hell were they? Just then, urgently in need of a wash, the council van trundled up the driveway and squeaked to a halt in front of the steps. He wriggled around in his harness and, giving the trunk of the tree a sympathetic slap, began his descent.

∽

When it came to it, the elm yielded to the saw's teeth without much trouble – not like some of the oaks and ash trees they had to deal with – but at the final instant it seemed to hold back before toppling, as though having one last look around at its domain. Then, in an accelerating crescendo of cracking and splintering, it fell, half-bounced once and collapsed with an immense sigh from its dying leaves on the soft bed of the lawn. A shocked, almost unearthly silence followed. The old man, who had stood at a distance to watch, stared up at the vacated space for a few moments, turned and walked back towards his fire. At the window, the woman's face shimmered and sank from view. The men from the council began to gather up their tools.

24

Fenton was in his parents' junk room having a leisurely hoke. Amid the chaotic jumble of broken lamps, defunct electrical appliances and busted picture frames were bags and boxes of his and Artie's childhood detritus (their mother, despite her astringent façade, had a sentimental seam). The air smelled of damp plaster, with an undertow of ancient kitty litter.

Against one wall, collapsed on its knees, was a crammed glass-fronted bookcase. He let the doors swing open and ran his eye along the shelves. *The Guinness Book of Records (1976), Little Women, A Choice of Poets, Strange Tales of Peril and Adventure, Treasure Island, Lord Byron's Poetical Works ... Rupert the Bear* annuals, a whole stack of them – some he remembered, others he didn't: *Rupert and the Enormous Pear, Rupert and the Mysterious Hole, Rupert and the Coloured People, Rupert and the Magic Toadstools, Rupert and Bill Get Caught.*

Fenton had always thought there was something odd about Rupert, something indefinably creepy about him and his friends, with their weird clothes, moving through their eerie version of the Home Counties. That Raggety thing had featured in more than one childhood nightmare.

He turned away and tugged at the knot of a bulging refuse bag, releasing an exhalation of fustiness. Groping around, he hauled out a soft expanse of silky turquoise and held it up, awed by its swag and shimmer: his Hammer pants. *Hammer time!* Had he really had the nerve to prance around the dancefloors of Caproni's and Milano's in these ludicrous bags? A gyrating genie. Aladdin Sane. How had he not got a kicking? He rummaged again. This time a navy serge hussar jacket with elaborate gold braiding. The New Romantic days! A set of fluttering vistas briefly lit up in his head. He tried it on. The buttons were now obsolete, but it felt good. He admired himself in the panes of the bookcase.

∽

Downstairs, at the kitchen table, his parents and Mihaela were engaged in a game of Scrabble. True to family form, there was a dispute.

'Fenton, your father won't let me have breadserver,' cried his mother, sitting back with petulantly folded arms.

'There's no such thing,' growled his father.

'Of course there is – someone who serves bread. It's not fair. If you're allowed *farmless*, I can have breadserver.'

'Farmless?' said Fenton.

His father looked up, did a double-take at the tunic and said, 'White Rhodesians who had their farms taken away – what were they?'

'Angry? Taught a lesson?'

'What? No, they, for God's sake – they were *farmless*.'

Fenton leaned over the board. 'Who's winning?'

'Mihaela,' his mother said sulkily, glaring at her husband. 'Clive, if you're at a banquet and you want some bread, who're you going to call?'

'A waiter or a waitress,' his father replied. 'Hazel, they don't have people who are trained specifically to serve bread. That's nonsense.'

'And we don't have a farm,' retorted his mother. 'But I've never heard you complain that we're farmless. It's not like being homeless, you silly old toad.'

Fenton began to feel a familiar, ancient tension in his stomach, recalling the family games when he was young; how Artie would always win, trotting out smart-arse words like *quixotry* and *syzygy* and *caziques*, and how often they'd had to abort when things boiled over, everyone strunting away from the table for a pink-faced sulk.

'Fenton, what are you wearing?' his mother demanded.

Brushing lint from his sleeve, Fenton said, 'I found it in the box room. I'm taking it home. By the way I think the plaster's about to fall down up there. You might want to get a wee man in to have a skelly at it.'

This precipitated a brooding silence. His mother stared at the floor, his father at the ceiling. Mihaela seemed to have another word ready to go, but was trapped in the impasse over the existence of baked goods sommeliers. Finally his father said, 'Bugger.'

'Where are we going to get a wee man?' said his mother. 'There are no wee men any more. It's all big firms who charge you an arm and a leg. Pixie Dixon had a tiny bit of dry rot in her joists last year and they hit her with a bill for ten grand. She nearly had a heart attack.'

'What about whatshisname from the village?' said Fenton. 'The guy who used to do the lawn and the drains, had a stutter or a stammer.'

'Willy? Willy Whiteside? Sure he died about five years ago from head cancer.'

'Really? *Head cancer?* Well what about that other fella who could fix anything – the man with the van?'

'Jack Russell?' His mother's expression was almost accusatory. 'Sure Jackie's been in the Salvation Army home for two years now, barely knows his own name.'

'You're just going to have to bite the bullet then,' said Fenton. 'You've plenty of money. What are you saving it for?'

His father performed one of his low, drawn-out throat clearances, a sound like the scrape of a dungeon door on stone. 'We might not be as well-off as you think, Fenton. I'll have a look at it myself and maybe Basil can give me a hand. How hard can it be?'

'You and Basil? Plastering?' Hazel was incredulous. 'It's a skilled job. *Getting* plastered would be more like it.'

Mihaela laid down her tiles, utilizing the final 'R' of *breadserver* to spell out a word that contained a 'V', an 'X' and a 'Z' on a triple.

'Bogdan, he can fix,' she said, totting up her score. 'I think maybe I win.'

Down at The Stoat, it was 5 p.m., and Fenton's old New Romantic look got a mixed reception.

'Fuck me, it's Adam and the Antiques,' said Bob. 'Where's your horse?'

'Fenton, that's quite a bold statement,' said Graham.

'*Qua qua, da diddley qua qua,*' went Liam.

'Envy's a terrible thing,' said Fenton, suddenly spotting the identical navy blue gilets that all three lads were wearing. 'Pint of Guinness, please ... Anyone else? And another stout there. Thanks.' He climbed up on the corner stool. 'So, what's happening?' Glancing around, he was relieved to see that the scary septuagenarian known as Mad Dennis was absent and noted that the Sevens & Fruits machine was out of order.

'End of a busy week,' said Bob, who was wearing a patch over one eye. 'We just fancied a bit of an oul' swaggle.'

'Fair enough. What are we discussing? And, by the way, what's with the eyepatch?'

'Laser surgery. One down, one to go. Stings like a bastard.'

'Actually,' said Graham, tapping a tabloid someone had left on the bar, 'we were just talking about this "agreed Ireland" thing. What do you reckon?'

'I think it's real. Not any time soon, but probably inevitable.'

'Nah,' said Bob, 'it'll never happen.'

'Why you so sure?'

'The Shinners.'

'The Shinners?'

'Bob's right,' said Graham. 'They're the stumbling block. Unpalatable. Even if there *are* people coming round to the idea, who see it as a price worth paying to stay in Europe or whatever, in the end the thought of the Shinners strutting around crowing about having won will be too much for them. They won't have the stomach for it.'

'Maybe.' Fenton took a long pull of stout. 'But maybe not. Say there *was* a border poll and it swung in favour of unity – what do you think would happen to us?'

'You mean the Prods?' Graham scrunched up his face and scrabbled at his beard. 'Well, that's the question, isn't it? In the short term – assuming the rocket men don't pop up again – probably just a lot of squabbling and wrangling to protect our new minority status. In the longer term, I suppose the fear is we'd be painted over. Erased.'

'M'm. Or it could be just fine, and we all rub along together like reasonable adults. Parity of esteem and all that.'

Graham snickered. 'Yeah, right.'

'*And righteous men must make our land,*' crooned Liam.

'Away out of that, Liam,' said Bob. 'Not going to happen.'

'*A nation once again* ... Who knows?'

'Nope. Anyway, I don't think you'd like it if it did.'

'Oh?' Liam set his hands on the bar-top; the air, minutely but perceptibly, tightened. 'And why's that?'

'You're one of us now. A solid citizen. No one's benefited from the British exchequer as much as you and your civil service mates. You've had the soup *and* the hairy bacon.'

'Is that so?' A tiny muscle beside Liam's right eye began to flicker.

'You really think you'd be as cosy under a Dublin diktat?'

'You're talking shite –'

Graham stepped in. 'Come on, guys, keep it country. We're all Ulstermen here.'

'Never fear, Bob,' grinned Liam, raising his glass. 'I'll put in a good word for you.'

Stevie, the longest-serving barman, leaned on the counter and surveyed the company with his heavy-lidded, yellowish eyes. Not for the first time, Fenton perceived a hint of amusement, as if Stevie knew something; as if Stevie was thinking Fenton and his ilk had made a huge and fundamentally incorrect assumption about the world and how it worked. Wee Davy sometimes had a similar look. 'Saw your name in the *Advertiser*,' he said to Fenton. 'Six-month ban for the morning after? That's rough.'

'Tell me about it.'

'You must've had a skinful.'

'It was my birthday.'

'Still, rough. Hope you enjoyed it. Same again, lads?'

'Will we try another one?' said Liam. 'Yeah, go on. My round ... Hey, who'd you think would win in a fight, Bono or Van the Man?'

They pondered.

'Well, Van would probably have the weight advantage,' said Bob. 'But wee Bono might be nippier ... dirtier.'

Graham demurred. 'I dunno. I reckon Van could take him. A lot of pent-up anger there looking for a lightning rod. Plus, he's from east Belfast, so he must've had a few scraps in his time.'

Fenton thought back to his encounter with the menacing motorist and what might have happened if there'd been a handy parking spot for him to stop and unleash his rage. Fenton hadn't had a fight since school (a 'serious' one at any rate. He'd had to shove a drunk once who was pawing at Carolyn during a picnic in the park – the guy fell over with a grunt of surprise and went to sleep). But he'd had a real fight back in fifth form, a new boy, name of Peacock, who'd transferred from another (rougher) school and decided he'd establish his credentials by, for some reason, putting Fenton in his place.

Billed as The Slog in the Bog, it was staged in the junior toilets one break-time a few weeks into the spring term, and Fenton had just about prevailed. His early attempt at a headlock choke-out was derailed by an upward punch to the clinkers, and then things opened up into a conventional bout of shirt-ripping, scrabbing and bruising collisions with sinks and cubicle doors. Peacock was wiry but tenacious and kept up a torrent of swearing throughout, which was surprisingly off-putting. In the end, though, the challenger, ostensibly tapping out to deal with a truly prolific nosebleed, showed no enthusiasm to resume. Deafened in one ear by a knuckly sidewinder, and unable to turn his head without yelping for a week, Fenton decided that pugilism wasn't really his thing (rugby-field scraggings didn't count).

'Any sign of that crazy old coot who gave me a hard time about the fruit machine?'

'Mad Dennis?' said Bob. 'Saw him the other day, funnily enough – on crutches. Said he fell down the stairs, but I suspect he got a hiding.'

'I heard he ran out of road with Big Roy,' said Liam. 'Small matter of a large unpaid debt.'

Fenton permitted himself a smirk, which was almost instantly dislodged by an icy ripple of anxiety. That word *debt*.

'So, Fenton, are you going to tell us why you're wearing an artefact from the distant past?' asked Bob.

Fenton slipped off the tunic. 'Found it in my old stuff up at the folks'; thought Andrea might like it. The youngsters are all getting into vintage.'

'Are they?'

'Oh yeah. Wouldn't surprise me if flares make a comeback. Hammer pants, even.'

'*Hammer time!*' cried Liam. '*Duh duh-duh duh.*'

They finished their pints in silence. The late afternoon sun hit the windows of The Stoat at an angle, like a shot off a shovel.

'Same again, lads?'

∽

Fenton took off his hussar jacket and slung it over his shoulder. The beers had spaced him out, put him into a kind of wistful reverie. He looked about him as he walked, listening to the soft crunch of his footsteps on the sandy path. Down on the beach, a couple of young people in hi-vis vests were picking up litter with grabber sticks and putting it into refuse sacks. At the pier, three middle-aged women had been in for a swim and now stood huddled in their towelling tepees, talking and laughing. One of them waved.

There were usually more of them, a gang who took a daily dip even in the depths of winter. It gave Fenton the shivers just thinking about it, but when he'd chatted to them once, they said it made them feel *fantastic* and that he really should take the plunge, and he had to admit they looked pretty perky on it – fresh and pink, sprightly, their eyes seemingly recalibrated, far-seeing, as though they were gaining some mysterious super-power. It was like fricken *Cocoon*, he thought.

He crossed over the tinkling outflow of the stream that began up the hill behind the park, and stopped and took in the sweep of Belfast Lough, trying to grasp its indifferent beauty. He was feeling a tad spiritual. 'This is where I live,' he whispered to himself. 'This is my home.' And he repeated, as though realizing for the first time, 'This is where I *live*.' He looked at the silver-green water and at the far mountains, mauve-grey in the dimming light, and he sniffed the familiar smells of sand and kelp and driftwood, and said again, aloud, 'This is my home.'

After a while he moved on. Coming towards him was the jogger he often saw on the path. She was thirty-ish and gangly, with a ponytail, and her running style was a kind of stealthy tiptoe, knees high, like someone fleeing a midnight crime scene. He stood aside as she tore by. Up ahead, sailing along on his bicycle, was another regular on the seafront, a man of advanced but strangely indeterminate years, with hair that tended to the bouffant. He had an English face and always wore a bemused smile that reminded Fenton of Sergeant Wilson out of *Dad's Army*. 'Beauteous evening, calm and free,' the man called out in a rich, happy tone as he passed.

'Yes.' Of course. Fenton wondered why he hadn't thought of it before: he would dust off his old bike, pump up the tyres and get back on the road. Better than walking everywhere. Graham had taken up cycling the previous year – they could go for jaunts along the coast together. (On the other hand, Graham was a serious biker, obsessive, one of those ageing alpha males forever munching energy bars and checking his beats per minute. Physically, he was approaching ninety per cent gristle, on the verge, it seemed to Fenton sometimes, of turning into a human-sized dog chew.) He strode on, cut along the lane and came to the gate at the bottom of his garden. Gazing up at his house, at the prow-like edge of the upper deck, warm lamplight flowing from its windows, he thought how like a ship it appeared, how solid.

25

It was the end-of-term concert – an event for which Fenton had annually to brace himself, an obligation, an endurance test, not least because of the mortality shock of being back at his old school, with its unchanging odours of floor polish, disinfectant and sulphurous rumours from the science labs. He was beside Bob, whose eldest son was due to play the drums in a band called Extinction Event. Andrea would be sulkily dummy-mouthing along with the choir.

'Do you think it'll go on as long as last year?'

'Hope not,' said Bob. 'Though I necked a couple of Una's Xanax to be on the safe side.'

'Any left?'

''Fraid not, mate, you're just gonna have to lie back and take it.'

It was sweaty in the assembly hall, and the moulded plastic chairs were rigidly unforgiving. To make matters worse, Fenton's skin condition was playing up. The rash was now uniform down to his knees, appearing when he was naked as though he were wearing scarlet knickerbockers, and was, he feared, mulling an incursion farther north. He wished he'd worn looser trousers and thought with fond longing of his Hammer pants. He'd started wondering of late whether he could actually get away with a kilt, or even one of those wrap-around sari things old Indian gentlemen seemed so comfortable in. How would that go down at The Toad? Safer than a kilt, which was sure to be wheeked up by some joker at the bar sooner or later.

Bob nudged him. 'See your woman there, with the blonde hair, three up, seven along? Didn't you get off with her once, at a party?'

'It's not Laura Hayes, is it?'

'Who? No, it's ... whaddya call her, Deke Beatty's sister – Ann, is it, or Anna? – she was on the netball team. You definitely did.'

Fenton craned forward, caught a flash of soft semi-profile, but not enough for a positive ID. A ripple of shushing reached them from the front rows and the headmaster emerged from the wings, hands operatically outstretched. The overheads were doused, and a yellow spotlight sought and eventually found him, smiling beaverishly behind a close-cropped full-face beard. After the customary squeals of feedback from the microphone, he looked the audience over benignly and embarked on his spiel.

'... a productive year ... much progress ... some challenges ... departure of Mr Wedge ... unfortunate business ... Symington memorial pavilion ... links to slave trade ... change of name ... new era ... community spirit ... academic excellence ... dedicated teaching staff ...

sporting achievements … better luck next season … times we live in … upholding of traditions … pride … And now, without further ado …'

After some further ado, a small boy in a black bow tie and over-long tails walked at a funereal pace across the stage and wriggled into position at a baby grand piano, arranging himself with much creaking and squeaking on the stool. Having stared at the ceiling long enough to trigger nervous coughing in the audience, he made a start on the 'Minute Waltz' and, after several faltering detours and panic-stricken reversals, completed it in just under three minutes.

This was followed by a saxophone quartet named, somewhat confusingly, The Saxtuplets, who played a modern jazz piece of their own composition, entitled 'Squeeze My Pips'. Skilfully executed and initially toe-tappingly melodic, it soon descended into a honking riot of nightmarish self-expression that raised the blood pressure of every man, woman and child in the place. Calm was restored with a three-girl a cappella version of Adele's 'Someone Like You', which garnered grateful and prolonged applause.

Unfortunately, the next offering was a fifteen-minute xylophone solo. 'What do a xylophone solo and premature ejaculation have in common?' whispered Bob. 'With both, you know it's going to happen but there's nothing you can do about it.' Fenton sniggered under his breath, but his mind was already on the interval and how he might engineer a conversation with the woman Bob had pointed out. Time was limited, and he'd have to give Carolyn the slip. He began to gird himself, his rash fully awake now and prickling northwards.

In the canteen everyone stood around drinking stewed tea, eating stale biscuits and lauding the high quality of the performances, while the headmaster circulated, shaking hands and cracking family-friendly jokes. Carolyn and Una were chatting with some other mothers they knew. 'Jeez, I could murder a pint,' said Bob, looking around as though there might have been a beer tap he hadn't noticed. 'Do you fancy a scoop on the way home?'

'M'm?' Fenton was watching the woman he may or may not have had a tryst with, who was at the far side of the tea dispensers talking to one of the teachers. Of medium height, with an erect posture, she had a round, pleasant face and pale, quizzical eyes. He couldn't place her at all. 'Yeah, good idea. Run it past the girls.'

The 'girls' swept by, announcing they were visiting 'the Ladies' before the concert resumed. Fenton saw his chance and wandered over to the woman, but, as he approached, she set down her cup and strode away, also in the direction of the toilets.

Carolyn, Una and the woman were in a queue. He passed on to the end of the cloakrooms, with their benches and colour-coded coat pegs, and diverted into 'the Gents', which was deserted. His nostrils flared at the reek of Jeyes Fluid.

Standing at a sink, he glanced over his shoulder and with some urgency pulled his jeans halfway down and began splashing cold water on his burning upper thighs. Then, he grabbed a handful of paper towels and entered a stall to dry himself. This accomplished, he urinated. The silence of these white-tiled, high-ceilinged spaces! The sound of his jet in the bowl was deafening. Images came back to him: many water fights, much flushing of junior boys' heads, numberless Players No. 6s dispatched while avoiding assembly. This had also been the venue for his Slog in the Bog with Peacock. There must have been thirty-odd boys packed in (possibly even a couple of teachers). And here he was again, pissing in the same bowl.

Outside, the corridor was empty and the queue gone. He swore to himself. He'd missed her. But as he passed the girls' cloakroom, there she was, rummaging in her bag. He took a moment. 'Hi there. It's Ann, isn't it?'

'Anna.'

'*Anna*, of course. It's been a long time.'

'Uh, actually, Fenton, I saw you here last year.'

'Oh. Really? I didn't ...' Nodding and smiling inanely, he studied her face. There was coldness in her eyes. 'You remember me then.'

'Of course.'

'I'm afraid my memory isn't what it used to be.'

'No? Alzheimer's?'

'Haha, God no. I hope not. Maybe.' A bell rang and they both glanced in the direction of the assembly hall. 'Listen, Anna, I, uh, do I owe you an apology?'

'How do you mean?'

'Back then. Did I, did we ... was I out of order?'

'Come again?'

'Did I take advantage? If you know what I mean. If I went too far, I'm truly sorry.'

She was staring at him hard, her lips twitching. 'The snog at Gemma McConkey's party – is *that* what you're talking about?'

Fenton was floundering. 'So it's not you?'

'Is what not me? What do you mean?'

'Ah,' said Fenton.

With a look of irked bafflement, she half-turned to leave, then, seeming to struggle with a thought, swung back and, addressing his sternum, said in a quiet voice, 'You know I was very keen on you, Fenton. *Really* keen. I think it's fair to say you were my first love. All those Valentine's cards. I worshipped you. And you barely knew I existed.'

'I'm sorry.'

She looked up at him with the pale quizzical eyes that flashed at him, unmistakable now, from the margin of his inner vision. 'You broke my heart, Fenton, but I suppose that doesn't mean much to people like you.'

Back in the hall, the lights were already down. The piano had been wheeled away and the stage decked out for a rock band, with drum kit and electric guitars on stands. 'What kept you?' said Bob. 'The lads are up.'

The lads appeared from the wings and swarmed to their instruments, sunglasses, headbands and heavy jewellery much in evidence. Clacking his drumsticks together, Bob's son Luke counted them in, and a juggernaut of decibels came crashing forth. People reeled back, swearing, in their seats. Two small girls burst into tears in the next row. Bob said something that Fenton couldn't hear.

In truth, he heard little at all of the progression of the second half – which included 'Spring' by Vivaldi, a song from *Frozen* and, inevitably, something by Ed Sheeran – lost as he was among the brute facts of his predicament. He entered into a strange kind of dream which involved him fighting his way, in mounting panic, through a dense crowd. People kept turning to look at him, but as he looked at them, their faces would dissolve into pixellated blurs of pink. When he came to, with a jolt, the finale was drawing to a close – orchestra, choir and band joining together for (ironically, one of his faves) 'Africa' by Toto.

26

Studying the list of handwritten names on the desk in front of him, Crawford Wylie took his pen and put a line through 'Liam McIlvenny'. Liam hadn't been so bad – had on one occasion even counselled for leniency and years later, in the pub, expressed regret for the actions of the others, albeit in a 'sure we're all eejits at that age' kind of way. No, Liam he would spare.

Conville, on the other hand, had showed no remorse, offered not the slightest apology, and seemed either to have forgotten entirely or deemed both Wylie and the torment inflicted on him to be neither here nor there. Well, he was almost certainly on the hook now and would shortly pay.

Wylie ran his eye over the other names: Bob Moffat, Graham Winter, Newton Stuart, Spud Murphy, Soupy Campbell, Mike Cruddy. He drew a wiggly line through the last two (Campbell, who had joined the cops, was thirty years dead from a Provo bomb under his Ford Escort; Cruddy, he had recently learned, was doing twenty years for killing his neighbour with a spade in a dispute over trellising). Fenton's sidekick Bob had been quite the sadist, chief instigator of the debagging that necessitated Wylie sprinting the length of the school playing fields (halting a girls' hockey final en route) in just his shirt and blazer (and it had been a very cold day). He had never moved so fast in his life. Despite this, the jeering and giggling went on for weeks. That guy Graham had rarely missed an opportunity for humiliation, and nor had Murphy, and as for that bastard Newton ... the superglue in the pubes could have been very serious indeed.

Panting slightly, his eyes stinging, Wylie shoved back from the desk, crossed to the open window and sucked at the air from the street. Those had been unhappy times. Even now, he wasn't sure why he had been singled out for the routine emptying of schoolbooks into the foul-smelling canteen bins, his shoes lobbed over the wall of the adjacent convent school. The regular hair-washes down the jacks. Because he was a short-arse? His briefcase? (He'd ditched it in third form.) His acne? (Beano Hynes's was much worse.) Sometimes – he knew, from unreasonable, even downright perverse, instruction from clients over the years – there was neither rhyme nor reason.

His misery had been greatly compounded by another factor – another singling out – and this had been the dedicated attentions of an extracurricular bully, an *ultra*-bully, who appeared as if out of nowhere at the start of third year. Itchy Billy was from the other school, the rough school at the back of the housing estate, where the wearing of a uniform was not enforced (was, in fact, unenforceable). Why he was 'Itchy' was a mystery, but he was called by no other name (although occasionally someone might ask the whereabouts of *the* Itchy Billy, as if he were a mythical entity, like 'the Abominable Snowman' or 'the Devil').

Every day for the best of a year, Itchy Billy lay in wait for him, rushing between speeding traffic, sprinting across any distance of parkland, leaping high fences just to deliver a few crunchy punches and a hearty kick up the arse for good measure. Every day, rain or shine, this hulking, dead-eyed figure would materialize like Grendel loping from the swamp. And then he vanished and was never seen again, and no one ever knew where he went or why, and gradually he faded into the mists of local folklore.

For many years, caught up in the G-forces of work and marriage and children, Wylie had consigned these memories to a deep vault – the kind of lumber room that has become so chaotic and onerous you can't bring yourself to open the door. But as life levelled out and became emptier again, he went in and reacquainted himself, and his anger became all-consuming.

Outside, in the street, some kind of altercation was taking place. He leaned forward and peered down. The yellow-haired bouncer-ish guy they called Big Roy was standing very close to and yelling at a much older man on crutches. 'What did I tell you?' Finger in the chest. 'What did I fucken tell you?' The old man mumbled something and Big Roy made as if to strike him but stopped short.

'Final warning,' he bellowed. 'You hear me? You fucken hear me?'

There was a soft rap at the door and the part-time secretary poked her head round. 'Crawford …? Everything okay? It's just, uh, Mr Conville's here.'

'Right you are, Janice. Send him in.'

27

According to Soupy's dad, the pond was actually a crater made by a German parachute mine that blew off course when the Luftwaffe was bombing the shipyard in 1941. Graham's dad said this was rubbish – the pond had always been there. It was deep in the woods at the base of the hills behind the village, and it came to Fenton's mind as Wylie was pressing home, once more, the horrible consequences of not paying up. He hadn't thought about it for decades and yet there it was in his memory, still and glassy among the trees, patches of cool green iridescence flickering under the ferns. He could smell the sticky black mud. He could hear the quick pops and splashes of sticklebacks and newts. At one end there was a fallen oak and you could shimmy along the trunk and sit and look down at insects skating across the reflected sky. There was a solitary moorhen, fugitive among the reeds. In spring the water would be thick with billows of frogspawn.

He dismounted, passed through the gate and bumped his bike along the root-veined path that led off the main track.

On his right, the ground fell away steeply into a ravine; to his left, the woods banked gently upwards, sunlight striping the undergrowth. A breeze riffled the treetops. He sniffed the bosky scents and tried to relax. Eighty-five grand! Eighty-five fricken big ones … In the scheme of things, given the large amounts of money he had handled in his time, this was not a wholly terrifying sum, but in the current circumstances, in one go, it was problematic. This he had explained to Wylie, who seemed surprised. More time was required. It was agreed that Fenton would deliver 'the compensation' by mid-October. Which left the matter of his loan, due a month later. In all likelihood he would have to talk to Victor about more time on that too. Arranging the deal on the phone had been straightforward enough – the man had been brisk, businesslike, a little bit stern maybe, but came across as reasonable. It shouldn't be a problem. He could handle Victor.

After a while the path descended to a wide, flat clearing of scrub where the outlines of stone foundations, ivy-covered, marked out the ruins of a mansion. It had been built on a grand scale by a whiskey baron in the nineteenth century and demolished in the twentieth after a combination of Prohibition and mismanagement wrecked the business. As boys, Fenton and Artie had spent hours collecting fragments of multicoloured mosaic from under the leaves. Once they found a rotted leather purse with coins in it, among them a gold half-sovereign and a solid silver army temperance medal. What had happened to those treasures, Fenton wondered. Had Artie nicked them?

Farther on, at the frayed edge of the old estate, the path resumed and entered another swathe of forest. He began to feel a little flutter of excitement at the thought of seeing the pond again. It had been an illicit pleasure back then, a no-go area, deemed by the adults to be too deep and dangerous for little boys. But they had gone anyway, sometimes to fish with a net for sticklebacks, sometimes just to throw stones and drop heavy rocks and logs in the mud and pretend it was quicksand.

He made his way through the trees towards the glade. It was just as he remembered: the creaking firs, the clumped vegetation, the spikes of pink foxglove, the otherworldly tangle of rhododendron. But as he stepped onto the ridge that sloped to the pond, he came to an abrupt halt. The twisted, trampled-down remnants of a barbed-wire fence greeted him. Beyond, where should have been darkly rippling water and reeds and flitting dragonflies, was an expanse of rubble littered with discarded shopping trolleys and broken bottles. A child's tricycle lay rusting on its side. The fallen oak was gone.

As he stared, a sensation of hot, sick despair fizzed in his kidneys. This is what happens when you turn your back, he thought. Why is the past always getting messed up? But the sight was dispiriting on another level, and it took him a minute to discern why. If he wasn't careful, it occurred to him, this was what his own life could look like. The money.

The house. His family. The whole shooting match, everything he had worked for could come down around his ears. Reduced to rubble and litter.

The silence was broken by a raucous exchange up in the canopy – crows or rooks, he didn't know. He stooped and picked up a stone and flung it as hard as he could across the dead surface of what had once been the pond.

28

'Just put that down over there for me. Thanks, love.' Pamela consulted her notepad and put a tick against *2 do*. *Brazilian hard wax.* She stared at the list, then underlined *UV LED Nail Lamps x 4* and put a question mark beside it. Behind her, the sound of drilling abruptly subsided and a man of about her own age, in work clothes and yellow Caterpillar boots, appeared and said, 'Have you a wee minute, darlin', to show me where you want this bed?' She followed him along the corridor, which was dizzy with sawdust and smelled of scorched electricity and freshly cut hardboard.

Back at the reception desk, she resumed her seat and picked up her packet of salt and vinegar, extracting the crisps with long chilli-red fingernails and popping them between her lips with leisurely relish. She was making good progress. Most of the new stock was in, four tanning machines had been taken away (she'd got nearly a grand apiece for them) and the conversion of the cubicles was almost done, apart from a lick of paint. She'd have the doors open again by the end of the week.

And what treats awaited her clients. They could get a tan, of course – still two sunbeds on the premises – but now also manicures (with shellac in all the colours), pedicures, facials (plus brows and lashes, and microblading – her nieces were dab hands), dermabrasion, scalp exfoliation *and* every wax treatment anyone could imagine. Waxperts? Would that be a good name? They'd have to rename. This was a whole new thing. Hair Today Gone Tomorrow? Tops 'n' Tails?

At times Pamela could barely contain herself, could scarcely believe her dream had coalesced so suddenly. And so easily. Fenton had practically leapt on it. She hadn't even got to the end of her pitch before he was grinning and nodding and holding his hands up and saying 'You win, Pamela! You win!' Of course, he *was* in holiday mode, and he felt bad about having to deny the pay rise (she'd seen the drift in takings with her own eyes and knew it wasn't a goer) but she'd expected more resistance, more scepticism, at the very least a 'let me think about it', but no, an instant green light. Mind you, she had all the costings and projections to back it up. The numbers were sound. That Women-Into-Business course at the community college had been a right slog, but it had paid out in spades. The clincher, though, had been funding the new stock with the proceeds from the excess sunbeds, she clocked that – it was like his whole face had kind of *gulped*. And now she was a partner in a going concern.

She'd kissed him – a big m'mmm wet one on the lips – and he'd ordered a bottle of The Arms's best sparkling wine to be brought over to the snug to celebrate, even though it was just lunchtime. She leaned across and dropped the empty crisp packet in the bin. A few streets away the rapid rattle of half-a-dozen snare drums was joined by an army of shrill flutes. She got up and closed the window.

He was quite the charmer when he wanted to be, that Fenton, not smooth as such, he could be awkward, but – what was the word? – she couldn't put her finger on it. He gave the impression of knowing what was what. Or something. A posh education, she supposed. And definitely a bit of a rogue. Her mind wandered back to the blur of the Christmas outing and the hot kernel at its centre, and her heart did a quick misfire. If her Ronnie caught him at that carry-on – not that Ronnie paid much attention to what she did, but still …

For Bod And Ulster? She knew a few people who'd like that one. Belles of Belfast City? Hell's Belles? No. What's New Pussycat? Probably best not to go down the pussy route. She wanted something classy. She looked around and pictured the salon in full flow: women in the tanning pods, women lying back in robes, a hive of women beautifying and being beautified – mud packs, emery boards, shellac rainbows – the buzz of conversation, the smells of coffee, Prosecco, moisturizer, the odd squeal from the waxing rooms. For a moment she let herself imagine what it would feel like to own the business outright, and then – she couldn't help it – she saw a map of salons lighting up across the city. A chain. Her own empire.

'Right, love, that's me.' The joiner was beside her. 'The wee lad will be round to start the paintin' after lunch.'

He put down his plastic briefcase of tools and holstered his drill. She opened the drawer and began peeling off notes. Outside, the clatter and squall of the flute band was coming closer. The tradesman, whistling under his breath, looked out the window. 'That's the traffic knackered,' he said.

Alone again, Pamela set about extracting a coffee from the machine. Eventually, she was thinking, Botox would be the way to go. There was good money in fillers. Lot of technical stuff, though, training, licensing and what have you. That was way up the road. Have to walk before you can run. She picked up the cup and sipped. Hair We Go? Not bad. From Hair to a Tan-ity? Her mother's contribution! Venus Envy? That was from her son Tyler but she didn't really get it. Smooth Operators? In the Buff? And then it came to her, a vision of the façade of her salon, the signage in flowing cursive, lit up in volcanic-orange neon. She would call it PAMELA'S.

29

The Convilles stayed in the same villa they rented every year – actually more of a luxury farmhouse – a mile inland from Majorca's east coast, with a view of hazy mountains and surrounded by lemon trees and hissing olive groves. It had a vine-latticed terrace beside a swimming pool and was just ten minutes' drive from the village, where a daily market proffered cascades of lustrous fruit and vegetables and mounds of vivid sweetmeats. Everywhere was colour. After the pallid hues of home, the Mediterranean was like waking up in the saturation of a Pixar animation.

Andrea brought her friend Zara, and the pair of them cycled out to the beach most days, leaving Fenton and Carolyn to bask by the pool or tootle round the coast in their hire car. One afternoon, they drove out to a lighthouse on the northern cape, along miles of a zig-zagging, vertiginous cliff road, and drank cold beers on the parapet.

Drenched in the blues of the sea and the sky, the purity of light, Fenton felt calm for the first time in an age, almost spiritual, momentarily cleansed by colour, buoyed by immensities of clear, warm, beneficent air. And, as he stood beneath the sparkling white tower and looked back at the impossibly steep twisting route he had driven (with a shaking foot on the brake) and saw all the other – dazzling, robot-built – cars successfully parked along its sides, it struck him that humans really were quite clever and that perhaps there could, after all, be hope.

From Fenton's point of view – drugged most of the time on cheap booze and charred meat – the fortnight was a much-needed respite from his worries. Only once was the idyll disrupted. They were on the terrace on the penultimate night, enjoying a starscape of dizzying scope and profusion. It had been the hottest day of the holiday and the teenagers had spent the evening in town, returning on the backs of scooters driven by two leering locals. Fenton was just describing a pork-and-clams dish he had once eaten in Portugal when Zara leapt up, rushed to the balcony and projectiled a fluorescent orange half-gallon of Aperol into the pool. This triggered Andrea, who disembogued a chute of identical colour and volume – a flame-tailed comet across the flickering turquoise – setting off a worse-for-wear Carolyn in turn. Even Fenton, a man of robust constitution, found himself gripping the handrail and bidding an explosive farewell to his evening's intake. The pool was a write-off.

◊

The lighthouse, the powder-blue villa, the blood-temperature evenings, the suckling pig (it made them feel like murderers but, oh, it was *so* good), the icy *cervezas* – those were fading now. He was back in harness, to the balance sheet, the numbers. Back on the Planet of the Vapes.

He ran his eye over the figures again and was impressed anew. Aaron had come into his own, quite the salesman, pushing new flavours, nudging the upgrades, shifting accessories hand over fist. Booked nearly a grand in a single Saturday during the Twelfth fortnight. Fenton clicked on the calculator icon and did some estimations. If he could achieve consistency – and that was by no means a given – and if Pamela's new enterprise gained enough traction, it might be doable. Just. But factoring in the mortgage and household expenses meant that, either way, it would be tight. Super-tight.

There was something else. He was trying not to think about it, and it took quite an effort, but there was another monster swaying in the blackness of the tunnel up ahead. He could hear it breathing. From time to time the bass notes of its alien heartbeat quickened and thumped deep down under the layers of soundtrack.

It was funny stuff, money, he thought. The root of all evil, so they said. Fenton had rejected this very early on: it was the *lack* of money that was the real troublemaker. It had never occurred to him to not have it. Growing up, there had been affluence all around him (although his father hadn't made serious dough until he was nearly forty). The alternative was inconceivable. In a way, it was the only thing worth having, it seemed to Fenton, for without the security it provided, he could see no viable freedom. His brother, on the other hand – and this he had never understood – showed little interest, indeed had for some time positively embraced squalor, prancing around in dead men's clothes from charity shops, living on baked beans and quoting poetry like some kind of mad itinerant. He sometimes wondered about Artie's place in the family gene pool.

Inasmuch as he allowed himself to perceive his recent predicament on a psychic level, it was, somewhere in his dream life, like bits falling off a spaceship. He was the lone astronaut inside the module listening to ominous groans from the hull, sensing power loss, no longer able to affect direction. Every few hours another bank of console lights would flicker and shut down. The comms channel was degrading into pure static. He did not like it.

Again, with the same sense of warp with which he was coming to view most of the modern world (and yes, he did fear he was sliding into that most dispiriting of subsets, Angry-Old-Mandom), even money, immutable for four hundred years, was taking on strange new forms, becoming alien. There was no doubt that regular cash was on the way out, what with the tapping and everything. Cheques seemed like something from the age of guineas and florins. And now, cryptocurrencies. He had tried to get his head round this one, but every time he thought he might have a grasp, it evaporated in a welter of dissonance, became a problem of language itself. How do you *mine* something that doesn't exist? How do you *spend* an incorporeal block of code? Who was the first person to buy some, and why? Nevertheless, there was a fresh one along every minute: Ethereum, Mydassium, PyRiteez, ObolCoin. It didn't make sense.

Yawning, he flipped open his laptop and clicked on a news website. Floods in Florida, suicide bombers in Kabul – he was distracted by an ad for a monocular with incredible powers of magnification – missile testing in North Korea, earthquakes in China ... Nothing to worry about there. More ads appeared, for hearing aids, orthopaedic shoes, elasticated trousers, depilatories – what kind of hellish target demographic was he in?

His phone tolled with a reminder that his car insurance was up for renewal. Which meant both the house insurance and the rates bill weren't far behind (always in threes). Which meant having to engage with menu options, and horrible on-hold music, and torrents of terms and conditions and what have you, just to do the dance: 'Is that your best price?' 'Let me just talk to my supervisor ...'

Time and money. It was becoming exhausting. He sometimes wondered how old people who didn't own a computer or a smart phone, or just couldn't work technology, coped with the automated interface of the matrix. The *paperless* world. Or did they just gradually give up on things like insurance, heating, income tax, electricity? The thought of it was distressing, not least because he suspected the day would dawn when he himself would have to concede that he no longer knew how *anything* worked.

࿊

He was minding the shop, Aaron having had to suit up (or at any rate, tracksuit up) for a long-delayed court appearance on a minor possession charge. Being behind the counter was a little strange, and for the first hour he felt weirdly self-conscious, as though he was in the shopping module of a low-budget English-for-foreigners video: 'Good morning, how are you today?' 'I'm fine, thank you.' 'And what can I do for you?' 'I would like to purchase some ...'

His first customer actually was a foreigner, a Spanish tourist in need of a power-point to charge his rig, which Fenton provided. When the man returned clenching a coffee, he spent a full twenty minutes sampling juices before buying a single bottle of the cheapest. '*Vaya con Díos*,' Fenton called as he departed.

Things picked up mid-morning with the arrival of a couple of hipsters in braces and flat caps who, in a previous century, might have been dropping by on their way to stoke a furnace in some satanic mill, but in this one were more likely to be taking a break from blogging about plaid, upcycling jam jars or reinventing already perfectly good cocktails. They tested his knowledge of ohm variance, correcting him thoroughly, advised him on growing a beard ('It's the only thing we have left that the women can't do') and spent a gratifying amount on coils, juices, drip tips and cables. There was a flurry over lunch hour, and then a lull in which Fenton settled down to a flaccid pasty from the bakery.

'What about ye?'

Fenton glanced up. 'All right, Roy, how's tricks?' (He was never quite sure whether to use the 'Big'.) Big Roy, wearing a white T-shirt under a loosely cut black jacket that was nevertheless tight across his massive shoulders, stood with his hands thrust into his pockets, appraising his surroundings.

He made smiling, slightly chilling eye contact. 'Lookin'
good, Fenton. How long you been open now?'

'Oh, just a few months.'

'Goin' well?'

'Not bad, not bad. Ticking over, you know.'

'No problems with supply, with the old Brexit and all
that?'

'Not so far, thank God. You thinking of taking up
vaping?'

Big Roy was examining the shelves with a bemused air.
'Nah, I'll stick to the fegs, thanks – too hairy-arsed to change
now.' Some moments passed. He smiled again. 'You've a
quare amount of stock, Fenton. Insurance all up to date?'

'What? Ah yeah. All up to date.'

'You heard about the wee fire at Kennedys' the other
week?'

'I did. That was bad luck. Bit of a mess. Do they know
the cause?'

'One of the barmen was careless with a cigarette was
what I was told.'

'Well, there you are, another reason for people to switch
to vaping.'

Big Roy cackled. Patting the countertop and not looking at Fenton, he said, 'Do you need anythin'? Like, for the
weekend?'

'The weekend? Oh no, I'm fine, thanks, Roy. Special
occasions only these days.'

'Wise man.' Roy tossed his yellow locks in the manner
of a Timotei model. 'Right, I'm away here. Abyssinia.'

30

August, which began hot and dry, with smoke straggling from gorse fires across the hills, disintegrated into one of the wettest ever endured. Towards the end of the month, storms brought flooding and power cuts. Bridges collapsed, cars were swept away, airports shut down. As the clean-up began, the airwaves filled with strident bleating about compensation and insurance claims. There was still no sitting government. The rain continued to hammer on caravan sites and esplanades, washing out every festival and fête. Wan and etiolated people peered out of windows and from under umbrellas at relentlessly opaque northern skies.

On the domestic front there was a flurry of heavy lifting. Jamie returned, tanned, blond and rangy, from the elephant orphanage, requiring a royal expedition's worth of equipment for his first term at university. This at last assembled, and somehow crammed into the car, Carolyn drove him to Glasgow. Andrea they had to negotiate out of the dormant (and, Fenton suspected, cannabis-infused) state she'd been in since a surfing weekend in Donegal in late July and coax her back into a school uniform. Carolyn began tending to her briefcase and fretting about work outfits for the next phase of the tribunal. And in this way the dog days of summer passed, and the yellow-tinged borderlands of autumn came into view.

Fenton was still skiting about on his bicycle. He was fitter than he had been in years and had shed half a stone. His perineum had achieved the texture of fine vintage leather. Most days he cycled into the village to shop for forgotten essentials and to check on Aaron. He rediscovered the reckless pleasure of cycling after a feed of pints, man and machine fused in effortless synergy, rollicking along the shore path like a drunken centaur. These rejuvenating effects alleviated to a small degree the slow corrosion of his viscera by impending reckonings.

One morning in the second week of October, Fenton biked up to visit the revamped Sunbirds, taking his life in his hands on terrifying stretches of carriageway where the cycle lane ran out. Pamela was nailing it, literally. The place was going a dinger. Booked solid. Even the two remaining tanning beds, thanks to the appalling dearth of direct sunlight the previous month, were back in demand. Pamela had brought in her nieces, Kylie and Kayley, and one of their pals to help out and had hired a specialist fresh from beauty school to deal with the, uh, topiary.

At the top of the stairs, Fenton stood agog on the threshold behind a shimmering force field of oestrogen, his nostrils twitching at warm thermals freighted with all the perfumes of Araby. There were women all over the place, sitting, standing, moving around, laughing, chatting, sipping fizz in a hubbub of contented industry, women in robes and towel-turbans, face-packed, bare-footed, attended by their handmaidens. Everywhere was the impression of stripping back and rebuilding, of *vorsprung durch technik.*

'Well, whaddya think?' Pamela was in front of him, flushed and bright-eyed.

'Looks busy.'

'We're out the door. It's unbelievable – the phone has never stopped ringin'. Didn't I tell you? Didn't I?'

'You did.'

A yodel of agonized disbelief came from one of the waxing cubicles. Pamela glanced over her shoulder and grinned. 'First timer,' she said. 'Always a bit of a shock. You want a wee cuppa coffee?'

'Actually,' said Fenton, looking uncertainly at the route he'd have to take, 'I thought I'd just nip into my office for a minute – do a spot of housekeeping.'

'Aye, I was meanin' to talk to you about that, Fenton. See, I had to make that into a storeroom, we've so much stuff. You don't mind, do you?'

'Oh, okay. Sure no probs. Well, I'll uh … maybe you could email the numbers to me when you get a minute?'

She reached out and squeezed his hand. 'Thanks for lettin' me do this, darlin'. I know I can make it work. You won't regret it.'

As he backed away, Fenton had a last gander through the closing door, imagining he saw, as though a curtain had been pulled aside, the sacraments of tribal ceremony, the convocation of a secret society. He also saw: money.

༄

Back at home, braced with a cafetière of monsoon-drain blend, Fenton knuckled down to a long hard look at the books. An hour later, the caffeine boost exhausted, he stepped away from his desk, sank into an armchair and closed his eyes. Behind his lids, rows of numbers dropped and sidled with mesmeric inexorability, sometimes melting or disintegrating in the manner of a computer virus, occasionally catapulting into hyperspace before returning in a different guise. At length, the numeral storm abated and he was able to discern the bones of his situation.

Roughly, it was this: his income streams were in better shape than he could have hoped. Averaging two dozen clients a day, six days a week, Pamela was bringing in more than twice as much as Planet of the Vapes – and he was on schedule to hand over 'the compensation' to Wylie. Factoring in his mortgage, household expenses and school and university fees, however, meant he would need an extension of at least three months for the repayment of Cecil's loan. And even that might require a raid on Andrea's college fund. A few more wax-and-nail salons on the Pamela model would solve all his problems – he had already identified possible locations in the north and south of the city (the west was terra incognita) – but all the capital was being sucked out of the window.

He picked up his phone.

'Hello, Victor? Fenton Conville here ... Cecil's son-in-law? Yes, that's right. About that loan ... I'm thinking I might need a wee bit more time ... Uh-huh ... Okay. I see. Yes, that should be fine. No problem. Thanks, Victor.'

He hung up and regarded the ceiling. Well, he thought, that had been surprisingly easy. And a couple of percentage points on top seemed reasonable enough.

31

Judge Murdoch McCoubrey throttled back and let the boat – *Iris*, named for his wife – slow to a drift in the middle of Belfast Lough. He cut the engines. There was no wind, and the sound of the current's gentle chop against the hull was pleasantly lulling. Therapeutic, even. He looked around. Out here between the two shores – the grumble of the city faint behind him, the lough becoming open sea at the horizon – he felt that he was in neutral territory, at peace and free of quotidian vexations. It helped to clear his head.

When this inquiry business was over, he was thinking, he would step back and take it easier: hit the links, spend more time with *Iris* (and, he supposed, with Iris); maybe even make a serious start, at last, on delving into the family tree. After all, it wasn't as if he hadn't put in the years – he'd been prosecuting terrorists in the 1970s, for God's sake – and his career could not be categorized as anything other than 'distinguished' (a gong, or so he was led to believe, was not far off). Sure, I know where the bodies are buried, he might say after a few drinks at the club, but generally didn't.

And the inquiry itself – a whistly sigh escaped through his nose. It was difficult to say with any certainty at this stage where it would go, but he had a fair idea of where it should go. Always dangerous unsealing the past, especially in this neck of the woods. Too many parts too easily set in motion. Destabilizing. There was something to be said, he mused, though he knew most of his junior colleagues would disagree given the rewards they currently reaped, for putting an end to all these inquests and tribunals, to drawing a line under the whole disgraceful mess. In the meantime – and the prospect caused an involuntary grimace – he could see this particular case dragging on for the rest of the year, and possibly into the next. None of the parties seemed to have their ducks in a row. He might well have to intervene. Make an executive decision.

He swivelled in his helm chair. Dirty cloud was building above Carrickfergus, and a breeze was springing up. He wondered whether he had time to smoke a cigar, but it meant going below to root one out and he was nicely comfortable in the chair's soft leather embrace. Anyway, probably better off not, after his most recent blood pressure score: a hundred and seventy-four systolic – 'rather impressive', according to Dr McKenna. (And then the old croaker had buggered on again about alcohol 'units' – why not just call them drinks? – a bit rich, seeing he, the judge, happened to know that the doc put away three bottles of Gordon's a week in the club bar.)

He nestled back. Yes, truth, justice, accountability – all fine words. But then again, at what cost? And what was the truth, exactly? In his experience of these things, everyone had their own version. Napoleon Bonaparte, what was that line of his? History is a set of lies that people have agreed upon. It struck him as about right, in a global sense, though the problem in this place was that there would never be agreement. On this point, everyone was agreed. And justice? Ah, justice … A luxury, not a right! a judge had once barked at him back in his barrister days, a cynicism that had shocked him at the time but that he now regarded as hard fact. And the third one – a much-used word these days – accountability? He squinted up at the sky. Like searching for a just man in a hall of mirrors …

Heavy weather was imminent. Scanning the southern shore he could see the collapsed scaffold of the old disused jetty and, farther along, the whitewashed façade and timbered eaves of the yacht club. If he got moored smartly, he reckoned, he might fit in a couple of large ones before lunch. He jabbed the ignition button and the twin engines snarled into life. As the boat heaved forward, a gust of cold rain spattered across the flybridge and the judge, feeling the sting of it, reached back and pulled the black hood of his yellow slicker over his naked head.

32

'Who should I make it out to?'

Wylie eyed the chequebook with open distaste. 'I'd rather it was a bank draft.'

'Sure I've the cheque right here.' Fenton waved his biro. 'Old school. Let's just get this done.'

'Well then, I suppose make it out to me.'

'Not her?'

There was the flicker of a smile. Or a grimace. Wylie leaned back, folding his arms. 'The thing is, my fee's to come out of it. It's not all ... It won't all go to her.'

Fenton stared at him. 'Tell me this: I *am* going to know who she is, right? Once I've paid?'

'No.'

'No? Come on, Crawford. I know it's Laura Hayes. Just blink twice if I'm right.'

'It's not called non-disclosure for nothing, Fenton — *she's* protected as well as you.'

'What!'

'Believe me, it's better like this. The NDA is signed; it goes into my safe in perpetuity. Done and dusted. She can have no hold over you ever again. Your debt is paid. Your carelessness is behind you.'

Fenton clicked the pen, his gaze fixed again on the watercolour scenes of the town that hung on the wall behind Wylie's head. One of them was of the church in whose graveyard his paternal grandparents and uncle were buried. It was small, this world he inhabited.

Wylie was watching him. 'Listen, I know it's a tough one, Fenton, but believe me, this is the only way. I'd a hell of a job persuading her to take the money rather than go to court. She wanted to see you squirm so badly, she could taste it.'

Fenton shook his head and tapped on the cheque with his biro. The first intimations of an 'extreme weather event' were worrying the office windows. Storm Ophelia, which had been bullocking around in the mid-Atlantic for days, was bearing down on west Kerry and would shortly make landfall and then head to the north-east, news reports said. There would be damage.

'I'm going to have to trust you on this one, Crawford.'

Wylie leaned forward, exhaled and folded his hands on the desk. 'Sure didn't I fix that preservation-order business for you? I think we both know I went far out on a limb on that one. They wanted your house knocked down, Fenton. I took a big professional risk greasing those palms. You can trust me.'

Fenton looked across at his solicitor in his prim blazer, white shirt and striped tie, the hair cut short and neatly side-parted, the cheeks well fed, and for a second saw the podgy schoolboy of thirty years before. He focused on the anomaly in Wylie's right eye, a distinct freckle-like blemish on the pale iris. A moment passed and there was no flinch.

'Fuck it. Let's do it.'

He signed his name.

෴

The storm rampaged across the island. Fenton observed the tempest, coffee in hand, from behind the triple-glazing of his upper deck, trying to savour his liberation from tenebrous terror. He was relieved, certainly, *tremendously*, but he had paid a very high price considering the lack of – what did they call it? *Closure*. He was still none the wiser. What had it come to, he wondered, when anyone could accuse anyone of anything, after any number of years, and if it leaked into the public domain, it would stick, regardless of due process. He had read only that morning of a Twitter furore around some famous writer who may or may not have brandished his todger at a party in 1965, and now people were burning his books on YouTube. In time the man and his work would be erased. It was surely disproportionate. Mind you, there *was* a pattern: it was always men. Women seemed to know better.

'I can't believe they're going in.' Andrea, sent home from school for fear of Ophelia, appeared at his side. She pointed. The all-weather ladies swimming gang, six or seven of them, were wobbling along the pier towards the steps. Fenton and his daughter watched as, one by one, the women climbed down and plunged into the wind-whipped swell, their seal-slick heads in brightly coloured swim hats rising and falling with the peaks and troughs of the waves, bobbing like buoys.

'Oh my God,' said Andrea. 'Are they mad?' On the deserted shore, the gale was flinging bits of flotsam and litter around like black confetti. An unsecured red towel took flight. The sky was as dark as the sea but exuding round its edges the peculiar bruise-yellow light of storms. Then a fresh surge of rain all but obliterated sight of the swimmers.

'It says on Instagram there's loads of power cuts down south,' said Andrea. 'Do you think we'll be okay? It's just I need the internet for my geography essay.'

'Should be. What's it on?'

'Climate change. Basically how you guys messed things up for my generation.'

Something tightened. Fenton sensed danger: interactions with his daughter had a tendency to accelerate into mystifying mayhem at lightning speed. 'Us guys?'

'Yeah, you old guys, with your plastic bags and big cars and, like, air miles, destroying the ozone layer, cutting down the forests, polluting the sea.'

Fenton couldn't deny that he had polluted the sea on more than one occasion, but he was confident he had never cut down a forest. He refrained from saying so. He glanced at his daughter. She had her mother's luxury cream complexion and the same forthright set to her chin. She was warming to her theme.

'Do you know how much, like, polar ice we've lost in the last twenty years?'

'I'm not sure *exactly*. A lot?'

'Thirty *trillion* tonnes. That's, like, about *six* Mount Everests.'

'Wow.'

'Yeah, wow. And you know what happens if all the ice melts?'

'Um ...'

'Sea levels will rise by two hundred feet. This whole coast would flood. This house would be, like, completely under water. We'd all be drowned.'

'That's a long way off though, surely,' he said, instantly regretting it.

'Oh my God! Are you for real?' Andrea did a restrained version of the two-step rage dance that had punctuated her childhood, earning her the family codename 'Michael Flatley'.

'Easy, sweetie,' Fenton began. 'I'll be buying an electric car as soon as they –' But it was too late. She was stomping from the room.

'And by the way,' she bawled, 'I'm going vegan again.'

The wind boomed against the glass and somewhere in the garden something big and metallic – the swing seat, he guessed – made a clattering dash across concrete and was swallowed by the tumult. He hurried to the freezer to root out some steaks for dinner.

33

In the east of the city, at No. 12 Schomberg Grove, Carolyn's parents, Cecil and Ruby, were monitoring with unease the sporadic dimming of lamps, and Ruby in particular the faltering reception on the television set. She was looking forward to an hour in the enervated company of the English upper classes and their doughty servants. It was a repeat, but that didn't matter – her appetite for ITV's consoling world of the gentry was pretty much insatiable. Cecil, on the other hand, hated everything about the English (apart from the Premier League – though that was 'hardly even English any more') and especially their fawning veneration of the aristocracy, but it had been a long while since he'd had a say in the viewing schedule.

Despite the elemental fury outside, the power held. Ruby, trying to concentrate on the screen, was vaguely aware that her husband was more restless than usual when forced to watch her programmes, shifting and sighing in his armchair. She also noted that he had set aside his M&S

traditional Cumbrian cottage pie half-eaten, which wasn't like him – he loved those pies, with their salty gravy and crusty topping. She glanced over. He was massaging his chin and dabbing at his phone. His face was an odd shade, she thought, a bit on the grey side even for Cecil. It was nearly the ad break – she'd get up then and pour him a nice big Scotch. That would put some colour in his cheeks.

'Cecil, love, are you all right?' He grunted. The lights dipped again. Upstairs, Lady Mary took off her hat; downstairs, Mrs Patmore clucked over a syllabub; in his dressing room, Lord Downton surveyed himself in the looking glass and fingered the tasselled cord of his robe. The ads came on. Cecil gave a jolt and hunched forward, staring into space as if receiving the astonishing key to an ancient riddle, and in the next instant it became clear that he was actually very far from all right.

34

The morning of the funeral, though bitterly cold, started off dry, but a couple of miles from the church flurries of sleety rain began to whip against the glass, and the driver flicked on the wipers. The occupants of the limousine, stiff in their formal clothes and having exhausted all logistical exchange, gave themselves over to the soporific rhythm and looked out at the blurred lights and slow-moving traffic of the waking world. The sky hung low and glowering over the city like a slab of rock.

Fenton was impressed by the size of the turnout. The church was packed, mourners standing ten-deep at the back, fifty more clustered around in the car park – noticeably more men than women. Despite the numbers inside, it was freezing, the air fogged with breath. 'I hadn't realized your dad was so popular,' Fenton whispered, attempting to blow life into his fingers.

Carolyn, pale but calm, glanced around. 'I don't recognize half these people, but I suppose he would have made a lot of friends in business over the years.'

'M'm.'

Carolyn's mother was beside her, frail and shrunken inside a camphor-scented fur coat, frowning as though trying to remember whether she'd left the iron on. A blocky man with bluish-black hair made his way down the centre aisle and stooped to her, clutching her hand and murmuring close to her ear. He straightened up, nodded gravely at Carolyn and retreated. He looked familiar.

'Who was that?' asked Fenton.

'That's the famous Victor. Surely you've met him before?'

'That's Victor?'

Oh yes. Fenton *had* met Victor. Or rather, had exchanged words with him. On a wet morning in the east of the city after a near miss on the carriageway. He remembered the barnet, the nasty dye-job. Other than that, he'd only ever spoken to him on the phone: to arrange a bank transfer and an extension of his loan.

An outbreak of shuffling, coughing and rustling anticipated the minister's ascension to the pulpit. Everyone settled in. 'We brought nothing into the world and we take nothing out of it,' he began. He had a soft, clean-shaven face and a chalky pallor and spoke in a lugubrious sing-song. 'The Lord gave and the Lord has taken away ...'

Fenton looked up at the stained-glass windows, at the darkly glowing cobalts and carmines, and sought to centre himself in the gravity of the occasion. Meditating on mortality was something he generally avoided. One moment you're here, the next you're gone, he thought – one minute you're scoffing a plate of chicken and chips and enjoying a Glenmorangie and Diet Coke, and then that's the end of it. Shutdown. No more signal. *Like the flame of a butter lamp in the wind of impermanence* – where had he heard that? Artie, probably, it was the kind of thing he'd say. (What, exactly, *was* a butter lamp?)

'For one, a stone, dark and immovable,' the minister intoned, his long black skirts swaying above his high-gloss slip-ons. 'For another, a scattering of pebbles ...'

It was the cholesterol that had done for Cecil. A catastrophic heart attack halfway through episode one of the fifth season of *Downton Abbey*. Dead in his armchair before the ambulance even arrived. Fenton had been shocked by the news, but at the same time strangely exhilarated, a response for which he later felt something like shame. His relationship with Cecil hadn't always been comfortable but he had admired him, the way he'd harnessed the streetfighter in himself and channelled it into the cut and thrust of business. Hauled himself up. It couldn't have been easy in the early days, with all those Rocky Dans and spidermen running around with their flags of convenience, the city a chequerboard of no-go zones. Carolyn said that for several years of her childhood she barely saw him.

'Then Jesus spake and said, "Verily, the Kingdom of Heaven is spread upon the earth, and men do not see it." And now ...' A huge collective reconfiguration was taking place and Fenton realized they were standing up for a hymn. In fairgroundish tones the organ led them into 'The Lord's My Shepherd'. Behind him, to his mild surprise, both his parents were giving voice like hardened church-goers, his father almost perfectly off-key. Fenton made the droning noise he used in such situations, mastered while having to sing the school song, moving his lips when he remembered a word or a line. The organ wheezed to a halt and the congregation settled once more. There followed a reading from Ecclesiastes.

He had so far avoided looking at it directly, but Fenton now contemplated the hard, gleaming lozenge of Cecil's coffin: top of the range, lots of metalwork. His earthly remains. That box was the last material object Cecil's money would buy for him, he thought. *Time's up – did you get it all spent? No? That's a shame.* He wondered if his father-in-law had believed in a hereafter. Cecil was quick enough to give a robust view on most topics but the subject of faith had never arisen (although he and Ruby did attend services on special occasions such as Easter). Fenton suspected not. Cecil was a realist; he knew the odds.

It would be comforting, though, to have that consolation, to be convinced this wasn't the end. Belief in God, he sometimes mused, would make things so much easier: just to hand your rucksack of fear and confusion over to the Big Man and write everything off to 'The Plan'. Don't worry about it – *He has a plan.* Even religious people, though, he had noted, didn't seem that chuffed when the time came.

'Whosoever believeth in him shall not perish but have everlasting life ...' Someone told him once there were more people living than had ever died, but he didn't think this could be true, and when he tried to compute it, his head ached. Either way, it must be getting pretty crowded up there, in the imaginary heaven. Or was it like that multiverse thing that Graham banged on about? That made his head sore too. The coffin was definitively black – varnished ebony, perhaps. He pictured it tumbling through the cosmos like the monolith in *2001: A Space Odyssey*.

'As for man, his days are as grass,' the minister was declaiming; 'as a flower of the field, so he flourisheth, for the wind passeth over it and it is gone.'

Fenton zeroed back to the status of his loan: had a wind passethed over *it*? Could he be off the hook? The phrase *compassionate grounds* had established itself and kept rolling and swirling around in his head like a screensaver. What a relief it would be if the debt could die with Cecil, the trail just go cold. His mind raced: it wasn't as if there was any paperwork; it was a gentleman's agreement and one of the gentlemen was no longer around; *and* it was family. *In view of the terrible shock ... at this dark time ... compassionate grounds ...* He heard himself saying 'It's what he would have wanted', croaky, like in films. Was it, though? He remembered Cecil's hard-ass speech in the clubhouse about a man paying his dues. But it was different now. Death changed things. And Victor, he recalled, had seemed quite relaxed about his request for an extension. Anyway – it suddenly struck him – it would all pass to Ruby now, sweet little Ruby, and she was hardly likely to bust his balls, was she? That was it then, he decided with a delicious sense of release, the loan was now on a finger so long it stretched almost out of sight.

They rose again, for 'Rock of Ages', and Fenton, his eyes unaccountably prickling, fumbled for Carolyn's hand and this time solemnly, earnestly, added his own voice to the human sound that swelled and soared as they, the living, prepared to face once more into the waves.

⌇

Outside, the rain had eased, and the sky had lightened from lead to zinc. Standing on the steps wishing he had a cigarette, Fenton noticed first one, then another police Land Rover parked fifty yards apart on the road opposite the church gates. Half-a-dozen uniformed cops were spaced in ones and twos along the pavement. Puzzled, he went over to the nearest one, recognizing her as the joker who had breathalyzed him. Had something happened? he enquired; why was there a police presence? She pointed him in the direction of 'the boss man' – with his North Face puffer over a shirt and tie, unmistakably a plainclothes officer – leaning on the railings.

'How's it going?'

The cop registered him but didn't speak.

'I, uh, I was talking to your colleague there about why there are police at my father-in-law's funeral and she said I should speak to you.'

'Did she now.'

'Yes.' Fenton waited while the man continued to scan the crowd.

He took his time, cleared his throat: 'Routine. Just keepin' an eye on the guest list.'

'I don't understand. Was Cecil involved in something?'

The officer gave Fenton a look and resumed his vigil. 'Mr McCracken had a lot of business associates. Some of the people he did business with would be of interest to us. As I said, just routine.'

Fenton surveyed the mourners gathered in small groups on and around the church steps, coat collars turned up and hats tugged down against the biting November air. 'I hardly know any of these people,' he said, 'but they look harmless enough.' (This wasn't true. Some of them looked like very mean hombres indeed.)

'Well, for example,' the cop said, 'see that big lad with the red scarf talkin' to the oul' doll? That's Ronnie Hogg. Major paramilitary. Controls half the drugs trade in this city.'

'Really?'

'Yeah. And that guy over there in the cap, with the golf umbrella? Brendan O'Murtagh. Top boy in the Dublin mafia. Very serious piece of work.'

'The Dublin mafia?'

'Crime gangs. You know what I mean.'

'Jeez. What's he doing up here?'

The cop made a sound that combined a grunt with a snort. 'Payin' his respects.'

Carolyn and Andrea, the diminutive widow between them, emerged from the crowd and beckoned to Fenton. Black cars were nosing into place to transport them to the burial ground.

✍

'I'm taking my ma up for a wee lie-down. She's a bit over-wrought,' said Carolyn. 'Maybe you could give a hand with the food and drink, make sure everyone's looked after?'

'Right you are.'

Fenton proceeded along the hallway towards the mumble of voices. The McCracken home was spacious, built in the sharp-edged style of the 1930s, with flower motifs and squares of coloured glass in all the doors and windows. High-quality chintz dominated. Valances and sconces were in abundance. In the living room, two mute, broad-backed men, still in their overcoats, sat in front of the television watching Crusaders take on Cliftonville, with the volume turned down out of respect. At the end of the room, the conservatory had been opened up and a linen-draped table set out with plates of sandwiches, cocktail sausages and pastries. Rain drummed steadily on the glass roof.

In the kitchen, he quickly found what he was looking for and poured himself three fingers. Women bustled around him, talking to one another in the bright, voluble way of those spared the lightning strike. *And silence shall have no dominion*. He gazed out at the garden, at the drenched rockery and dripping ivy, at a red wheelbarrow almost brimming with rainwater. The malt diffused into his core, blooming like a big warm flower inside him. (If nothing else, he thought, funerals were great for daytime drinking.)

The cemetery had been a classic scene in windswept black and white, complete with spooked umbrellas and a keening widow. The lowering of the coffin, the patter of earth on the lid, that was when it became real. Clean and final. There was no way round it: death was a shocker.

He refilled his glass and held the honey-gold liquid up to the light. Cecil knew his whisky. Had never scrimped on the old *uisce beatha*. Fenton breathed a fumey benediction. The kitchen was filling up with mourners back from the cemetery and in search of hot beverages and discreet alcohol. The kettle was doing overtime. Fenton moved around, shaking hands and exchanging the phrases of bereavement. Cecil's younger sister arrived and held his fingers in an icy grip for several minutes without speaking, until finally he suggested a gin and tonic. His parents came, drank tea and departed for another funeral. A while later, having downed his third king-size Glenmorangie and challenged the minister on a point of Darwinian incompatibility, he realized soakage had become a matter of urgency.

In the creaky wicker armchairs behind him, as he loaded his plate, two elderly women – neighbours, he presumed – were conversing in the low timbre of tragedy.

'Apparently it happened durin' the ad break. He was tryin' –'

'Was it the one where that Irish chauffeur puts a bomb in the soup?'

'No, that's next week. Anyway, he was tryin' to send a message on his new phone and the next thing, Ruby said, it was like he'd been plugged into the mains.'

'Poor Cecil.'

'She said his legs shot up in the air and his slipper flew off and knocked over one of her Staffordshire spaniels. Smashed it.'

'Poor Ruby. It's just awful.'

'Terrible.'

'Though you never know, she might get another one.'

'How's that?'

'To make up the pair. It's very lonely-lookin', the one sittin' there on its own.'

'Oh, yes. Yes, you never know.'

'He was a lovely man, so he was.'

'He was. He'd a great head of hair on him.'

'He did, and such a smart dresser. Always looked the part.'

'Spruce as you like.'

'Did you get a sandwich yet?'

'Not yet. I was waitin' to see could I get a cup of tea. Tell me this: do you think she'll keep this place on? It's some size of a house for one person. A lot of upkeep.'

'I don't know. Maybe she'd move in with her daughter and her family' – Fenton looked up sharply, his spoon stalled over the coleslaw – 'I hear they've plenty of room down there. And it would be nice for her by the sea ...'

Fenton crammed another fistful of mini-quiches onto his platter and retreated to the sofa near the television. The match was over and the two men had gone. In the television studio, a pair of identically dressed pundits were moithering over the possibilities of things being otherwise. Carolyn plumped herself into the space beside him and exhaled.

'How's she doing?' he asked.

'She's ... *okay*. She's going to come down in a minute. I think it's just the shock's worn off – it's finally hit her that he's gone and she's on her own. They were together for, what, fifty-odd years?'

'And what about you? Do you want a cocktail sausage, by the way?'

'No, I'll get something later. I'm too sad. And I keep thinking we should have insisted the boys come home for this.'

'Hey, they're young, they've got their own stuff going on, and Jamie has exams coming up.' He chewed and swallowed a miniature egg sandwich. 'I was wondering – do you think she'll keep this place on?'

'I don't know. It's a big house for just one person. But we'll deal with that later. I'd better go and say hello to some people.'

Fenton stared, unseeing, at the television and tried not to let the prospect of his mother-in-law moving into his man cave spoil his lunch. Back in the kitchen, bothering the whisky bottle again, he turned, with a start, to find Victor standing in front of him.

At this proximity, he was struck first by the man's breadth – he was almost literally as broad as he was tall – and second by his eyes, which were the colour of wet slate but devoid of any glimmer or shine or, indeed, humour or curiosity, as though masked by some form of membrane. His vinyl-black hair and the shoulders of his velvet-collared Crombie glistened with rain.

'Could I get a drop of that?' His tone seemed to imply that Fenton was selfishly or otherwise deliberately keeping it from him.

'Sorry. Of course.' He poured a double measure. 'It's Victor, isn't it?'

Victor sniffed his drink, then dropped his head and for several long moments stared at Fenton's shoes. 'D'I know you?'

'We've spoken on the phone. I'm Cecil's son-in-law.'

'You're Fenton?'

'Yes.'

Victor straightened up and slowly appraised the rest of his interlocutor. 'D'I ever meet you before?'

The glass in Fenton's hand wobbled. He took a pull. 'As I say, we, uh, talked on the phone.'

'Aye, about extending your loan. But I never met you?'

Fenton looked around, hoping Carolyn might be in the vicinity. He contrived an elaborate cough. 'It's very sad about Cecil,' he said. 'It's a big shock. A big loss.'

Victor nodded and resumed his footwear inspection. 'There's not many left like Cecil,' he said. 'A true gentleman. A man of honour.'

'Yes, it's always the good ones.' They both studied his shoes, which were unremarkable black Oxfords. 'Anyway,' Fenton said, 'I should probably go and see if I can ... It was nice meeting you at last.'

'Right.'

For the next hour Fenton went out of his way to avoid further contact with Cecil's lieutenant, but was several times aware of his strange blank eyes on him from across various rooms. He mentioned it to Carolyn who said, simply, 'Don't mess with Victor.'

He sat on the sofa with his mother-in-law, doll-sized in her black twinset, her freshly washed hair almost the same colour as her pearls, and felt a twinge of genuine tenderness. He held her hand. She was already in nostalgic mode, burbling about her late husband's many endearing quirks and foibles, fretting about what she should do with his tie collection, his twenty-five Harris Tweed jackets, his gun.

'Sorry. His what?'

A long sniff. 'His wee pistol. I never liked havin' it in the house, but Cecil, you know, with all the cash, it gave him peace of mind, but I don't want the nasty old thing hangin' around now. What will I do with it, Fenton? Would you ever take it away with you?'

For a moment he gave it serious consideration, imagined tucking it into his waistband on the way into The Stoat, getting a little respect from Mad Dennis and the like. 'No, I don't think so. Best probably to hand it over to the police. For disposal or "putting beyond use" or whatever they call it. That's what they're there for.'

She expressed lavishly into her hanky and examined the result. 'No. Not the police. It was never ... there's no, you see, there's no licence.'

'You have an illegal firearm in the house?'

Ruby sniffled again, dabbed at her empinkened nose and peered around. 'I'll get Victor to take it; that's the best thing. He'd know what to do with it.'

I bet he would, thought Fenton.

The widow shifted on her cushion, sat up a little and, squeezing his hand, said, 'You know, Cecil thought the world of you.'

'He did?'

'Oh aye, the bee's knees. Said you were a man after his own heart.'

'Really?'

'Oh aye, true blue. He was so pleased when you and Carolyn got married, chuffed to bits.' This was not Fenton's recollection. 'He said he couldn't have wished for a better son-in-law.'

'*Really?*'

'My Cecil didn't always show his feelings, I know that – he could be a tight wee man, so he could – but underneath he was a big softie, a wee dote. That was the Cecil I knew, that's the man I loved, Fenton, for fifty-five years. Mind you, it wasn't, you know yourself, it wasn't all plain sailin' – there were times I could happily have strangled him, so I could – but he always looked after me,' the chin began to crumple, 'and now I've no one.' Fenton put his arm around her. 'What am I goin' to do, Fenton? What's goin' to happen to me?'

'Don't you worry, Ruby,' he crooned. 'You have us. We'll look after you.'

∽

It was decided that Carolyn would keep her mother company overnight, so Fenton phoned a taxi for himself and Andrea, and presently they said their goodbyes and began looking for their coats. Just as he was about to follow his daughter out into the mizzling darkness, a voice hailed him from the foot of the stairs.

'Yo, Fenton.'

In the refracted light of the hallway, Victor's jowly face looked grimy and un-nourished, almost bloodless, his eyes smears of shadow. With a stiff forefinger and cocked thumb, he pointed.

'You need to come and see me.'

35

Nothing about these places ever changed. It was the same tableau preserved in the same aspic of harsh white light. The old guy with the tobacco-blond quiff in the 1950's suit was still in the corner chewing on his little pen, the floor was still a litter of broken dreams, the atmosphere one of studious desperation. Televisions flickered and fizzed with names, colours, probabilities; dogs and horses in perpetual motion. Actually, something *had* changed since Fenton was last in a bookies: it was possible to breathe. No more squinnying through bands of smog to see if your horse was ahead or even, in fact, whether you were watching the right race. Somehow, though, the absence of fag smoke made the place even more desolate.

He approached the glass. A young woman assessed him with bored khaki-coloured eyes, waiting for him to speak. 'Hi, I'm here to see Victor.'

She lifted the receiver of an old-fashioned beige phone. 'Does he know what it's about?' He nodded. She mumbled into the phone, then said, 'Mr Dougan's up the stairs, end of the corridor. That door there. I'll buzz you in.'

Fenton climbed steep uncarpeted stairs to a maze of partitioned nooks containing people and computer terminals, and found Victor behind a desk in a large office beyond, his shirtsleeves rolled up to reveal thick furry forearms. In one hand he gripped a coffee mug whose logo asserted, in anarchistic red and black, that Brexit *meant* Brexit. He had a laptop open on one side of the desk and was talking to someone on the screen. He gestured for Fenton to sit.

'Yeah,' he was saying, 'it's due in on Tuesday.' The voice on the other end – Fenton caught a glimpse of long, lugubrious features and a receding hairline – said, 'Is that the noyun-tee-unth?' Victor nodded. 'And what about our friend,' the voice continued, 'Mr Hogg?' 'Nothin' so far,' said Victor. 'But, Brendan, we're goin' to need a united front on this one.' The voice said something Fenton didn't catch. 'Anyway, mate, I'll head on here, I've a meetin'. No rest for the wicked, you know yourself.'

Victor took his time disengaging from the laptop, even appearing to peruse a fairly lengthy email before turning his attention to Fenton. 'So here we are, and where are we?' he said at last.

Not knowing quite how to respond to this, Fenton went straight into his 'compassionate grounds' speech, hesitating now and then for nose-breathing pauses suggestive of unresolved grief. It had hit him hard, he told Victor. Cecil had been like a second father to him, he explained. A role model. A stern but affectionate dispenser of hard-won wisdom and golfing tips. He had been his moral compass when the path was unclear. Fenton faltered slightly here, suspecting his portrait of Cecil was turning into an unlikely composite of Gandhi and Uncle Remus, but he pressed on. Replaying the scene in his head later, Fenton had the impression that he had then talked, indeed jabbered, for a very long time while Victor watched him with those curiously lustreless eyes and said nothing at all. At one point, Fenton thought he may even have pleaded for leniency on the basis of his rash.

When he was done, there was a lengthy silence, until Victor said at last, 'You know what pisses me off most about your type?'

Fenton was taken aback. '*My* type?'

'Aye, the haves-and-have-yachts. Yiz think you're above it all. Yiz think the rules don't apply. Yiz think you can do whatever you like and nothin'll ever come back at you.'

'That's not true.'

'Sixty-five K. Next week. In full.'

'Now hold on a second, Victor … Wait, *sixty-five?* That's not what I agreed with Cecil.'

'Cecil stepped back a long time ago. There's new management here, new partners, new rules. Anyway, in case you hadn't noticed' – with a stubby finger, he snapped shut the lid of the laptop – 'Cecil's tatie bread.'

∽

Cecil *was* dead, it was true. And when people died, they more often than not left a will. Cecil had left a will. It specified that his worldly goods be divided equally between his widow and his only child. This was exciting news for

Fenton, who envisaged a stupendous boost to the household finances. These things didn't happen quickly, however – probate, inheritance tax, capital gains and what have you, and of course the solicitors would want to rack up their billable hours. No use for present purposes. He tried calling his own solicitor for counsel but was refused access. The third time he rang, he was told that Mr Wylie had gone on holiday, to Sri Lanka, for a month.

Fenton finally had his licence back and was spending a lot of time in his car, just driving around, parking in quiet spots, sitting, thinking, listening to the radio. In his car he felt relatively safe. After a while he stopped listening to the radio – the news was too stressful; it aggravated his sense of helplessness. He was able to understand less and less of it and this caused him to wonder if it was the world that was going mad or himself.

His despondency at this juncture was such that even Carolyn, despite her own preoccupation with work, noticed.

'Fenton,' she said at breakfast one morning, 'is everything all right?'

'Yep, all good. Why do you ask?'

'I don't know, you just seem very … withdrawn.'

'I might be coming down with a cold or something but, no, fine.'

'Nothing worrying you?'

'Nope. Pass the jam, would you?'

He anointed his toast and munched it, trying to ignore the hard stare coming his way.

'Listen,' he said, 'I was just thinking. Do you remember a girl called Laura Hayes, went out with my old mate Spud Murphy?'

She shook her head. 'No. Do you mean Lorna Hughes, the one he ended up marrying?'

'Lorna Hughes?'

'Yes, she was in my yoga class for a while before they moved to Canada. What's this about? Who's Laura Hayes?'

'Oh, nothing. Just couldn't remember. Getting bad with names. You'd better hurry up, you're going to be late.'

He took his plate over to the dishwasher, his head fizzing. Of course, he thought: Laura Hayes doesn't exist. *She doesn't exist.* Spud's girlfriend *was* Lorna Hughes, a petite, pixie-like presence who was a year older than them, and Fenton had never had anything to do with her. Baxter, long addled no doubt by all the rum and ganja, had mis-recalled.

This realization in turn activated another thought, and it was this: what if his accuser, whoever she was, didn't exist either. What if there was no 'client'? Thinking this made him dizzy. Surely ...? Why would Wylie risk it? Every last household in the village was on his books – he was absolutely minted. Why would he resort to fraud?

⌒

One afternoon, parked on the shore road, staring at the sea and scratching his affliction – in its scaly reptilian phase now and turning his elbows silver – he began to entertain fantasies about filling the tank and just taking off. He could vamoose, hide out somewhere where no one knew him and no one would ever find him. A line from the song 'South of the Border (Down Mexico Way)' became lodged in his head and he thought: the wilds of Kerry, perhaps, or the misty bogs of Westmeath. Or maybe Leitrim – he'd never heard of anyone ever going there. It was practically a mythical place.

The day of the deadline loomed. Fenton pulled himself together. He'd pay Victor back in his own sweet time, and Victor could like it or lump it. Who the fuck did he think he was – a jumped-up bookie's assistant, a bagman – menacing him like that? This wasn't *Goodfellas*. Fenton couldn't give what he didn't have. Fuck the wee shite. What was Victor going to do about it?

36

No matter what anyone said, it never really got any easier. The coldness and the shock of it. Some essential part of you, your soul or whatever, just for an instant, fled from your body in disbelief. The trick was to keep moving, gain control of your breathing and endure long enough that your flesh began to tingle with that marvellous, magical heat. And then, before you knew it, you were back on the pier, swaddled and sipping hot sweet tea, with your whole system rebooted and ready for anything. It was worth it.

Flailing her legs, Joyce Mehaffey twisted around to face the shore. Not too bad today, the water temperature – about fifteen degrees, she reckoned, and hardly any breeze. Ten feet away, in her crocus-yellow cap, Maureen was doing her high-chinned breaststroke and making that burbling noise, like a Trimphone, against the cold. The others were still dawdling on the steps, goading each other, having a laugh. What were they like? In their flipper-like neoprene socks and gloves, half-women, half-fish, submerged in the freezing sea. People must think we're mad, Joyce thought.

If only they knew. Doing this daily swim with the women had changed her life, there was no doubt. She should probably have planned it better, had a few more plates spinning before taking early retirement, but she'd had enough of admin, and marking, and tests, and bolshie kids questioning the *actual point* of trigonometry, and of more and more strictures about what she could and couldn't say or do, and of praying by Tuesday for Friday to *hurry up*. But then, rather than relief, and boundless freedom and leisure, had come silence and an emptiness that, try as she might, she could not fill. Having jumped ship, she was drowning.

Now she had a gang, a cohort. They swam, they went to the cinema, they had a quilting club. Three of them were learning to paint with acrylics. They were all roughly of an age, retired, mostly divorced or widowed (though she herself had never married) and in no mood to go quietly. They might, she supposed, be some class of a cliché, but so what?

The women were also, she noticed, evolving, becoming more alike in other ways. They had the same fondness for warm fleecy sports gear in pastel shades, worn over the same black Speedo swimsuits. They had the same cropped silver-grey hair, the same vein-marbled white skin. And they were growing in number.

Joyce moved her arms and legs around and made a quick calculation: three more minutes – any longer and her core would be too chilled. The shivers. Too hard to warm up again. Too stiff. She scanned the coastline, with its gradations of sand and grassland receding to wooded hills, the people walking their dogs along the shore path. A mechanical digger was at work shifting sand farther up the beach. Something to do with erosion. The houses, set back among the winter trees, were large – actual mansions most of them.

That big boxy one there that was out of whack with the style of the others, she saw its owner around quite often: he had stopped to chat to them once. A long time ago – so far back it seemed another lifetime – she had taught his brother, a good-looking boy, a dreamer, useless at maths. She thought, What happened there? Her eyes stung, and the outer rims of her goggles blurred. *How* did it happen? How could she have *let* it happen? *He was older than his years.* It was wrong. It was a terrible mistake, and she had paid a price. Though it was difficult now and painful to access the details, shut away for so long and with so much effort. Better to let it lie.

Her limbs were burning and her body surrendering to this watery immolation. One more minute. She felt the exhilaration of weightless immersion, sought and found the sea swimmer's moment of affinity with vastness, with fluid otherness, and dipped her head under briefly to hear the muffled hubbub of the current. When she came up, she looked again at the land mass, hard and solid against the smoky sky. Around her, Belfast Lough was liquid silver, a melted entity. Beneath its surface was a hidden litter of broken, foundered things, lost, discarded, sunken in the depths, hulks rotting and rusting, forgotten on the sea bed. Concealed by this absolving water. And now there was Maureen, robed and turbanned, waving from the wooden pier and holding up the beacon-red flask.

Joyce struck out for the dry land and the hot sweet tea.

37

Here's what Victor did about it.

The following Friday morning, two days after his loan was due, Fenton had just set down his phone and was about to buckle up when a white van with dark-tinted windows lurched round the corner of the driveway and skidded to a halt in front of his car. Two large men emerged. As he scrabbled for the locking button, one of the men wrenched open the door and hauled him out by his lapels. The other man jumped in. With an immensely strong hand gripping the back of his neck, Fenton was propelled at high speed to the rear of the van and turfed inside. The door slammed. Both vehicles surged from the premises.

Stunned and winded, Fenton managed to get up off his knees and crash sideways into a seated position on a narrow ledge over the wheel arch. The only available light was leaking through holes in the grille behind the driver's cabin, and in the gloom he could make out, stacked opposite him, cases marked Krapovnik Vodka and what looked like miniature hay bales wrapped in shiny black plastic. The cold air was greasy with diesel fumes and cigarette smoke. He rubbed his bruised knees, massaged his neck. His ears were almost bursting with the blood-thump of his heart. He was having trouble processing what had just occurred. Then, a flash of instinct – his hand flew to his pocket – followed by a sickening jangle of realization: his mobile was still on the dashboard of his car.

By the motion of the van, its swings of direction, he could tell they were out on the carriageway heading towards the city. He managed to gain some control over his breathing and listened. From the front came the plaintive holler of country-and-western music playing at low volume: *When yore legs are all shakin' an' yore teeth are a mess, ah sweah ah'll still lurve you in yore ole yeller ...*

Victor was on the phone. 'Beemer, Seven series, all the bells and whistles. Leather in the rear could do with a once-over but ... Now? Speed your Séan drives at? S'probably already south of the border ... Yeah, we have him in the back, just goin' for a wee drive ... No, just me and the nephew ... Aye, Itchy Billy ... The other thing? Dead on. I'm happy, Ronnie's happy, and I take it you're happy? ... Right you are, Mr O'Murtagh, I'll be in touch.'

They drove for about twenty minutes or so, stopping at five or six sets of lights, before entering slower, heavier traffic. Fenton guessed they were somewhere in the vicinity of Pamela's. The conversation in the front was sporadic and one-sided, Victor doing the talking. Occasionally the big

lad at the wheel responded but his words were indistinct –
he had an odd feminine, cooing voice that reminded Fenton
of Michael Jackson, or a wood pigeon.

After a while the van pulled over and the engine stopped.
Fenton could hear the sounds of a busy street. He grabbed
at the door handle and heaved. It didn't budge. The driver
got out.

'You all right back there?' called Victor. 'Just havin' a
wee break and then we'll be on our way.'

'Victor, what the fuck?' yelled Fenton, but there was no
reply. Ten minutes later the driver returned and there was
murmuring and the rustling of paper and the snap of ring
pulls. For a horrible moment Fenton thought he could smell
urine but then realized it was vinegar, vaporizing in the
heat of deep-fried food. The bastards! They'd stopped for
fish and chips. 'Where's the mushy peas?' he heard Victor
ask. 'What? Ah, ye fricken spanner. Nah, forget it, doesn't
matter.'

Despite himself, Fenton's mouth was watering, and his
stomach growled. Breakfast – a vegan white-pudding sandwich – may as well have been a week ago. Indeed, everything seemed to have rushed into the distant past: there was
only now and what was about to happen next, and whatever
way he crunched it, the options were limited. People talked
about out-of-body experiences and, for the first time without the aid of alcohol and/or drugs, he was having one. His
mind was bouncing around the walls of his metal prison,
unable to reconcile his situation with any non-fictional
reality.

Up front, wrappers were crumpled, drink cans crushed. One of the men discharged a heartfelt Tyrannosauran belch, and the van started up again. After another half-hour, the traffic thinned and the engine reached for the higher gears. Fenton had lost all track of direction. Presently, they slowed for a series of ramps and came to a stop. The rear door swung open. Shielding his eyes against the sharp, levelling rays of a mid-November sun, Fenton peered out at the hulking silhouetted figure of Itchy Billy, who was in the process of lighting a cigarette. Victor appeared in the background. 'C'mon,' he said to Fenton, 'let's take a wee dander.'

They walked, the three of them — Victor in the lead, Itchy Billy behind Fenton — as though on a leisurely afternoon hike, along a springy bark-chipped path through the woods of a country park. Somewhere off to the side and lower down was the gurgle of running water. Birds called from the foliage. Victor whistled a few bars of 'The Teddy Bears' Picnic'. More than once Fenton had to ask himself whether he was in some kind of waking dream. He saw a glossy auburn squirrel scampering along a branch. It halted midway and sat up, peeping at them with its Richard Gere face and wringing its hands under its chin in a parody of agitation, or anticipation.

Eventually, the trail sloped up and out of the trees to an area of grassland, in the centre of which was a children's playground enclosed by railings. On the western skyline Fenton could make out the hunched shoulders of Black Mountain, and it occurred to him that he recognized the view, the angle he was at to the city: he knew this place. It was long ago. His grandparents had brought him and Artie here on a couple of outings when they were kids, in the days before playgrounds were health-and-safety-ed up – rubberized and stripped of danger, and fun.

Somehow this one had been overlooked, left to its own devices. Rusting here, out of sight, was still a vertiginous metal slide with razor-sharp sides, a spine-jarring seesaw, a gravity-defying swingboat, and the most deadly and thrilling of them all: the Witch's Hat, an unstable, clanking, unpredictable contraption whose awesome centripetal and centrifugal forces at full tilt were capable of flinging a small child into the treetops.

Fenton considered making a run for it: a public road couldn't be more than a mile away; he was relatively fit from the cycling; Victor, he reckoned, was no sprinter, and Itchy Billy, apart from weighing at least eighteen stone, had already sucked down an impressive number of fags since leaving the van. 'Don't even think about it,' said Victor. Itchy Billy again placed a massive paw on the back of Fenton's neck.

They entered the playground through a gate that was hanging on by one hinge and proceeded across the chewed-up tarmac to the Witch's Hat, where Fenton was seated and instructed to stretch his arms out to either side. Itchy Billy then took from his anorak a couple of cable ties and, one after the other, fastened Fenton's wrists to the cold metal struts. Victor headed for the only swing still on two chains and wedged his arse into its tiny seat.

'Used to love this wee park,' he said, looking up at the crossbar. 'Me and my mates had the best fun here.' He gave a little shove with his feet and the chains whinged in their eye-bolts. 'Mind you, someone was always comin' a cropper. Lots of bumps. I remember Turbo, one time, flyin' off that round-about and takin' all the skin off the side of his face. Should've heard the squeals out of him.' He smiled to himself.

'Victor,' Fenton began. 'We need to –'

'And another time, Scobie fell off the top of the slide and cracked his head open. It was wild. He was never the same after. He'd to go to a special school and everythin'.'

Itchy Billy, who had not moved from in front of Fenton or taken his eyes off him, lit another cigarette. His stare, Fenton noticed, had the same lifeless, incurious quality as Victor's, though, unlike his uncle, his slabby face was almost totally free of lines, oddly ageless. A breeze whistled through the playground and the Witch's Hat groaned and swayed. Apart from the rhythmic squeak of the swing, there was no other sound in the broad cold space of the afternoon.

'Victor,' Fenton began again, 'this is insane.'

'Shoosh up, Fenton.' Victor was doing the thing where you twist around and tangle the chains and then let them spin you as they untangle. 'You know somethin'? I knew I knew you. Soon as I seen the car. It was you on the car-riageway that time, nearly had me off the road. Coulda killed me.'

'God's sake, Victor, it was very slippy that day. I lost control. But this is mad; you can't be serious. What do you think Cecil would have said about this?'

'Cecil? Cecil thought you were a prick.'

'What? … Look, you're going to get your money. I'm good for it. There's no problem. So please, tell me: what the fuck are we doing here?'

'Ach,' said Victor, sticking his legs out and pulling on the chains to get the momentum going, 'just havin' a bit of fun.'

Itchy Billy grasped the wooden skirt of the Witch's Hat and heaved. The mechanism creaked and clunked and slowly, arthritically, began to move. Fenton saw heathland and trees, distant chimneys, the mountain, Victor swinging. He heard Itchy Billy grunt with effort as he went past him again. He began to feel the familiar childhood playground nausea, mixed with authentic grown-up fear.

The Hat gathered speed, the landscape becoming more blurred with each revolution, and at last the old whirligig was spinning without effort, at ease with gravity, fulfilling its function. Itchy Billy now stood back. Shrugging off his black puffer, he angled himself and cocked his huge arm, ready to aim the first of many blows. The fag never left his mouth.

38

Sometimes, days don't go the way they're supposed to. That is, not the way the person starting out in the morning expected them to go. Sometimes this is for the better, sometimes for the worse. Fenton, for one, had definitely had better and probably never worse. There are days like this.

Sometimes people are not where they're supposed to be, or where others *suppose* them to be. Jamie Conville, for example, while his father was in orbit around the centre pole of the Witch's Hat, was not attending a lecture on plate tectonics in Darwin Hall, Glasgow – had not, in fact, attended a lecture anywhere on campus for at least six weeks. He was in the basement of a club behind Sauchiehall Street, sound-checking a multi-deck system ahead of the early evening session, furthering his fledgling career as a DJ (stage name: MC Pachyderm; specialty: Nairobi neo-soul).

Carolyn, to her relief, was not in a swelter of stressed boredom at the Royal Courts of Justice but, the hearing having adjourned early, swilling Veuve Clicquot in the bar of the Merchant Hotel in the company of Stewart and six other tribunal lawyers keen to spend as much of their day's fees as possible before closing time. Seafood platters had been ordered and would be served presently. There was talk of cocktails up on the roof garden, with its panoramic views of Black Mountain and Cave Hill.

And they would see where things went from there.

In the offices of Cavill & Gould Solicitors LLP on Crockett Street, Ruby McCracken, accompanied at short notice by her oldest friend, Ivy, was receiving the details of Cecil's will. 'That's the situation as it stands,' the solicitor was saying. 'But you're not to worry, we'll do the best we can for you. This can be sorted.'

Rather than finishing a service on Judge McCoubrey's Jaguar SUV, Wee Davy, still in his overalls and without leave even to wash the oil off his hands, was in an interview room deep in the interior of Palace Barracks, engaged in a session of Q&A (though without much forthcoming in the way of A) about people he may or may not have known in the east of the city in the mid-1980s. His memory, it was becoming monotonously clear to all involved, was 'not the best'.

In Edinburgh, late for his afternoon lecture on Linear Perspective in the Fifteenth Century, Artie Conville was lingering over a coffee on Buccleuch Street and staring at a job advert on his phone for a position as Head of Visual Innovation at the Belfast Metropolitan School of Art.

The salary, to which his slightly wild eyes kept returning, was almost twice what he currently earned.

Ottoline Symington would probably have just been leaving the consultant oncologist's office at the clinic had she not decided, around lunchtime, that she simply couldn't be bothered. Instead, she was standing at the window of her lost daughter's bedroom, looking out at the garden, her eyes drawn to the absent space where the great elm had been.

Fenton's faithful young servant Aaron *was* at Planet of the Vapes, but he was not manning the till. He had flipped the Closed sign over at three o'clock and was in the storeroom with Tilt and Lamp, vaping a sample of cannabis wax that Lamp's brother's mate had smuggled back from Amsterdam inside a tin of beard balm. An initial round prompted the verdict that it was a bit mild, so they double-loaded and had another. This time there was general agreement that it was starting to work, so they went again and sat back to relax.

Pamela, meanwhile, had left Kylie and Kayley in charge of reception and stepped out to supervise Sunbirds' new shopfront signage. This she was now admiring with a triumphant smile: her own name in cursive volcanic-orange neon.

As for Crawford Wylie (Litigation, Matrimonial, Wills and Powers of Attorney), he was not in Sri Lanka. He wasn't even, indeed, out of the country. He was in his office above the furniture showroom, on the phone to his broadband provider demanding for the final time that a technician come and restore the Wi-Fi, which had been down for four days. An abject apology received and another solid promise secured, he poured himself a cup of coffee and got back to work. He was preparing a letter to a man called Bob that began:

Dear Mr Moffat,
I am writing to inform you of an allegation made against you by my client ...

39

The oldest part of the hospital was built of red brick, with yellow stone brackets and Italianate turrets and cupolas. Situated in the heart of west Belfast, it had once been home to hundreds of casualties sent back from the trenches of France and Belgium during the First World War. Among these men was Fenton's paternal grandfather, who was treated for a suppurating shrapnel wound in his hip – debris from a German artillery shell that exploded above a mud-choked gully north-east of Ypres in August 1917. He had been walking up the line to deliver cigarettes to the commanding officer and had just paused to light one for himself when he heard the telltale whistle overhead. The infection was effectively subdued, but a shard of metal had fused with the bone and he would walk with a slight limp for the rest of his life.

Over two decades later, in April and May 1941, the Luftwaffe carried out bombing raids on Belfast. Its intended targets were the shipyard and the aircraft and munitions factories, but the ferocity of the attacks, combined with poor defences, resulted in the devastation of half the city. More than a thousand people were killed. The hospital received many of the injured – victims of blast burns and flying glass and masonry – among them Pamela's aunt Josie, then five years old, her cheek pierced by a section of copper piping when a bomb ripped through the family home in Carlisle Street. She was left with a horseshoe-shaped scar that make-up would never quite conceal.

During the Troubles, the hospital became renowned throughout Europe for advances in tissue trauma surgery, thanks to the skill-honing opportunities provided by victims of paramilitary punishment shootings. Among these was Victor's older brother Wesley, who was stretchered in one Friday evening in 1976 with low-velocity rounds in the backs of both legs, after he had ignored warnings not to trespass on the drug-dealing turf of a local commander. Despite successful surgery and the clenched tissue-clamping grip of 'the Belfast Fixator', a game-changing device created by an enterprising orthopaedic consultant, Wes's gait thereafter gave the impression that his kneecaps were somehow on back to front.

And here now, availing of the hospitality on the top floor of the latest addition to the complex – a seven-storey critical care and fracture block opened by His Royal Highness the Prince of Wales in 2003 – was Fenton.

လ

'So the nurse says, "But doctor, it's a case of second-degree burns, why the Viagra?" – Hello, Mr Conville, how are we today? – And the doctor replies: "It'll keep the sheet off his legs".' A couple of the male students sniggered; one of the young women winced. The consultant, a large, smooth, spume-haired man in an immaculately cut pinstripe suit, complete with gold watch chain, perused Fenton's chart. 'Oh dear oh dear, you *have* been in the wars, haven't you? My word.'

With his one good eye Fenton regarded him over the wedge of his bandaged nose and said nothing. Speech was severely hampered by the wiring of his jaw and by the economy of breath imposed by four broken ribs. There was also a persistent loud hum in his left ear which made it difficult to hear himself when he did try to speak. The missing teeth didn't help either.

'Uh-huh,' went the consultant. 'Okay, let's have a look at these legs. You won't mind if my students observe?' He whisked the bed cover aside to reveal a complicated arrangement of splints and calipers. With a strapped-up hand, Fenton attempted to tug down his gown over his testicles.

'Right, that really is quite some rash,' the consultant said after a pause. 'Most impressive. Can anyone tell me the name of this condition?'

The students leaned in, several of them openly appalled. 'That bit there looks like Peppa Pig,' one of the young women said.

'Eczema?' someone ventured.

'Nope. Try again.'

'Psoriasis?' another piped up.

'Yes, and one of the worst cases I've seen since Michael Gambon. More or less rules out the use of plaster casts, which will inevitably slow the healing process. Any suggestions for treatment?'

'Steroids?' someone said. 'Ultraviolet?' said another. 'Coal tar?'

'Coal tar?' the consultant roared. 'My God, are we in the Middle Ages? Fetch the leeches! No, this requires something quite radical.' He replaced the sheet and began scribbling on Fenton's chart with a gold-nibbed fountain pen. 'I'm prescribing a new treatment: a monoclonal antibody called Scrofatrexate. You can't drink any alcohol with it, that's vital, and it will, I'm afraid, cause hair loss – on all parts of the body – but you should see an improvement with your skin in just a few months. Do you need any help with the bowels?'

Fenton mumbled a denial. He thought he might be about to cry. The consultant handed the clipboard to the nurse. 'Better double up on the laxatives,' he told her in a stage whisper. 'The morphine's very binding.' And, with that, the great silverback swept from the room, his white-coated disciples scurrying in his wake.

From his bed, when propped up and angled so he wasn't in agony, Fenton had a view of the city looking towards the river. He could see, across the never-ceasing traffic of the Westlink, the blurred outlines of familiar landmarks – the Obel Tower, the cathedral, the Europa Hotel – to the trees-cape of Botanic Gardens and the rooftops of the Holyland, but could only imagine, given the current limitations of his monocular vision, the horizon beyond, where the cement works and breakers' yards gave way to farmland and equestrian centres, trout fisheries and country parks.

Somewhere in that direction, at dusk, an elderly springer spaniel had come sniffing across him, barely conscious, still crucified on the silhouetted scaffold of the Witch's Hat, and the dog's equally elderly owner had eventually managed – with Fenton first having to rouse himself from excruciating pain to explain how to switch it on – to use her mobile phone to call an ambulance.

He was finding this new perspective, this dislocation, very strange – to be plucked out, suspended, sidelined from his own life. Put on ice. How far away it all seemed: his comfortable light-filled house, his warm car (that was particularly far away, with new number plates, the keys having been handed over to a pleased pig farmer in north County Wexford), his lovely wife, his darling daughter, his fine sons. He thought of the lads in the pub, sinking cool pints and talking shite; of leisurely Saturday-night get-togethers round the dinner table – the bubbling casseroles and bountiful vino, the craic; of free-wheeling along the shore through a silky evening breeze. How immeasurably precious all these things suddenly seemed. What he would give just to stroll into a café and order a burger. (Christ, after three days of compost soup through a straw, he'd even choke down a couple of Andrea's chicken-free 'chicken wings'.)

He pressed the button with his thumb and the little emerald light winked, and soon the opioid was melting like butter through his synapses. The drugs helped – especially when his mother arrived in a lather of indignation and disbelief (and flanked by Mihaela and Bogdan, who seemed neither indignant nor surprised to see him in this condition). What his mother couldn't get over was the apparent randomness of it. Why him? Why now? How could this happen in this day and age? And, more to the point, in *their* neighbourhood? It was outrageous. Her friends, he was informed in a tone that implied it was his fault, were living in fear of their lives. Mihaela and Bogdan, who stood respectfully back, kept silent but it was clear from their faces that they also apportioned to him some level of blame.

'This gang could strike again at any time, Fenton. Who knows who could be next. Pixie Dixon's had a quote for a new security system and it's going to cost an arm and a leg. She's terrified. And Basil's even talking to an ex-UDR friend of his about getting a firearm, and, Fenton, you know Basil, he wouldn't be afraid to use it. What have the police said? Have they got any leads? Have they found your car yet?'

He managed a minimal shake of his head. 'Where's Dad?' he whispered.

'What? Speak up. Oh, he's back at home playing war games with the professor. He said to tell you he's thinking of you and to get well soon. You know your father – he doesn't like hospitals.'

Fenton gazed up at the television on the wall – *Dickinson's Real Deal* was on – and wondered who in their right mind actually *did* like hospitals, that's to say, actively enjoyed being in them, apart from highly paid consultants and nuns.

'Anyway,' his mother said, rising from her chair, 'you'll be allowed home soon and Mihaela and Bogdan have volunteered to help out with, well, you know … *that* side of things.' Mihaela nodded at him, and if he was not mistaken, smirked. Bogdan definitely smirked. 'You're not to worry. You'll soon be up and about. And, Fenton, the animals that did this will be brought to justice, I'm sure of it.'

After his visitors had gone, he drifted between brain states, mulling the elusive nature, the arbitrary luxury, of justice. In its conventional sense it meant little to psychos like Victor, that was for sure. For them, it was what they did to other people if they didn't do what they wanted them to do, and if it was the other way round then, presumably, it was simply *getting caught*.

The cops wouldn't be troubling Victor or Itchy Billy on Fenton's account. The consequences had been made very clear (as had the revised, elongated timescale of the payments he would be making). His statement, such as was intelligible through clamped jaws and a haze of concussion, cited four short men in balaclavas, a glimpse of a black car, possibly a Mondeo, and a blindfold. He could come up with no possible motive – despite the half-hearted probings of the (apparently fifteen-year-old) officer who perched on the end of his bed, his eyes wandering every few seconds to the nurses' station – other than 'mistaken identity'.

Carolyn remained sceptical and asked him again, 'Why would they steal your car *and* beat the shit out of you? They already had what they wanted.' She was on her way to the airport, dressed in her scarlet power suit, with a pleated white blouse and freshly aerated hair. 'It just doesn't make sense.'

Fenton moaned. He was struck in a woozy way by how young and *real* his dressed-up wife looked, as if he was seeing her for the first time after a long absence. It was beginning to seem incredible to him that he hadn't told her everything from the very start. She would surely have been on his side. Wouldn't she? Maybe he would tell her everything when he could talk properly. But, then again, maybe he wouldn't.

'Anyway, some good news,' she trilled. 'It looks like my ma will be coming to live with us as soon as her house is on the market. I've already started clearing your den. Her solicitor says if we get the asking price, it'll just about cover Daddy's debts.'

She nibbled her lower lip and scuffed with a lacquered fingernail at an invisible blemish on her skirt. 'It's a mystery. He was always so good with money. How could this have happened?' She stared at the wall. 'The main creditor's a Dublin company apparently – Omerta Security, or Securities, or something like that – and they sound dodgy to me. What on earth was he thinking?'

Fenton fumbled for his new best friend, the drug pump. His pain was various, and inventive, and came at him in different pitches, like an orchestra: bass notes in his legs, trebles in his chest, screechy and violin-like in his jaws and skull. He had sneezed earlier and nearly fainted from the hoo-ha between his ribs.

Carolyn assessed her watch. 'I'd better get going. Stewart's waiting in the car.'

An image of floppy-haired athleticism shimmered in Fenton's brainpan and he felt a new pain start up, a sickening ache that radiated from his abdomen and licked at his heart.

Carolyn reached out to touch his face, thought better of it and patted his shoulder instead. 'I'll be back in a couple of days and, with any luck, you'll be allowed home soon. You'll feel better then. Okay? And listen, we're staying at The Connaught if you need to contact me for any reason. Okay? Ah, come on now, Fenton, don't cry.'

Gradually, he grew accustomed to the rhythms and routines of his environment, the clatter of the food and drug trolleys, the clicks and clanks of beds being adjusted, the brisk, soothing tones of the nurses. Hospital time was slow, as slow, he imagined, as prison time. In between mini-comas, he watched a lot of daytime television. He became addicted to *Homes Under the Hammer* and to the whole genre of people finding, bidding for, buggering about with and selling houses in general. The shows where scared late-middle-aged couples in elasticated shorts attempted to do roughly the same thing except in sweltering heat without a word of the local language – *Bankruptcy in the Sun* and the like – were particularly entertaining. He was also absorbing a great deal of information about Hitler and sharks.

Bob popped in for a visit, with an account of an epic session with the lads that included 'a few lines of banger', 'a clatter of pints' and the gatecrashing of a wedding reception at the yacht club.

'It was a free bar all night – anything you wanted. You know me, Fenton, I'm not a greedy man but Jesus. It was one of those hangovers – it was weird, I couldn't get my right eye to sync with the left; I looked like Marty Feldman, remember him? – where the only thing that's going to alleviate the suffering is a glass of wine at five o'clock *and you're not even looking forward to it.* Do you know what I mean, Fenton? Are you awake? By the way, any more word on the shop?'

Fenton had received news that Planet of the Vapes had been broken into and all the stock taken – every last rig and bottle. (He had settled on Big Roy as the chief suspect.) The perpetrator had even taken a dump on his leather sofa. The police didn't hold out much hope for recovery of the goods and seemed reluctant to pursue the DNA side of things. Fenton, who had a nagging doubt about the status of his insurance, thumbed at his drug button.

'Right, Fent,' Bob said. 'I'll head on here and leave you in peace. I'm meeting Una for a bite at this new place, Connolly's – apparently the steaks are phenomenal. It's okay, mate, don't get up … Hey, you're looking good; you're doing fine.' He tweaked Fenton's big toe through the sheet. 'No surrender. D'you hear me? It'll all be over by Christmas.'

∽

The days drifted along through banks of fug and fog, interminable 'bargain' hunts and incomprehensible quizzes. As the pain in his jaws eased, Fenton had his first semi-solid food – mashed potato, spaghetti hoops, rice pudding (they all tasted the same) – and was able to speak a little, albeit in the style of an apprentice ventriloquist. Despite his protests, they insisted on dialling down his morphine intake, and while this led to an improvement in his *Countdown* scores, it made him simultaneously more resentful of what he was missing in the outside world and more uneasy about what might await him there.

They hauled him out of bed and made him try a few tentative steps using a frame. This was traumatic and painful (he was asked to moderate his language). The opioid deficit meant he required sleeping tablets at night to block out the snoring and screaming of his elderly ward-mates, and this messed with his head to the point of him hallucinating a visit from his dead grandmother, who told him, without much conviction, he felt, that everything was going to be all right.

40

The ward sister who came to see him on the day before he was due to be discharged was an unusually tall, matronly woman who wore a snowy apron over her grey uniform and an old-fashioned, it seemed to Fenton, white cap atop crimped silver-marl hair. She had sombre grey eyes and a palely luminous complexion – a face that struck him as made for the era of black-and-white film. She towered over his bed.

'Haven't seen *you* before,' he mumbled. She had settled herself and was engrossed in his chart. 'M'm ... Been in the wars,' she said quietly, as if to herself. She continued reading while Fenton dozed off. When he came round, he found she was gazing upon him with an intensity that slightly startled him.

'If you feel up to it, we just need to go through a few questions.'

Fenton wasn't sure he did. There had been some kind of urinary fracas in one of the other beds during the night and his drugged-up circadian rhythm had looped back on itself, leaving him muzzy and disoriented.

They established his full name (Fenton Thomas Basil Conville) and date of birth.

'Nationality: British or Irish?'

'Um, Northern Irish.'

'That's not actually an option.'

'Oh. Really? That's where I'm from.'

'It's not on the form.'

'Can I put European?'

'Not really, we'd need a specific European country. Which one?'

'Ireland?'

'So … Irish?'

'Northern Irish.'

'Again, that's not on the form.'

'Is there a "None" box?'

'No. Come on, you must have a nationality. Where were you born?'

'Belfast.'

'So …?'

'What's the next question?'

'Religion: Protestant, Roman Catholic, Other or None?'

Fenton glanced past his interrogator at the sky beyond the window. Vast plains of dark cloud were ponderously arranging themselves over the city, black scribbles of rain already visible in the gaps. It was turning into an Old Testament kind of day.

'Protestant, I suppose.'

'Good. Now ...'

'No, wait. Put "Lapsed".'

'That's not an option.'

'Okay, "None".'

They moved on to the topic of access to bathroom facilities in his house: were they upstairs or downstairs? Would there be someone at home to supervise toilet visits and help with bathing? Through gritted teeth, he named them. They discussed his care plan, including physiotherapy visits, and a long list of required medications and their frequency.

Outside, the rain was pouring down in earnest, cascading across the glass, pounding on the aluminium sill.

'Right, now let's go back to nationality – you know, I don't understand why these details weren't filled out earlier. You must have fallen through the cracks. It's really just a case of British or Irish.'

Fenton's head was aching. He dabbed at his button but no infusion was forthcoming. 'The problem is,' he said, 'I don't feel like I'm either of those. Do you know what I mean? That's to say, not completely one or the other. I'm ... I'm a PONI.' The ward sister looked blank. 'You know, like they put on meat and dairy exports? PONI? A Product of Northern Ireland.'

She regarded him with a mixture of puzzlement and pity. 'I'll just write "Patient unfit to respond",' she said finally, 'and we'll blame the sedatives.'

She shuffled the papers together and set them aside, then leaned over him and began straightening the bedclothes, pulling the sheet taut and tucking it beneath the mattress. When she had finished, he was tightly swaddled, effectively pinioned, apart from the hand that held the drug trigger. While she worked, he had an urge to tell her everything that had happened to him, about the battalion of sorrows that had marched into his life, about all the blows that had been inflicted on him, about the pain, the fear, the loss, about how he had come to this. Instead, he clicked on the button until at last it gave him his allowance.

'Yet man is born to trouble, as the sparks fly upward,' she murmured by his ear.

'Excuse me?'

'Book of Job.'

'What?'

She turned and walked slowly over to the window where she gazed out at the rain, sweeping now in great dark curtains across the skyline. There was a pulse of lightning, and a profound, billowing drum roll of thunder made the double-glazing buzz. 'Honest to God,' she said, 'it's like the end of days out there.' Another strobe X-rayed the clouds and Fenton shut his eyes. When he opened them, she was gone.

The hot-drinks trolley had arrived, and from farther down the room drifted mumbled to-and-fros about biscuit choices and the plinking of crockery. This was the dead hour, the hour of nothingness, the slow hinge of the hospital day. Tea and a ration of digestives were set beside him, but Fenton had no use for them. Instead, depleted, and with the first warm-bath wave of narcotic washing through him, he lay and watched the torrents descending on the city. He was fading out. Becoming vapour.

The last of the afternoon light was receding, and splashes of icy blue and white neon were beginning to appear on the sides of buildings, spots of red on the tops of the tallest ones. Everything was drenched, the vista through the window blurred and warped by rivulets of water. The shops and offices would be emptying out soon. He pictured bullets of rain bouncing off umbrellas and car roofs and all the everyday people moving through the downpour, waiting for trains and buses, wiping down bike saddles, heading for home, to familiar shelter somewhere beyond in the darkness.

He thought of the rain falling on the crags and gullies of Black Mountain, rushing down the hillside, soaking the bog meadows, swelling the streams. It was falling on the domes of City Hall, and the satellite dishes of the BBC, on Royal Avenue, on Sailortown and the docklands; lashing down on the Dublin Road, and Shaftesbury Square, on the dark red-brick façade of the university, the panes of the great Victorian Palm House, the slate roofs of the little industrial terraces. It was splashing down on the statues, on C.S. Lewis and his holy lion, on Edward Harland, and Lord Kelvin, and Edward Carson with his defiantly raised arm, and on the Monument to the Unknown Woman Worker. On The Balls on the Falls, and on the Big Blue Fish.

It was falling on the Linen Hall Library, on Cornmarket, and the Albert Clock, and the white parliament on the hill, on the Custom House, and the Courts of Justice, on schools, and shopping centres, parks and playing fields, on the banks, and the churches, on the memorial gardens, on the cholera victims and the Famine dead buried in Friar's Bush, and on all the gravestones in all the cemeteries. He saw the deluge dancing on the glittering black surface of the Lagan, and his mind swayed along the river's looping length to the edge of the city where it spilled into Belfast Lough.

Tomorrow he would be leaving the hospital. He would be going home. Back to 'the village'. He had an image, a bird's-eye view of himself crossing the Queen's Bridge. He was on his new crutches. It was early morning, the sun not yet fully risen. There was no traffic. The air was cold and still, a pearl-grey mist rising off the water. It was one of those winter days when the light itself is a kind of mist. He was not alone. There was a crowd of everyday people walking, and he was among them, and all of them were flowing over the bridge together.

Acknowledgments

I would like to thank my agent Jonathan Williams for his generosity, skill, and guidance in bringing this novel into the light. Thanks also to Sean Farrell for his deft editing; to Emma Dunne and Susan McKeever for their eagle-eyed copy editing and proofreading, and to Antony Farrell, Enejda Nasaj, Stephen Reid, and Liam Maguire at Lilliput Press.

I'd also like to thank Cian Cafferky, Mary Rose Doorly, Carlo Gebler, Hugo Hamilton, Julie McDonald, Eve Patten, Patrick Ramsey, Nigel Townson, and my parents, John and Maureen Smith, for reading early drafts.

I am grateful to the John Hewitt Society for permission to use lines from 'The Coasters', and to David Higham Associates for permission to quote from 'Bagpipe Music' by Louis MacNeice.

And finally, my love and thanks to Eve and Esme, always.